P9-DMI-211

ONE LITTLE LIE

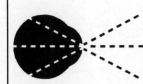

This Large Print Book carries the
Seal of Approval of N.A.V.H.

THE PELICAN HARBOR SERIES

ONE LITTLE LIE

COLLEEN COBLE

THORNDIKE PRESS
A part of Gale, a Cengage Company

Thorndike Press® Large Print Christian Fiction.
The text of this Large Print edition is unabridged.
Other aspects of the book may vary from the original edition.
Set in 16 pt. Plantin.

LIBRARY OF CONGRESS CIP DATA ON FILE.
CATALOGUING IN PUBLICATION FOR THIS BOOK
IS AVAILABLE FROM THE LIBRARY OF CONGRESS

ISBN-13: 978-1-4328-7595-4 (hardcover alk. paper)

Published in 2020 by arrangement with Thomas Nelson, Inc., a division
of HarperCollins Christian Publishing, Inc.

Printed in Mexico
Print Number: 01   Print Year: 2020

For the wonderful England family who helped so much in the research of this novel! You guys are the best!

PROLOGUE

May

Button eyed the compound's exit and forced herself to trudge behind her parents as the pain intensified in her belly. She stifled a groan and filed into the Mount Sinai meeting hall.

State forest surrounded the compound, and the breeze blowing through the door held the scent of pine. The white-board structure had once been a Methodist church and still turned blind stained glass windows toward the road. The church held about forty people, and Button slipped onto a bench by the door while her parents proceeded to their spot on the front pew.

The small community was all she'd ever known, but as the pain in her back grew and wrapped around to her enormous belly, she wished she'd been able to talk her father into taking her to a hospital. Indecision had filled his eyes, but her mother's quick refusal to her plea had hardened his gaze, and he'd shaken his head too. Their leader never allowed anyone to leave, least of all for something as basic as childbirth.

But she was afraid. The pain made her tremble inside with the uncertainty of what else she'd face. Her best friend had died in childbirth just last fall. What if Button died, too, and someone else had to raise her baby?

She wanted to hold her child herself, and she'd spent countless nights wondering if it would be possible to escape with her baby. But even if she managed to get outside the compound gates, where would she go? How could she care for herself and a baby? It seemed impossible.

Moses Bechtol rubbed his hands together as he approached the podium. The place quieted as the group leader started his sermon, a thunderous harangue that shook the windows. Button cringed and closed her eyes. The man wasn't the godlike figure he thought he was, and Button grew more and more weary of listening to him.

Was she the only one here who saw through his posturing?

She'd tried to talk to her mother a few times, but Mom loved the man. Maybe more than she loved Dad.

Button's awakening had started about six

months ago after she'd recruited two girls in a nearby town. They'd brought some books with them, and she'd been particularly captivated by *The Princess Diaries*. It had opened up the possibilities of an entirely different world from the one she inhabited.

Button's woolgathering shifted to the growing pain in her midsection. She stifled a groan and wiped perspiration from her brow. The walls seemed to slide toward her, and her stomach roiled. She had to get out of here. She wanted her mother, but Button didn't dare try to get Mom's attention.

She slipped out the old back door into the cool Michigan air. Last fall's dry leaves scudded across the remains of the spring snowstorm. The chill on her cheeks was a welcome relief from the heat washing up her skin.

Half crouching, she stumbled toward the cabin she'd been assigned. The enclave of twenty or so cabins and tents cluttered the clearing around the church, and hers was on the western perimeter. The viselike grip on her back eased slightly, and she hurried.

She fumbled at the doorknob and practically fell inside as another pain gripped her. Liquid pooled at her feet. Was she dying? She gasped as the pain moved from her back to her belly. The baby was coming *today.*

She found her way to the hard cot in the bedroom and fell on it. As the pain came in waves, she lost track of time. What felt like hours later, she felt a firm hand on her forehead and looked into her mother's face.

"It's the baby," Button whispered through dry lips.

"Yes, it's nearly here." Her mom dipped a rag in water and wiped her forehead. "You're doing great, honey. I've sent word to Moose."

The baby's father was the last person Button wanted here. She'd never even seen his face clearly. Her parents had betrothed her to him when she was twelve, and Moses had tied their hands together a year ago when she was fourteen. He'd come to her twice before she found herself increasing, and he would be no comfort now.

She clung to her mother's hand. "It hurts so bad, Mom. I'm scared. I want to go to the hospital."

"I know it hurts, honey." Her mother soothed her with a calm hand on Button's forehead. "Breathe through the pain. I'm going to deliver it now."

The world narrowed to this room, this pain blotting out everything around her. It seemed an eternity before the thin, reedy cry of a newborn emerged. Button had no strength left to ask the baby's gender.

"It's a boy!" Her mother plopped the baby on Button's breast. "He's good sized too. And listen to those lungs. He needs to nurse."

Button had seen the procedure plenty of times over the years in the community, but her mother had to help her figure out the actions to get him to latch. She smoothed her hand over his thick cap of black hair. "He's beautiful."

His skin was pink and perfect. She ran her finger along his arm. So soft. An overwhelming love for him surprised her by its intensity. She closed her eyes and breathed in his scent as her mother snapped several Polaroid pictures. There had to be a way to give him more than she had in this compound.

Button was barely aware of her mom finally moving the baby to the small box prepared for him, and she fell asleep.

A loud sound outside awakened her and she sat upright. "Mom?"

No answer. She caught the whiff of smoke and heard screams from outside her cabin. Then more loud noises. Gunshots? Were they under attack? Moses had warned them it could happen anytime.

11

She rolled out of bed and went to grab the baby from the box, but he wasn't there. Maybe her mother had taken him to bathe or to show him to her father and Moose. Weak from the ordeal, she lurched out of the bedroom into the living room. A curl of smoke drifted around the door, and flames licked at the frame.

"Mom!" Where was her baby?

Frantic, she darted her gaze around the small cabin, but there was no sign of her son or her mother. The smoke burned her throat all the way down to her lungs. She coughed and backed away from the fire shooting up the cabin's front wall to the window.

She had to get out.

The glass shattered in the window behind her, and the flames intensified with the fresh insurgence of air.

"Button!"

She turned at the sound of her dad's voice. He'd broken out the window and was holding out his arms. "Hurry, there isn't much time."

She rushed to him, and he helped her through the window and out into the fresh air. "My baby. Where's Mom and my baby?"

"Come with me." He swung her into his arms and carried her through thick smoke.

Flames crackled from cabins all around, and the acrid stench made her cough again. More screams and gunshots rang out. A bullet whistled by her head, and she buried her face against her dad's chest. What was happening?

He reached his old Jeep, a dented green vehicle that was a good thirty years old. He put her down by the passenger door and opened it. "Get in."

She shook her head wildly. "No! I have to find my baby. And Mom!"

"Your mom refuses to come. She's staying with Moses."

Button's eyes widened in horror. "She took my baby? She can't keep him here. He's mine!"

Dad looked at the ground. "Honey, the baby died. We have to get out of here or we're all going to jail. You need to get in the Jeep." His words were gentle.

Dead? Her perfect little son had died? "I don't believe you," she whispered.

Her dad held her gaze. "I saw him, honey. He was blue and cold. Your mom gave me this photo for you to keep to remember him by." He thrust a Polaroid picture into her hand.

Tears filled her eyes, and she fell into the Jeep barely conscious as her dad drove through the inferno to safety.

ONE

Fifteen Years Later

"Last net of the night, Boss."

Alfie Smith nodded at Isaac, his sixteen-year-old helper, and started the hoist motor to bring up the nets. Nearly eighty, he'd plied these waters aboard his boat *Seacow* for more than sixty years. The lights of Gulf Shores shimmered in the distance and more lights passed to his starboard side, other shrimping boats pulling up their last nets of the night before heading for a berth at Pensacola, Gulf Shores, or Mobile.

Sunrise pinked the clouds in the eastern sky and spread an iridescent shimmer over the waves. This was Alfie's favorite time of day, when his muscles ached from good use and shrimp filled his hold. Most people said the smell was bad enough to gag a maggot, but to Alfie it was the aroma of money.

He glanced at Isaac, who looked like a surfer with his vivid blue eyes and his

15

tanned face. His hair was streaked blond by the sun and tousled by the sea air. In spite of his good looks, he had a mariner's soul and a natural aptitude for shrimping.

Isaac pulled out his phone. "Your daughter said this is your last trip. Maybe we should commemorate it somehow. I'll take a picture."

"She told you that?" Alfie scowled and stared out at the horizon. "Put that blasted phone away. Dr. Cosby is an old busybody, and she's got her knickers in a knot over it. I'll be out here on the water as long as I'm still kicking. She wants me to plop down in my recliner and die right there. I plan to keel over right here on my boat."

Isaac gave him a doubtful look, then stuck his phone back in his pocket. "If you say so. Your daughter was pretty adamant."

"She's not the boss of me." She was a good girl, much like her mother, who'd gone to glory ten years ago. But she was too big for her britches when it came to trying to dictate his actions. "I'm going out tomorrow, and you can take that to the bank along with your paycheck."

Isaac pushed his curly hair out of his eyes. "You still want me then?"

"Yep. When you see me in the casket, you'll know your job is done."

That old goat of a doctor claimed Alfie's ticker was having problems, but he felt fine. A little more tired maybe, but he was an old coot.

A harsh whine in the engine caught Alfie's attention.

"The engine is straining. We must have a good haul," Isaac said.

Alfie nodded and maneuvered the net over the sorting table, then dropped the contents. Something heavy banged on the table, and he flipped on the floodlights.

Isaac groaned. "There's a big cooler in here, Alfie. It's damaged the net."

The big Grizzly cooler, one of the four-hundred-quart ones, was nearly five feet long. Alfie had always wanted one, but they were dear. The one he'd priced had been nearly seven hundred dollars. Mother Ocean had brought him a nice gift today.

It made Alfie madder than a wet hen the way people dumped things right in the shrimping grounds. They took their trash just far enough offshore to toss it overboard unnoticed. Sometimes he thought people did it on purpose to snare the shrimping nets.

Alfie turned to look at the big hole. "We're done anyway." The net would take some mending before he could go out again.

Isaac grunted as he pulled the cooler toward him. "Too heavy to be empty." He struggled with the lid and managed to open it.

When Isaac cussed and stumbled back, Alfie hurried to the boy's side. "What is it?"

Eyes wide, Isaac's hand shook as he pointed. "I-I think there's a dead woman in there."

Alfie approached the cooler and peered inside. A bloody wedding dress was bunched inside. No, wait, not just a dress. A human torso. He backpedaled, spun around, and retched over the side of the boat. After he emptied his stomach, he reached for his phone.

Jane Hardy sat in a chair in front of the five executive committee members seated at a shiny curved table. Her golden retriever, Parker, lay at her feet. Her mouth was dry, and she wasn't sure why she was even here. They couldn't seriously be considering promoting her already, could they? But the group of three men and two women seemed to regard her with some sort of approval in their eyes.

Jane's gaze met the pale-blue eyes of Victor Armstrong. He wasn't smiling.

Armstrong cleared his throat. He was a

big man in his fifties and the only city council member to wear a suit and tie. He sold commercial real estate and was well known in town.

She realized he'd spoken while she was daydreaming. "Excuse me?"

His eyes narrowed. "I hope we're not keeping you from something important."

"No, sir." She clamped her mouth shut because any kind of excuse she offered would make the situation worse. Jane tucked a strand of light-brown hair behind her ear and sent a nervous smile toward Mayor Lisa Chapman, who was seated beside him.

Lisa had befriended Jane the day she'd come to town. Lisa also owned Petit Charms, the beignet and pastries shop, but after being elected mayor, she'd given over running the shop to her daughter. Though in her fifties, Lisa appeared to be in her thirties with her unblemished dark skin and trim figure.

Lisa smiled. "We're appointing you chief of police, Jane. Congratulations."

Chief of police. Jane sat up straighter. "I-I don't know what to say. I'm humbled by your trust in me."

"You're well qualified for the job. We conducted extensive interviews with the department. Your management skills are

19

excellent, and you're organized and highly intelligent. All of us" — Lisa glanced at Armstrong and put a slight emphasis on *all* before she continued — "know you'll represent the department as well as your father has all these years."

Jane felt woozy as the blood drained from her head. She hadn't dared to hope for a permanent appointment. "Thank you so much, all of you. I won't let you down."

Armstrong frowned. "I must say I'm not sure about appointing a woman to this position. I'm sure it's politically incorrect for me to voice my concerns, but I've never cared about being PC. You're a small woman, Jane, and your appearance isn't likely to put the fear of God into criminals. And you've made no progress with the vigilante cases over the past two months."

Jane's smile died on her lips, and she barely bit back the gasp of outrage gathering in her throat. "The vigilante is hardly a priority, Victor. We have a small police force, and putting drug dealers and criminals in jail has taken more of my attention."

Lisa leapt to her defense. "Victor, I can't believe you'd say something like that. Jane has acquitted herself well in every role she's filled at the department from patrol to detective. As a detective she made more arrests than anyone we've employed."

Armstrong shrugged. "The mayor has the final say, but I predict we'll be back here in a few months reversing our decision."

Lisa moved her paper and pencil around, a sure sign of her anger. When she spoke, her voice was careful and modulated. "I don't want to hear anything more from you, Victor. This meeting is adjourned." She rose and came around the table to shake Jane's hand.

Jane clung to her hand for a long moment. "Thanks so much, Lisa."

"My pleasure. We have full confidence you'll do an outstanding job. I'm proud we have such a wonderful officer to step into that position." Her eyes gleamed. "I'm sure the news of this will get around."

Jane's smile faded. Was the publicity of being female the reason she got the job?

She barely registered the congratulations and well-wishes before she escaped into the heat of the Alabama spring with Parker. *Chief of police.* Paul Baker would not be happy at this turn of events.

Could she do the job? Was Armstrong right about the challenges she'd face as a woman? She gave a slight shake of her head. Her town was riding on her ability to do this. She'd rise to the challenge. In a larger police force the chief ruled from the office, but with only five officers including her on the force, she had to be a hands-on chief of police.

Pelican Harbor sat along the blue water of Bon Secour Bay between Oyster Bay and Barnwell. The town had mostly escaped the influx of tourists heading to Gulf Shores for many years, but times changed when Pelican Harbor's beignet shops and shotgun houses had appeared in *National Geographic Traveler*. The tourists brought prosperity to the village of two thousand souls, and the residents had begun to spruce up the wrought-iron balconies and paint the quaint French homes. The town reminded visitors of New Orleans' famous French Quarter.

This was her town to protect now, and she intended to do it to the best of her ability.

She turned toward the coffee shop and bumped into a man who reached out to steady her. "Sorry, I wasn't watching where I was going."

His eyes crinkled at the corners as if smiling was his usual expression, though his lips were flat now. He towered over her five feet two inches, and she guessed him to be six foot. His shaved head made his large brown eyes even more expressive and compelling, and he exuded controlled energy and power under his very attractive surface. His muscular arms and face were tanned as if he'd spent a lot of time in the sun. Her immediate attraction to him made her take a step back. She steered clear of relationships. Losing someone you cared about hurt too much.

Those dark eyes smiled down at her. "You're Jane Hardy."

"Guilty as charged. You look familiar."

A flush flared under his tan. "Maybe you've seen my picture around." He held out his hand and shook hers. "Reid Dixon. You might have seen some of my documentaries." He released her hand.

Of course she had. "You did the piece on cults a few years ago."

"I did. I was about to grab a cup of coffee. Care to join me?"

She didn't want to agree, but he was here for a reason, and she had a feeling that since he'd sought her out, she wouldn't like whatever had brought him to town. Better to be prepared than blindsided.

"I was about to get coffee as well." She walked beside him to Pelican Brews and had her dog settle in the shady overhang outside before she stepped into the building. The fresh aroma of the Guatemalan roast put a spring in her step. She ordered and paid for a coffee, then found a small table next to the window to wait for him.

He ordered black coffee and joined her. She took a sip of her coffee and waited for him to tell her what he wanted. When he didn't speak, she filled the silence. "I'm not sure where you live, but I'm sure it's far from our little burg."

"I live in New Orleans. I'm here for a few weeks for a new documentary." He gestured to the south. "I rented the Holbrook place."

The brick mansion on the Bon Secour River hadn't sold yet. Not many could afford its price tag. "Nice place."

"Yeah, it is." He sipped his coffee and glanced out the window. "You live here long?"

"Most of my life."

"Nice area. My boy and I are going shrimping in a little while."

What did he want with her? "It's best at night."

"Yes, but Will finishes his basketball camp in a couple of hours, and he's jonesing to get out shrimping." He glanced at her and opened his mouth to say something else, but her dispatcher called.

"Chief Hardy."

"Jane, we've got a murder," Olivia Davis

24

said. "You need to get down to the pier. A shrimper pulled up a dead body."

"On my way." She grabbed her coffee and rose. "Nice to meet you, Reid. I need to go."

"Of course. I'll be contacting you later."

It felt more like a threat than a promise.

Two

White boats bobbed along the finger piers of the marina, and Jane motioned for Detective Brian Boulter to follow her and Parker down the swaying path to the shrimper *Sea-cow*. Brian could intimidate suspects by his sheer size, and he played up his resemblance to Dwayne Johnson by working on the size of his already-massive arms. She had often been grateful for his strength, though he dwarfed her small frame.

The knot in her belly only grew when she caught sight of the boat, a decrepit relic she'd seen many times over the years. The body must have shown signs of violence for the dispatcher to call it a murder.

She spotted Paul Baker and walked toward him. About six two, Paul strutted toward her like a man used to turning female heads. She knew him to be about thirty, and he had ambition. He'd wanted to be appointed chief instead of her, and he wouldn't be happy to still play second fiddle. Especially to a woman.

"What's the story?" she asked.

"The shrimping trawler was on its last load of the day and pulled up an old cooler. The torso was inside." Though his voice was cool, he must not have heard about her appointment yet or she would be able to feel his anger.

She winced. "Only a torso?"

Paul nodded. "The ME just got here, but I took a peek without touching the body. No head or limbs. Probably to muddy ID." He hesitated. "She's in a wedding dress."

Jane winced. "I haven't seen any missing brides come across my desk."

"Nope."

Two male figures sat on the dock with their feet dangling off the edge. She recognized Alfie Smith immediately. She liked the old codger, and he'd often given her free shrimp. He stared blankly out toward Pelican Harbor. His teenage sidekick, Isaac, threw bread to the gulls fighting over the crumbs. They both wore long-sleeved shirts over long pants stuffed into rubber boots that used to be white.

Seeing a bride's torso was bound to rattle the most equanimous person.

Her steps sounded on the wooden decking, and Alfie turned his head. He stood and shoved his hands in the pockets of his khaki pants.

"You okay, Alfie?"

His faded blue eyes gave her a hard once-over, and he seemed smaller this morning — shrunken and spent. His Adam's apple made a jerky movement. "I'm plumb tired, Jane. I never seen nothing like this."

"Where is the cooler with the body now?"

"Still aboard. Starboard of the sorting table. I can show you."

"What else can you tell me about the body you found? Did you touch it?" She went over the usual questions, though Paul would have already interviewed him. Alfie liked her, and he was apt to open up more to her than to anyone else.

He shook his head. "At first I thought it was just a wedding dress until I realized how heavy it was. I-I could see parts of the arms in the sleeves. There's no way a whole body could fit in that size cooler, even though it's a big one. There's n-no head either. Just what looks like a torso."

Jane's stomach gave a slow roll, but she controlled her expression. "Any identifying marks on the cooler or the body that you noticed?"

"No. But like I said, I didn't touch it. I

28

think whoever put it in the bay wanted it to be found. This is prime shrimping water. If they didn't want it dragged up, they would have taken it out to sea."

"Unless the killer is someone who doesn't know anything about shrimping." Jane glanced at the boy. "How about you, Isaac?"

He shifted and stared down at his dirty white boots. "There wasn't much to see, and I didn't want to look." His face carried a green tinge. "I called Alfie over and then threw up. He did too."

The body itself would reveal more information than these two who had found it. "Thank you for your time. I might have more questions after we examine the remains."

Alfie straightened and touched the boy's arm. "You know where to find us."

Robert Yong, the ME, appeared, and Jane led the way aboard the boat. The reek of shrimp and sea life made her nose burn, but she walked to the large cooler with more confidence than she felt. She stepped back for Yong to kneel by the cooler, then peered over his shoulder as he gingerly did a preliminary examination with gloved hands.

The wedding dress had once been a pearly white and looked expensive with its lace and sequin detail. Locating the shop that sold it might help identify the bride inside even though her head and hands were missing. If she wasn't in the DNA database, she'd be hard to identify, though a missing bride on the day of her wedding would surely have been reported missing.

Yong had held the position of medical examiner for the past three years, and Jane liked him. His calm pragmatism was appreciated at a scene like this. In his early forties, he had black hair with no gray yet, and his brown eyes usually held a genial expression. Married to a schoolteacher, he and his wife had two grade-school kids and lived down the road from Jane.

He gasped and jerked back far enough to fall onto his backside on the deck. "I wasn't expecting that," he said in a shaky voice.

Jane moved closer. "What is it?"

"Our victim isn't female. It's a man."

"In a wedding dress?" A cross-dresser? A transvestite?

"Definitely male." Robert stood and shut the lid. "I'm going to request an autopsy in Mobile, of course."

"Of course." She nodded.

Robert didn't conduct autopsies himself. If he felt a case warranted it, he could request one from the Alabama Department of Forensic Sciences. If ever a case required an autopsy, this one definitely qualified.

The net spilled its catch onto the sorting table and mixed the odor of shrimp with the stench of diesel fuel. The afternoon sun was hot on Reid's arms as he and Will had motored out into the Gulf of Mexico. A pod of bottle-nosed dolphins escorted them away from shore. Gulls squawked from the boat's railing and waited for their chance to snatch discarded shrimp. A pelican and some blue herons flapped by overhead and added to his sense of a perfect day.

Reid frowned at the mixture of shrimp and detritus brought up by the seine. It was more trash and fewer shrimp than he would have liked. Maybe because he'd found it hard to keep his mind on shrimping now that he'd met Jane Hardy in the flesh this morning.

She was no longer a callow girl and had turned into a very beautiful woman.

Perdido Key rose in the distance, and several boats moved past in the choppy waters. Shrimping was best done at night, but his boy had begged to come out and Reid couldn't say no. What teenager still liked to hang out with his old dad?

He motioned for Will to help sort the ball of sea life and trash. Will was nearly six feet tall with developing muscles. Soon Reid wouldn't be able to pin him in their wrestling matches.

"Not much here, Dad." Will began tossing trash into a bucket. "I think we should move into Pensacola Bay and see what we find."

Will had a sixth sense about shrimping, and Reid had learned to trust his son's innate sense of where to drop the net. "Whatever you say. I'll finish sorting while you change our course."

These precious hours out on the shrimp boat with his son didn't happen often. As Reid's documentaries had become more and more sought after, he traveled more than he liked.

Reid's phone buzzed, and he glanced at the number. He didn't recognize it, but the area code indicated it was from a cell phone in the area. It could be a customer he hadn't programmed into his phone, but producers and people pitching stories were often strangers. "Reid Dixon."

A long pause followed before the caller spoke in a husky voice. "Reid?"

Her voice was the first thing that had attracted him. He held the phone away from his ear and looked at the number again. Was he dreaming? He glanced at Will, who stood at the helm. With the wind and waves he'd be unable to overhear.

Reid put the phone to his ear again. "Lauren?" His throat squeezed shut. *It can't be her. No way.*

"In the flesh." Her throaty chuckle was so familiar, so sexy.

"You're alive." Stupid thing to say. Of course she was alive or she wouldn't be talking. "I mean, I had you declared dead a year ago. Where have you been?"

"As soon as the law allowed, right?" An edge sliced through her voice.

He didn't answer, and she blew out a breath. He could almost smell the scent of tobacco wafting his way. She loved her cigarettes the way a cocaine addict loved the straw.

Where had she been, and why was she calling after all these years? He grabbed hold of his scattered thoughts. "I tried to find you for years. You just — vanished. What did you expect me to do?"

"How are you, Reid? And, um, Will?"

The thought of his son made his knees quiver. Lauren's sudden reappearance would rock him, and that reaction was exactly what Lauren wanted. "Fine. We're both fine. What do you want?"

The shape of Will's shaggy dark hair moved in the pilothouse, and Reid gulped back his terror. If she tried to take Will from him, he'd fight her tooth and nail. He never should have let her adopt him, but she'd hidden her true nature from him until it was too late.

"I hear you're very successful these days. I've hit a bit of a rough patch, and I need money." She stated her request with a bored tone, as if she knew he'd do whatever she wanted.

And he'd done that once. Tried to give her everything she wanted. But nothing he did or bought was ever enough. He knew better than to try now. "No."

"Fine. I'll talk to Will and see what he has to say about how you're treating me."

"You deserted a seven-year-old who needed you. You're not fit to even talk to him. Motherhood bored you then, and I'm sure you haven't changed. You won't take my boy from me."

"He won't cry and hang on to me now. I'm sure we'd get along just fine. And I know you, Reid. You'll want to protect him from his big, bad mommy. You won't want him to know how much I hated being a mother, how I shoved him away when he wanted me to pick him up. You won't want him to know about the times you had to take him before I threw him to the floor, will you? I get that, but protecting him is going to cost you."

She had him cold. In the beginning she'd seemed to truly love Will. Once Reid had married her, he'd helplessly watched her change toward his little man. He'd do anything to keep Will from knowing the truth about Lauren. In Will's mind, she had been a wonderful mother and something tragic had happened to her. It would devastate him to know she'd walked away willingly. And to know she wasn't his real mother would be even more traumatic.

It would lead to questions Reid wasn't prepared to answer.

He exhaled. "How much?"

"Five hundred thousand."

"I can't possibly raise that kind of money. I can scrape together a hundred grand, but that's it." And even that would be a stretch. Coming up with that amount of cash wouldn't be easy after Gary had stolen money and equipment from him. Reid had to spend quite a bit of his savings to replace the expensive cameras and editing equipment.

She must have recognized the truth in his voice because she sighed. "Fine. I need it as soon as I can get it."

He'd have to sell some stocks, raid his

401k. "It will take me a few days to get it together."

"You have until Wednesday or I make myself known to Will."

"I'll text you when I have it."

The phone went dead, and he looked at the screen. She'd ended the call. Typical. He palmed the back of his neck with a shaky hand. He couldn't even talk to anyone about this. Will could never know.

The game was afoot.

He saw the spring in Jane's step as she left the meeting and smiled. It wouldn't be there for long. Something about the shape of her face and her size always reminded him of Reese Witherspoon. Petite and small-boned, Jane walked with her head high and an I-can-take-on-the-world expression. She would find out she was no match for the adversary she didn't know existed.

Jane had no idea how much he was going to mess with her life. It had been a long time coming. *Retribution* was an exciting word, one he'd rolled around and around in his head for years. It would be a freight train coming for the Hardys at full speed. None of them would understand his purpose until it was too late.

He'd managed to rope in other help, and

now that they were working together, the cases being thrown her way would keep her occupied until it was time to strike. He pulled out his 1964 Kennedy half-dollar and flipped it through his fingers. He'd leave it where she'd find it, and she would think it was a lucky find when really it was the face of destruction.

It was just the first move in a deadly game of chess. Checkmate and game over.

THREE

"I hear congratulations are in order."

Jane looked up at the sound of Olivia's voice in the doorway. In her late forties, Olivia Davis was the department's head dispatcher. She'd been here as long as Jane and had taken her under her wing the moment Jane met her when Dad got a job with the police force.

Jane smiled and set her pencil down. "Thanks, it was a shock. I just made coffee. Want some?"

Olivia had been a widow since her officer husband, Chris, was killed in the line of duty when he was thirty-three. Jane had often wondered why her friend had never remarried since she was a bubbly brunette who made everyone feel like her best friend the moment they met her. Jane adored her.

Olivia shut the door behind her. "I need to talk to you."

Jane frowned. "Uh-oh, what'd I do now?"

Olivia's smile didn't reach her dark-blue eyes. "It's not you — it's me." She sank into one of the visitor chairs. "I've got ALS, Jane." Her voice trembled, but she held Jane's gaze with the strength and steadiness that made her so endearing. Parker must have heard the stress in her voice because he got up and came to push his nose into Olivia's hand.

Jane struggled for something comforting to say. She'd never known anyone with ALS, though she knew it was deadly. She squatted in front of Olivia and took her hand off Parker's head. "Tell me all of it."

Olivia's fingers were cold as she held to Jane's hand. "My muscles have been twitching and felt funny. My right leg has been weak, and I've fallen several times." She gestured to the elastic bandage on her ankle. "After falling for the third time, I went to the doctor thinking I might have MS. He sent me to a neurologist."

"That's why you were off work last week for a couple of days? Why didn't you tell me?"

Olivia swallowed. "I didn't want to worry you. The doctor ran a bunch of tests to rule out other possible causes. Nothing else showed up, so she's calling it ALS."

"Well, that's a crazy way to diagnose

39

something! Maybe it's not ALS at all. You need to get a second opinion."

"I can do that, but she's certain that's what's wrong. She will run more tests in six months to see how far it's progressed. She put me on some new medicine to slow the disease, but 95 percent of the time, it's fatal in two to five years. I'm praying I'm in the 5 percent who can live twenty years with it."

Jane froze and fought the tears forming. Olivia needed her to be strong right now, to help her get through this. "Oh, Olivia."

Tears hung on Olivia's lashes. "I know. It's overwhelming. I haven't told Megan yet. Would you be with me when I tell her?"

"Of course."

Megan was fourteen and had been a baby when Olivia's husband died. The two were very close, and this would hit Megan hard. "Have you thought about what to say? Maybe she doesn't have to know all the details."

Olivia shook her head. "I've got a lot of peace about it. I can't lie to her, and she has to be prepared for the worst. What if I only live the average of three years? Megan would not even be out of high school."

Olivia's parents were missionaries to Cambodia, and Chris's parents lived in

Canada. They only saw Megan every four or five years, and she wasn't close to any of them.

Jane squeezed Olivia's hand more tightly. "I'll take care of her, no matter what. You just concentrate on getting through what you have to do. I'll research and see what I can find out about how to beat it."

"You promise you'll take care of her? She's got no one but me."

"I promise."

The clouds cleared in Olivia's blue eyes. "I'm not sure how long I'll be able to work. Right now the muscle weakness isn't major, but that could change at any time."

"We'll figure it out a day at a time." Jane's mind whirled with thoughts of how to help. She could bring in food and help Megan with schoolwork. She could take Olivia to and from doctor visits too.

"Stop it."

"What?"

"Quit thinking you have to fix this. This is above your pay grade. You can walk with me through it, but you can't change it. I know how you get. You take the weight of the world on your shoulders and try to micromanage everything. That works great for your job, but it's impossible when it comes to something like this."

"Why you?" Jane blurted out. "Why would your God let something like this happen when you do so much for him and others? You've taken in how many kids from the streets in the past five years?"

"Seven," Olivia mumbled.

"Seven. And one of them stole from you."

"And six of them are doing fine now. Those are pretty good odds."

"Exactly. So why punish you?"

Olivia tightened her grip on Jane's hand. "Life isn't supposed to be all moonlight and roses, Jane. We're just here developing our character. And none of us get through this life without facing death. It comes to everyone. I'm just not ready to leave Megan."

"And your character is pretty darned great. I'd like to tell God what I think of the way he treats his servants. You're the *best,* Olivia. It's not fair."

Olivia's smile emerged then, a real smile that crinkled the corners of her eyes and stretched across her face. "Hey, I call it progress that you actually want to talk to him, even if you are mad."

Jane rose and paced the gray tile of her office. "I still think it's the wrong diagnosis. This makes no sense."

Olivia stood and grabbed Jane in a hug. "Life sometimes doesn't," she whispered in her ear. "That's what faith is all about."

Faith wasn't something Jane could wrap her head around. How did you trust something you couldn't see?

He kept hearing Lauren's threatening voice in his head. Reid stripped off his wet clothes and stepped into the shower. He wished he could wash off his worries as easily as he did the briny odor of the sea.

Clean and with the scent of Dial soap in his nose, he toweled off, then pulled on shorts and a T-shirt before he wandered back to the living room to find Will. This place was just a rental, and it showed. The walls were still without pictures. The place overlooked the Bon Secour River and had the barest of furnishings. Will deserved better, but Reid had only planned to be here long enough to satisfy his curiosity about Jane Hardy. That investigation had started this morning with coffee.

The bigger problem was, what was he going to do about Lauren? The more he'd thought about it, the more he worried that paying her off wasn't the right answer. Her insatiable nature would bring her back for more and more demands.

If only he had someone to talk to about this, but he didn't dare voice his predicament. Not if he wanted to keep this from Will. And he'd checked his accounts. There was no way he could get that much actual cash without dipping into his 401k.

He trailed through the living room to the big screened-in porch overlooking the river and dropped into a chair by his son. "You order lunch?"

Will nodded. "I ordered some po'boys and crab bisque. Food should be here in half an hour."

Reid didn't like to cook, though he tried most days because Will shouldn't live on restaurant food, but it felt like too much today. "Sounds good."

He listened to the frogs croaking and insects chirping out on the river. A splash just off the pier came right after the roar of a bull alligator. The solitude out here usually soothed him, but he was jumping at every sound. He didn't trust Lauren, not one bit. In spite of their agreement she was apt to show up on their doorstep at a moment's notice. If she'd gotten his phone number, he was sure she'd managed to find his residence too.

The unpleasant scenario played out in his head. Will's shock and hurt. Lauren's smug smile and fake sympathy. Reid's own feelings of abandonment.

44

He'd never been enough for her, and he'd tried so hard. She used him just like his dad. No matter how hard he'd tried to live up to his father's standards, he'd fallen short. Every time. If his dad were still alive, would he be proud of the work Reid had done? Probably not.

"You okay, Dad?"

Reid snapped out of his thoughts and managed to shrug. "I'm fine. Just tired."

Will rose and walked to the windows to look out on the slow-moving black water. "I like it here, Dad." He turned to Reid. "What if we didn't go back to New Orleans?"

Reid studied his boy's pleading gaze. "What's brought this on?"

"The football camp is really cool, and the other guys are including me in everything. It's a slower pace here. Not so busy."

The pinch of the kid's guilt card was enough to make Reid listen. "What about your friends back home?"

Will shrugged. "What about them? It's not like New Orleans is Mars. They can come visit, or I could visit them."

But they wouldn't. Relationships were fragile at this age. And Will had already been making friends here. He'd gone over to a friend's house to lift weights three nights this past week.

"I know I'm asking a lot." Will's voice was tentative. "I mean, you probably want to get back to Miss Saunders."

Reid had dated Will's French teacher a few times, but he couldn't say he really missed Amanda. They'd talked a few times in the past month, but it wasn't anything serious. Nothing was really keeping them in Louisiana. He could make trips for his documentaries when needed, just like he did now. Mobile's airport was close. And like Will said, New Orleans wasn't that far.

When Reid didn't say anything, Will turned away to look at the river again. "You don't have to answer now. Just think about it, okay?"

Love swelled in Reid's chest. When had Will become so adult that he didn't push? "I don't have to think about it. If you want to stay here, I'm game. I like having more time with you, and you'll be off to college before I can blink. I'll put the house up for sale, and we'll search for something here. Now that you're older, you can travel with me more too."

Will swung back around, a grin spreading across his face. "This house is for sale. We could buy it."

"We could." His job paid very well. "I'll call and see if we can come to an agreement

46

on price."

And just like that, life shifted even further. But his biggest problem could still walk right in that front door. "Tomorrow is your last day of football camp. Want to hang with your old man the rest of your spring break?"

"You bet!"

Reid never took his son's love for granted. Will was a great kid — the best. Reid kept waiting for him to turn into the proverbial teenage monster, but it had never happened and he was grateful.

The doorbell rang, and Will turned. "I'll get it. It's probably our lunch."

Logically Reid knew Will was right, but he imagined his boy opening the door to Lauren. "I'll do it. I'll need to pay for it."

He only relaxed when through the front door window he saw a young delivery guy. Was this what life would become — a knot in his stomach every time someone came to the door or called? He should have hung up the moment he'd heard Lauren's voice.

No one can dance to the devil's tune and expect to survive. He had to call her and tell her any deal was off.

Will held out his hands for the food, and Reid drank in the sight of his face. The boy might have to hear the truth. But not today.

Reid picked up a po'boy. "After lunch I'm

going to run into town and get started on my documentary. You okay here or you want to come?"

"I'll stay here. I thought I might fish from the pier."

"Watch out for gators. There seem to be a lot around."

Will rolled his eyes. "Dad, I'm not five."

"Point taken."

Reid scarfed down his sandwich and soup. The sheriff would hit the roof when she realized why he was here. He'd wanted to tell her about the documentary over coffee, but it was clear the mayor hadn't spoken to her.

FOUR

Jane parked her SUV in the driveway behind the flashing lights of a patrol vehicle and got out, the rising sun glaring into her gritty eyes. The call to investigate another body had sent her straight to her vehicle without a shower. Two bodies in twenty-four hours . . . Was she really equipped for this job?

She let Parker out of the back before she walked toward the shotgun house with its neat spring flower beds lining either side of the red front door. She spotted a woman standing off to one side with her arms clutched around her. It was probably the neighbor who'd made the 911 call, and Jane would talk to her next.

A figure moved in the brush at the side of the house, and she caught the shine of something metallic. A gun? She pointed at the bush. "Take down, Parker!"

Her dog's ears flicked forward, and he

bounded for the line of vegetation. The leaves shook as the person tried to escape the dog's attack, but Parker was an experienced K-9 officer, and his bark coupled with the man's yell for help told her the prey was on the ground. Most goldens weren't used for protection, but Parker was large for his breed at ninety pounds and had easily learned how to protect her.

She pulled her gun and hurried into the shadow of the trees, where she found Parker's paws firmly planted on a man's chest. She immediately recognized him as the man who'd invited her for coffee yesterday morning. Reid Dixon. She didn't see a weapon on him, but a video camera was tangled in the brush.

She holstered her gun. "Release, Parker."

The dog got off Reid and returned to her side. "Good boy." She narrowed her eyes at Reid as he stood. "What are you doing here?"

He brushed dust and debris from his tan slacks. "The mayor has given me permission to follow you around for the next few weeks, Chief. I'm doing a documentary on small-town police departments. You're one of the few female police chiefs around, so I'll be focusing the bulk of my video on you."

50

So that's why he'd sought her out in town. Heat rushed to her cheeks. "That's not possible. Lisa would have told me. I want you to leave."

"Call her yourself." He glanced at Parker, who was staring him down. "I'm okay, buddy. I'm not going to hurt her." The dog showed no signs of relaxing.

It was only five in the morning, but Jane had no choice but to check out his story. She called the mayor and moved out of earshot. "Lisa, there's a journalist here who claims he has permission to follow me around. This is a crime scene. He shouldn't be here."

"I told you there might be some news interest in your appointment." Lisa's voice was groggy with sleep. "He's very well known, Jane. It's a great opportunity for Pelican Harbor."

"You knew this when you appointed me, didn't you?"

"Yes, but I didn't think he would show up so fast. He called last week, and I knew he'd be even more interested in doing a documentary when he found out we had a female chief."

"So this was all a publicity ploy for the town? I don't want to do it."

"I'm afraid you don't have a choice. It's

51

only for a few weeks, and it's great exposure for us."

Her hard tone told Jane that arguing wouldn't get her anywhere other than fired. She ended the call and glared at Reid.

He had retrieved his video camera and was taping. She wanted to grab it and smash it to the ground. "No cameraman? I assumed you'd have a crew."

"I usually have a cameraman, but I had to let him go and haven't found another one yet."

The skin on her back prickled. She hated being photographed. It was going to be a long two weeks. "Stay out of my way."

She left him and walked toward the house. The crime scene was in the middle of the yard, and Jane's detectives had already roped it off with yellow tape.

A naked woman's body sagged in rough stocks, and she was covered in feathers sticking to some kind of black substance. Tarred and feathered like some kind of medieval punishment. A crudely painted sign with the word *Homewrecker* was attached to the stocks with one rusty nail.

Jane winced. Nicole Pearson. She'd always liked Nicole, who was about her own age and never seemed to know a stranger.

The vigilante again? If so, the stakes had

been raised to murder.

She approached Paul. "What do you have so far?"

"A neighbor called it in." He indicated a woman sitting with her back to them near the trees. "She showed up to go to breakfast with Nicole."

He didn't even try to hide the snark in his voice. He'd heard the news about her new job title, but nothing would make him congratulate her. She ignored his tone and approached the scene.

Robert Yong was kneeling by the body, and she stepped next to the ME. "I didn't think I'd see you again so soon."

"This one will need to be transported to Mobile too. It appears she died of asphyxiation, but it will take an autopsy to know for sure."

"Asphyxiation? Strangled?"

Yong rose and shook his head. "She might have been allergic to the feathers. She's covered in hives, and it's a common enough allergy."

"So the vigilante might not have meant to kill her."

"Maybe not. Whoever did this could have tarred and feathered her, then left her to be found and humiliated. She could have had an anaphylactic attack and been unable to breathe."

Jane looked again at the woman's face. "This is Nicole Pearson. She works at the library."

"Yes, I recognized her too."

Jane stepped over to talk to Brian. "See if you can get in the house. We need her phone and any electronics. Anything else you find that might point to who did this."

"I'll take care of it, Chief."

"I'd better talk to the witness."

Jane moved across the wet grass to the woman. "You're Gail Briscoe?" She didn't recognize the woman or the name, which was surprising in their small community, but maybe she was a newcomer. A brunette in her early thirties, the woman wore spandex capris and a sleeveless top that showed off muscular arms.

Gail's green eyes were wide. "Have they taken her yet?"

"They're putting her in the van shortly." Jane moved around so Gail didn't have to face the house and the gruesome scene in the yard. "How do you know Nicole Pearson?"

Color flooded Gail's face. "She's dead, isn't she?"

"Yes, I'm sorry to say she is. Were you

friends?"

Gail nodded. "I moved to the neighborhood last month, and we met at the library my first day in town. We made plans to go jogging before breakfast this morning, which is why I'm here."

"Any idea who might have done this? Or why?"

Gail's gaze darted away, then rested on the toes of her Adidas sneakers. "I might know the why." Her hand went to her throat. "Not to judge her or anything, but she was seeing a married guy. The sleazebag's wife is eight months pregnant, and they have a two-year-old as well." She gave an outraged huff.

"Did his wife know?"

"I don't know. I saw them together at the library once."

Jane nodded. "Do you know the man's name?"

Gail's lip curled. "Detective Paul Baker."

Jane struggled to maintain a neutral expression as her gaze went to Baker, who was helping load Nicole's body into the medical examiner's van. Baker should have told her immediately.

"Thank you. I'll check it out. Did you see anyone hanging around? Any vehicles?"

Gail shook her head. "No one was here

when I found her. I touched her and re-alized she was cold so I-I called 911 im-mediately."

"You did the right thing. Let me know if you think of anything else." Jane was itching to berate Baker, but she was all too con-scious of that blasted video camera taping. She turned her back on Reid.

Baker approached Jane.

Camera or no camera, she couldn't let this ride. "I hear you were sleeping with the victim, Paul. You should have turned over the investigation immediately."

He blanched and clenched his meaty fists. "Who told you a story like that?"

Jane knew guilt when she saw it plastered on his face. "All it would take is a strand of hair or a speck of body fluid, and your DNA will appear on her. You might as well tell me the truth. When did you see her last?"

His deep-blue eyes darted to the left and then to the right. He pressed his lips to-gether. "I didn't kill her. I was supposed to meet her at ten last night, but when I ar-rived, she wasn't there. I was about half an hour late. Our little girl wasn't feeling good."

Jane wasn't sure she believed him. "Where'd you go after that?"

"Home. My wife will verify it."

"We still don't have a time of death," she reminded him. "I'll have to speak with your wife."

"Tina took Ivy to urgent care at five." He glanced at his watch. "An hour ago. I can call and see when she'll be home."

"No, don't do that. I don't want you to tell her what's happened." She fixed him with a stern stare. "If you try to coach her, it won't go well for you, Paul."

His cheeks grew ruddy, and his jaw flexed. "I didn't do this, Jane."

"Then prove it."

He glared at her for a long moment. "Fine. Have it your way. If you stop by in a couple of hours, she should be home and have Ivy in bed."

"Until we know more, I'll have to put you on leave. I don't have a choice."

He ground his teeth together before he spun on his boots and stalked to his car. She rubbed her forehead. This all felt overwhelming. She never should have let the committee appoint her to this job.

FIVE

Reid gave Jane as much space as he could for the next two hours as she and her officers combed through the crime scene, but things would have to change. "Chief!" He jogged to catch up to her as she and her dog ducked under a water oak tree draped with moss to rush toward her SUV. She was fast moving for such a small woman.

She turned and skewered him with a glare. "You're delaying my investigation, Mr. Dixon."

"Look, Chief Hardy, I have every right to be here. You've got your orders. You might as well let me ride along with you instead of following behind."

She braced her hands on her hips. "Absolutely not."

"It's what I was assured would happen. I can place a call to the mayor if I have to. I suspect you'd rather not get reamed out your first week on the job."

He had her over a barrel, and from the expression in her eyes, she knew it too.

He didn't wait for her to acknowledge her predicament. "I did some research before I arrived and saw the accounts of a vigilante in the county. One woman was forced off the road and trapped in her car while the masked assailant cut off her hair and wrote *Liar* on her forehead in black tar. She admitted she'd falsely made an attempted rape report. I saw another incident involving a man who was boarded into his bedroom for two days. Rescuers found the word *Thief* written in black paint on the boards. He was distraught enough to admit he had stolen two hundred dollars from his employer. This looks like it could be another vigilante incident."

"It's too soon to know that."

He focused the camera on her face. "Do you think the vigilante is a local person?" He would have to find a new videographer. Getting all this on camera with someone else filming would be much more seamless.

She shrugged. "We don't know. The person strikes in the middle of the night, and witnesses have seen nothing. We had a report of an old pickup in the neighborhood when the victim who was labeled a thief was boarded into his room, but the elderly woman who reported it didn't know the make or model. Just that it was a dark color."

"Where to next?"

She gave him a long look. "This is what you wanted to talk to me about at the coffee shop, right?"

That and other things. He nodded.

"You could have told me right up front instead of pretending you wanted to get to know me."

"I was going to, but you got a call."

She tilted her head. "It made a convenient excuse, didn't it? You could have told me before we even reached the coffee shop. That would have been more honest."

He held up his hand, palm up in a placating gesture. "Look, can we call a truce? I'm just trying to do my job while you're doing yours. I'll get a videographer as quickly as I can, and things will feel much less intrusive."

Jane lifted a brow. "I doubt that. How'd you like having a video camera stuck in your face all day long?"

He gave her his best smile. "I'm used to it, and you'll be surprised how quickly you don't even notice."

He liked her spunk and the way the gold in her hazel eyes gleamed when she was animated. The opportunity to get close to her when she didn't know who he was had been the impetus behind this documentary, but he hadn't expected so much animosity from her.

He still didn't know if he'd ever tell her who he was.

Thunder rumbled and the wind freshened, bringing the scent of rain to his nose. "It's going to storm. We'd better take off. I'll follow you to your office and leave my SUV."

"Fine." Her tone said the opposite.

He slung himself behind the wheel of his SUV and headed into town. At the station he parked in the visitor lot. Jane didn't go inside but left her SUV running. The storm let loose as he dashed for the passenger seat with his camera bag, and he dripped water onto the seat when he climbed inside.

She handed him a napkin. "This won't do much good, but it's all I have. You could always go home and change."

"Not a chance." He mopped his face with the napkin, but water still trickled from his head. "You still haven't told me where we're going."

"To speak to Paul Baker's wife."

"The detective you just put on leave?"

"Yes."

She clearly didn't want to talk about it,

but that was all right. He'd heard enough to know Paul might be off this case permanently. He might even be a murder suspect.

The storm had let up by the time they reached Paul's house, and Jane's stomach rumbled. She hadn't had anything but coffee since last night, and there'd been no time for breakfast. She stood on the porch of Paul's French-style house with its arches over the windows. He'd done a lot of work to it over the years, and his wife's rose garden was in full bloom.

Parker stood at her side with his ears forward, Reid behind him. She'd told Reid he couldn't record this interview, and he hadn't protested. Had Paul kept his promise not to tell his wife she was coming? Jane didn't trust him. He was hiding something, and he surely warned his wife not to tell her anything.

The door opened, and Jane smiled at Tina. Jane tried to look reassuring when the pregnant brunette stepped into view.

Tina pressed her hand to the small of her back. "Jane. Is everything okay?" Her gaze darted past Jane's shoulder to Reid. "Is Paul okay?"

"He's fine. I needed to speak with you for a few moments. Could I come in?"

Relief lit Tina's blue eyes, and she stepped out of the way. "Of course. Have you had breakfast? I've got pancakes ready to eat." She didn't ask about Reid, probably assuming he was another officer who was out of uniform.

"I'd love some." And maybe Tina would lower her guard over a meal. She didn't seem prewarned by Paul.

"Rest," Jane told Parker. He settled on the tile floor by the door, his head relaxing on his paws.

She and Reid followed Tina through the living room and into the kitchen in the middle of the house. A stack of pancakes sat on a plate beside the stove.

Jane sniffed. "Smells fantastic."

Tina beamed. "Thank you." She served the pancakes on three plates, then gestured to the white table abutting the living room seating area. Real maple syrup and butter were already on the table.

Jane didn't want to start with the questions until after they'd eaten. She sat at the table and tried to ignore Reid's presence in the chair beside her. "Ivy is napping? Is she feeling better?"

Tina nodded. "The doctor said it was just a virus. She'll probably be down another hour." She set down her fork and fixed her eyes on Jane. "So what's up?"

Jane's appetite evaporated. How did you tell a pregnant wife her husband was a murder suspect? And that she might be as well?

She cleared her throat. "Do you know Nicole Pearson?"

Tina blew out a breath. "Is that what this is all about? Paul's affair? She isn't the first and probably won't be the last. I've come to some kind of peace about that." She shrugged. "He's a good man in a lot of other ways. Ivy adores him, and so will our son. He's a good provider, and he has ambition. We won't live in this little house forever."

A very pragmatic view that Jane recoiled from. Marriage shouldn't be like that, should it? If she ever married, she wanted to be able to trust her husband with every piece of her heart. If there was one thing that broke trust, it was lies.

"When did you find out about Paul's affair with Nicole?"

"I saw them together one day when I went to the library. I could tell by the way they were whispering." Tina bit her lip. "He told me yesterday he wanted a divorce, but I talked him out of it. I reminded him how this always blows over. We'll be fine."

64

"Is this the first time he's asked for a divorce?"

Tina nodded. "But it's the pregnancy messing with his head. He admitted that and said he'd tell her he was staying with me."

"Was he going to inform her of that last night?"

"Yes. He left here around eleven."

"What time did he get back?"

"About midnight. He wasn't gone long, and he didn't want to talk about it when he came home. I'm sure it wasn't pleasant." Tina's eyes flashed. "Women shouldn't go after other women's husbands. It's not right."

"Nicole Pearson was found dead this morning." Jane watched the bald facts register in Tina's widened eyes. "The medical examiner has yet to rule on whether it was murder, or maybe manslaughter."

Tina sat back in the kitchen chair. "And you think Paul did it? He would never hurt anyone."

"We don't have time of death yet. Did Paul leave after he got back at midnight?"

Tears tracked down Tina's face, and she sniffled. "No. We were both up and down with Ivy all night. She had a fever and threw up several times. He was here the whole time."

Which gave Tina an alibi as well. Jane struggled to keep her relief from showing. If the time of death came back before midnight, Paul wasn't out of the woods yet, but Jane hated to think about having to haul Tina down to the jail.

Tina reached for a paper napkin in the center of the table and mopped her face. "You believe me, don't you?"

"Yes, I believe you. Did anyone else know about Paul's affair with Nicole?"

Tina twisted her wedding ring around her finger. "Well, my small group at church. I asked for prayer."

"I'm going to need a list of names. This appears to be punishment for her behavior." Tina didn't need to know about the sign. Jane ripped out a sheet of paper from her notebook and slid it across the table to Tina.

"None of my friends would kill Nicole!"

"I'll still need those names."

Tina frowned but began to write on the paper. Jane rose and took Reid's plate with her own to carry them to the sink, where she rinsed and put them in the dishwasher. "Thanks for breakfast, Tina. And for being honest with me." She took the paper Tina handed her and glanced at it. Jane recognized several names, including Olivia and her father's girlfriend. She hadn't realized they went to the same church.

She stuffed the list in her shirt pocket. "If you think of anything else, here's my card."

Tina pushed it away. "I have your number in my phone. I hope you find who did this. I wanted her to stay away from my husband, but I didn't wish Nicole any harm."

Jane heard a cry from the hall. "Sounds like Ivy is awake. We'll let ourselves out." Parker rose and followed them to the door.

The heavy clouds parted, and sunshine began to heat the moisture on the streets into steam. Reid hadn't said a word inside.

He thrust his hands in the pockets of his Dockers and followed her to the SUV. "What's your take?"

"Suspicious. Until the autopsy gives time of death, Paul's still our best suspect."

"Where to next?"

"The bridal shop to see if we can ID the dress yesterday's victim was wearing."

"You had another murder? When?"

"The body was found early yesterday morning. A shrimping boat pulled up a male torso in a wedding dress. We still don't have an ID on the body. That might take a while with no fingers."

"No fingerprints to identify him?"

"Exactly."

"And why did you get the case?"

She shrugged. "The shrimper docks in Pelican Harbor and brought his boat in with the body for us to take. We've notified the Coast Guard as well, but they're letting us handle it for now unless we need them."

"You think the wedding dress can be identified?"

She buckled up and started the vehicle. "Maybe. There's a bridal resale shop in town, and the owner is a friend of mine. The coroner has probably already removed the dress from the body, and I'll see if I can get pictures of it. Maybe Fiona will recognize it or at least know the brand."

Six

By the time Jane pushed open the door to the Tropical Weddings shop, she'd received the photos of the dress. She stepped into the bright store. Fiona was a one-stop shop including flowers that spilled their scent into the shop to mingle with that of handmade soaps and candles.

She had Parker sit by the front door, then glanced at the photos to make sure there were no gruesome ones to make Fiona blanch.

Reid's long legs had kept up with her fast pace to the store, and he stood quietly looking around. "Nice place."

She darkened her phone and nodded. "Fiona's shop is well known across the Gulf Shores area. She carries designer dresses for everyone from the bride to the flower girl. Lots of wedding accessories too."

Several customers glanced up as Jane made her way toward the back where Fiona was assisting a young woman. Jane didn't recognize her, but patrons came from as far away as Pensacola and Mobile so that was no surprise.

Fiona looked up and smiled, then guided the bride-to-be into the dressing room with an armful of dresses to try on. The girl's mother went with her.

Fiona was about thirty, and the two of them had become acquaintances when Jane came into the shop about five years ago looking for a cocktail dress for a function her dad wanted her to attend. Fiona always wore her blonde hair up in a bun, and Jane had never seen her in slacks, only skirts and dresses. She was a throwback to the fifties and was as nice as June Cleaver.

Fiona slid her interested gaze from Reid to Jane. "Jane, what a nice surprise. Are you here to whisk me away for lunch with this handsome fella?" She held out her hand. "Fiona Hamilton."

"Reid Dixon."

Her smile widened. "I thought it was you. I saw your documentary on sex trafficking in Cambodia and Thailand. Heartbreaking with so much needed information."

"I always hope exposing darkness will send the rats scurrying."

Jane shifted restlessly. "I need your help

identifying a dress." She told her about the murder and watched the light fade from her blue eyes.

Fiona shuddered. "Do I have to look at the body?"

"No, I've got pictures of the dress only as well as the label. I was hoping you'd recognize it." Jane pulled up the pictures on her phone and handed it to Fiona.

Fiona flipped through the photos without speaking until she'd seen them all. She handed the phone back to Jane. "It's a Vera Wang."

"Expensive?"

"Not bad. This one is in the White line and costs about twelve hundred dollars new. It's a ball gown style with a T-back."

"Have you sold anything like it?"

Fiona's gaze flickered. "I had one just like it come up missing a couple of days ago."

Jane frowned. "I don't remember that report."

"I didn't report it. It was the only thing missing, and I honestly wondered if I'd sold it and forgotten to mark it down or something."

"You have a memory like an elephant."

Fiona smiled. "I've been a little distracted since I found out I'm going to have another baby."

A pang clenched Jane's chest. She forced a smile. "Congratulations! When are you due?"

"Around Thanksgiving. I'm still feeling a little green."

The bride-to-be exited the dressing room in a frothy white confection of a dress, and Fiona glanced that way.

"Go ahead. We're done here," Jane said. "I might want to look at any surveillance video you have in the store."

"Help yourself. The monitor is in the back."

Jane moved with Reid toward the back of the store. "We know the brand, but I'll bet it was the stolen dress, so it doesn't help identify the body."

He was staring at her with an odd, contemplative expression.

"What?" she asked.

He blinked and shook his head. "Nothing. I don't think I've ever been in a wedding shop before."

"You've never been married?" Such a stupid question was none of her business, but she couldn't take it back.

"I didn't say that. My marriage was a little outside the norm."

Though she didn't know what he meant, she wasn't about to ask. She opened the door to the back room and led Reid to Fiona's small office. A pile of wedding dresses lay across the only armchair in the room, and Jane had to move dresses on the desk to get to the monitor. She fiddled with the controls and scanned through the last few days of video.

Reid took a spot in the corner of the room where he could video her at the monitor, but she barely noticed as she fast-forwarded through the frames. She recognized some of the customers, including Brian with one of his many girlfriends.

She wrinkled her nose. He was probably buying one of his women some lingerie. Sure enough, the woman carried an armful of lace teddies into the dressing room. Paul Baker made an appearance too. He was with Nicole Pearson. Jane slowed the flickering video and watched them a moment.

"You've got something?"

"Nothing I didn't already know."

Nicole tried on several cocktail dresses, so maybe Paul was helping her choose something for a cruise. The background changed to nighttime, and she slowed the frames even more. A bulky figure moved in front of one of the small lights along the floor, but she couldn't make out any detail. A flash of white came, and the recording went to snow.

"Malfunction or something more sinister?"

"I don't know." She copied the file and emailed it to herself. "I'll have the forensic team examine it."

Reid followed her back into the showroom and to the front door. She patted her thigh so Parker joined her before she pushed open the door and stepped out into the rain. "Might as well grab lunch while we're here, and maybe the weather will clear."

And it was safer to talk about food than about relationships. She didn't want to get to know this infuriating man anyway.

The aroma of tomato sauce and spices hit Reid in the face when he slipped in the door of Pelican Pizza behind Jane as the skies let loose in a deluge. He shook the water from his head. "Whew, that's a downpour of biblical proportions."

Jane's hazel eyes flicked over his wet face. "Need another napkin?"

"I'll dry."

She didn't reply and spent a few moments settling Parker down by the front window out of the way of other patrons.

Reid went to the counter, and she joined him. "What kind of pizza you want?" he asked.

"I can buy my own."

"You can buy next time. I think I'll try a seafood one."

"It's fabulous. The shrimp, lobster, and crab are all local. I'll have the same." Jane grabbed a paper towel from the counter and wiped her wet face. "I'll have sweet tea too."

"Already have it for you, Jane." The man behind the counter handed a glass to her. In his thirties, he had sleepy brown eyes and an easy smile. "I hear congratulations are in order, Chief Hardy. Well done."

"Thank you, Troy. I'm still trying to absorb it."

"How's your dad doing? I haven't seen him for a few days."

Jane smiled. "I haven't seen him in a few days myself. He's probably busy enjoying retirement."

"Your dad's a good man. I'll never forget how he helped me get this business started."

"He was glad to do it." Jane wandered over by the big windows and pulled out a chair at a table for two.

The man handed Reid his tea. "I'll bring the pizza to your table."

Reid thanked him and joined Jane. "Your dad helped him start his restaurant?"

She nodded. "Troy's dad went to prison for murdering one of Dad's deputies, and his mother and sister were killed in a car accident when Troy was in college. Troy and his younger brother were left without a family. This place came up for sale while Troy was assistant manager. Dad spotted him the down payment, and Troy paid it back within a year.

"And my best detective, Brian, is his brother. Troy helped put Brian through school, then asked Dad to give him a job. Best decision Dad ever made. Brian's womanizing makes me want to pull out my hair, but he's a terrific detective. He can sniff out clues like Parker sniffs out squirrels."

"Your dad's retirement was a surprise?" He kept his tone light so he didn't give away his interest.

"It came out of the blue a month ago. He's so larger than life I forget he's getting older."

Her gaze drifted to a group of four teenage boys at the next table. The longing and fascination on her face caught Reid's attention.

"You have any kids?" Her lashes swept down, but not before he saw a flash of pain in her eyes. "Sorry, that was probably too personal."

"It's fine. No kids, though I love them."

He pulled up his video camera and trained

it on her face. "So what's next in your investigation?"

To her credit she didn't frown or grimace. "We wait for the autopsy report. Brian will get it and forward it to me. We take what we can find out from it and begin to interview people who might be able to help us identify the victim."

"You don't think the autopsy will give you the victim's identity?"

The camera loved her angular bone structure and the long column of neck. She seemed to relax in spite of his videotaping her every movement.

"We could get lucky and catch a hit on DNA, but that doesn't happen often. It usually takes a lot of hard grunt work, talking to people and combing through missing person's reports to discover the victim's identity."

"How long have you been in law enforcement?"

"It feels like all my life." She looked up and smiled as a boy barely out of his teens brought their pizza. "I inherited my dad's love of justice and graduated with a degree in criminal justice from the University of Alabama. It was near enough that I could come home on the weekends sometimes."

"Sounds like you and your dad are close."

She wrinkled her nose. "Not as close as you might think. Not for lack of trying on my part, though. Dad is . . . difficult to get to know."

"I think we have that in common."

Her gaze flicked up to lock with his. "You had a difficult father?"

"A lot of people respected him, almost worshipped him. He expected more out of me than a kid could give, and in the end he failed a lot of people, including me. I constantly feel like I need to atone for what he did." Reid shook his head. "I've often wondered if there's something to that whole biblical thing of sins of the father affecting my life."

He'd never voiced that fear to anyone, but Jane was easy to talk to.

"My friend Olivia would say that's crazy talk, that God doesn't work that way."

"And what do you say about it?"

"I'm not the person to ask." Her voice held a warning to back off.

The aroma of seafood made his mouth water, and he realized he was famished. The crust was thin and crisp, just the way he liked it, and held exactly the right amount of cheese. Instead of tomato sauce, the pizza's white sauce was a perfect complement to the seafood.

"Best pizza ever," he mumbled past a mouthful.

She nodded. "It's my favorite."

They ate in companionable silence for several minutes. He wiped his mouth and fingers, then picked up his camera again. "Why'd you decide to try for the chief's job? There aren't many female police chiefs. Did that play a part?"

"Not much actually. I have a strong sense of justice, and I hate to see crimes hurt good people."

"How did that dedication toward justice start?" At her pensive expression, his heart began to thump. Would she tell him about her earlier life?

She took a sip of her tea and peered at him over the top of her glass. "Did you ever see the movie *Armageddon*?"

"Sure. Great movie. Bruce Willis is one of my favorite actors."

"That was the first movie I ever saw. It sounds stupid, but it made me want to be someone who steps forward to help when all seems lost. All those guys who were willing to go up to space and try to destroy the asteroid were not the hero type. Most of them had majorly messed up their lives. But that one act of courage changed the course of history." She stared down at her glass.

"How old were you when you saw it?"

"Nearly fifteen."

His pulse throbbed in his throat. "No Disney princess movies before that?"

He could see the wheels turning behind those beautiful eyes, but she wasn't going to tell him anything more. As far as he could tell, she didn't talk about her past. He'd hoped she'd open up about it, but it was locked inside like an iron vault.

He clicked off his camera. "I won't use any of that, but I think it's great to want to be a hero. Did you have major mess-ups you wanted to atone for?"

She looked up, and her hazel eyes went wide. "Very perceptive. I'll admit I was recovering from some trauma when we came here. I've felt like a major failure for a long time. I couldn't even —"

When she stopped, he leaned forward. "You couldn't what?"

"Nothing. It's not important. I just want to help people. That sounds corny, I know."

"It actually sounds great." Aware his stare was too intense, he reached for his glass of tea. "So you don't want political power or anything like that?"

She grimaced. "I hate politics. That's the worst part of this job — I have to play by the mayor's rules, which is why you're here.

I can't stand insincerity, and the thought of putting myself out there like that gives me hives. But if I want this job, I have to do it. And I do want it."

"What do you think about being a role model for young girls who want to go into law enforcement?"

"I don't think it's a gender thing at all. It's more a heart thing. All of us need to do what we feel called to do."

"And this is your calling? You could have continued to be a detective and brought law breakers to justice."

"As chief I have the ability to oversee many more projects and make sure things are done right."

"Your dad didn't do things right?"

Her cheeks reddened. "My dad was a great chief, and he instilled that sense of justice in me. I want to continue his great work here."

"So lots of reasons to take the job of chief of police for you."

"Yes, I guess there are. I never really thought about it in such detail. It seemed something I was supposed to do."

"God-given task maybe?"

She shook her head. "I don't know that God played any role in it. He doesn't seem to listen to me."

"You don't believe God plays a role in human events?"

She picked up a napkin and began to tear it into strips. "Let's just say he's never been there when I needed him." She tossed down the napkin. "How'd we get on a topic like that? I think I'll go back to my office and see if the autopsy results have come through."

Reid rose. "I've got some errands to run, so think I'll leave you to it. Let me know if you hear anything interesting."

SEVEN

What was he doing outside her dad's property? After Reid had left Jane in her office, he hadn't been able to resist the impulse to come out here. He drove up to the compound's big iron gate. It was a beautiful afternoon with birds chirping and puffy clouds floating across a blue sky. There was an access-control system at the gate, so he rolled down his window and pressed the speaker button.

"Who are you and what do you want?" the disembodied male voice demanded.

"Um, I'm Reid Dixon, a journalist. I'm preparing a piece on your daughter and would like to speak to you."

The man didn't answer, but the gate swung open, and Reid drove through two more gates without codes before he was able to park in front of the house. Charles was clearly very security conscious. Nice place, though. Moss added a delicate touch to the water oak trees lining the drive, and more oaks interspersed with pine and cedar trees appeared in the forest to his left.

He still wasn't sure what he was going to say.

The house was a large two-story four-square built in the 1920s from the look of it. A new green metal roof topped the brick home. The porch looked like it had been built with the new composite or plastic that was supposed to last forever. Charles had spent some money out here on his prepper compound. The fever to be prepared had driven him all these years.

Reid shut off the engine and waited to see if Charles would come to the door with a gun. A burly man Reid recognized instantly stepped through the screen door. His thick, shaggy white hair touched the tops of his ears. He had a bushy white mustache and eyebrows, and he wore overalls without a shirt. Not exactly the normal cop image.

Charles shaded his eyes from the sun and put his hand on the butt of a gun at his waist. "Step out where I can see you."

Once a lawman, always a lawman. Reid pushed open his door and got out. "Thanks for letting me in, sir. I'm working on a documentary about small-town police departments and have spent most of the day with your daughter. I wondered if I might ask you a few questions."

Charles moved his hand away from his gun and grunted. "I guess it's all right. I've worked for a small police force for a lot of years. Have a seat on the porch."

Reid retrieved his video camera and brought it with him. The porch held several rockers with side tables and a swing. Charles chose a rocker, so Reid settled in the one beside him.

"Mind if I video our interview?"

Charles shrugged. "Fine. What do you want to know?"

Reid secured his camera on the tripod. "What are some of the challenges of working in a small force?"

"Biggest thing is there's no real downtime. When you're one of five officers, every break-in, every minor infraction results in a call to home after hours. There's never really any off-time. And when you know everyone, it can be hard if you need to arrest your friends and neighbors. We often don't have the budget for supplies to protect us. I've been lobbying for patrol cameras for a long time. We just got some portable mics, which is a step in the right direction, but there are so many things we don't have that would make officers safer."

"Your retirement came suddenly. Got tired of all of that?"

"I'm getting older. It's time to spend my time fishing and enjoying life." Charles narrowed his eyes a moment, then he looked away.

Could a medical diagnosis have pushed him this direction? Even Jane seemed surprised he'd retired so abruptly.

Charles leaned back and propped a boot on the porch railing. "I think I've seen some of your documentaries. The one on cults was interesting. You seemed to ask all the right questions."

Reid's pulse stuttered. "I had some good input." He gestured toward the big barn in the distance. "I heard you're one of those preppers. People say you have enough supplies to feed the town if disaster strikes."

"Maybe not the whole town, but I can take care of my family."

"You just have your daughter?"

Charles nodded. "For now. I keep thinking she might marry one day and give me grandkids, but the girl doesn't even date. Her early life —" He stopped and looked toward the barn.

"Her early life?" Maybe now was the time to reveal more about the past and why he was really here.

"Not important." Charles rose. "Getting on toward dinnertime. I hope you got enough for your documentary."

Reid lowered his camera. "It was very helpful. Thank you." Now wasn't the time.

Charles crossed massive arms over his chest. "Don't forget to shut the gate when you leave."

"I will." No more small talk. Charles had had enough of a stranger prying into his life.

At least he hadn't pressed Reid on his knowledge of cults.

To keep from worrying about Olivia, Jane spent most of the afternoon going through paperwork and organizing different investigations. She'd sent the video from the wedding shop to forensics at the state police department, but it would be a while before they could tell her if it contained any evidence.

What had gotten into her to reveal so much to Reid? She wished she could take it back, and when he left after lunch, she'd been glad to see the back of him.

Her office began to take shape with Post-it Notes stuck onto a bulletin board outlining the two crimes she was investigating. Her dad might have a heart attack if he knew she'd littered his perfectly organized space. When quitting time rolled around, it looked transformed. Her final action was to put a picture on her desk. It was of her mother and dad standing on either side of her when she was about three. They were standing on the porch of their cabin and smiling. They seemed happy.

Jane touched her mother's face. Where was she now? Dead like her father claimed? She'd tried to find her mom over the years, but she had no luck. Her dad told her to leave it alone, but it was like a splinter festering under her fingernail — something that needed to be tended to and dug out.

Someday she would find out.

It had been a long day, and she was about to head for home when her phone rang with a call from the Alabama Department of Forensic Sciences. Finally.

"This is Chief Hardy."

"We were able to slip in your torso autopsy this afternoon, Chief. I have those results for you and your detective, but I thought I'd call you directly. We got an immediate hit when we did rapid DNA. I emailed the results over to you."

A DNA hit? She had been sure they wouldn't be able to identify him. "I really appreciate you getting to him. Could you tell how he died?"

"We can't make a definitive ruling without the head, but I'm willing to say I think he was beaten to death with what I think was a golf club from the cuts and contusions."

"The dismemberment was postmortem?"

"Yes."

Rather than continue to question the tech, she thanked her and ended the call.

City hall was quiet at seven o'clock at night. Most employees had left by five, and though there were only four other officers on the police force, one or two might be hanging around listening to Dispatch. She hoped for a quiet night.

Jane scanned through her inbox and found the autopsy report. Her victim was Gary Dawson. He'd recently been arrested for skimming money and equipment from his employer. She'd look up the arrest documents when she got back from talking to the widow. She ran a search for his address and found it in Mobile, then went back to the autopsy.

Two details stopped her short. A Kennedy half-dollar had been found tucked in the front of the gown. What was that all about? And a note had been pinned inside the gown that read *Vow Breaker.* Her pulse quickened. The vigilante? Since this Dawson was accused of being a vow breaker, maybe the wedding dress implied he'd broken his wedding vows. Adultery maybe?

Detective Boulter's large frame filled the open doorway, and he entered her office. "Hey, Boss, you're here late. We got the autopsy results."

"They called me. I was just looking at them. We need to notify the widow and see what she knows about this." She saw Brian's gaze sharpen, but he said nothing, even though he knew that would be his job. None of them liked that tough task. "Did you see the notation about what was found tucked in the front of the gown and the note?"

Brian nodded, went to the coffeepot, and began to make coffee. "Weird, huh? Maybe the old geezer, Alfie, wasn't as far off as I thought. That body might have been planted here on purpose like he said. I'd assumed the guy's head and limbs were removed to make it hard to identify him, but anyone with even a little bit of forensic knowledge would know the DNA database would pull him up immediately since he'd been arrested. Maybe the killer just wanted to slow down identification a bit."

"Could be. I checked out the dress." She told Brian about the make and the theft of a dress like it. "I saw you there with a lady friend looking at lingerie."

Brian grinned. "The women love that store."

The coffee finished brewing, and she went around her desk to get a cup for Brian and her. "What are you doing here so late? Your date stand you up?"

"Yeah, can you believe it? Tourists." He shook his head. "Like the real Dwayne Johnson was going to walk up to a strange woman on the beach and ask her out."

"You play up that resemblance too much."

He ran his big hand over his head. "At least I've got hair."

She smiled and handed him his coffee. "There's that."

He'd asked her out a few times when he first came to work for the department, but her refusals had finally sent him searching in another direction. She hadn't been ready for a relationship when she was twenty-five, but now that she was nearly thirty, she was beginning to notice handsome men. And Brian was a fine specimen. But dangerous. Very dangerous. She doubted one woman would ever be enough for him.

She gulped down her coffee and turned for the door. "Let's go grab a sandwich, then head for our vic's house."

"You're tagging along?"

"Hearing it from a woman might be easier for the widow. And I'm sure you'd rather not do it alone."

He flashed her a smile, but she wasn't susceptible to him. An image of Reid glowering at her popped into her mind, and she frowned. Where had that come from?

She grabbed her bag as her phone rang, and she answered a call from the mayor. "Hi, Lisa."

"How's it going with Reid?" Lisa's voice was overly chipper.

"Awkward. A civilian shouldn't be tagging along on a murder investigation."

"You have an ID on the torso yet?"

"We do." Jane told her what the autopsy revealed. "I'm heading there now."

"With Reid, I hope?"

Jane grimaced. "He left hours ago."

"Go grab him. He'll get to see how quickly you've started to nail down what happened. This is great press, Jane, and I don't want it to slip away from us."

Jane sighed. "Fine, I'll call him." She ended the call and told Brian about the mayor's request. "I'll text him after we eat. If we don't give him much time, maybe he'll bow out."

EIGHT

She glanced at his boy's profile from the front seat. Nice kid. Will seemed respectful and well behaved. Jane guessed him to be around sixteen, and she suspected Reid looked exactly like him at that age.

She parked in front of a neat white house and glanced at Brian. "Ready for this?"

"As ready as anyone ever is for something like this."

Reid spoke from the backseat. "Wait a minute. This is Gary Dawson's house."

Her chest squeezing, she stared at Reid. "You know him?"

"He was the videographer I fired. He was stealing from me to pay gambling debts, and I had to turn him in to the police."

Great, just great. She had a possible suspect in the vehicle with her. "You can't be here." That should be obvious even to him. She turned the vehicle back on and flipped

93

the blower to high. "I'll leave the air on for you."

He held her gaze in the rearview mirror. "I know his wife well. It might help if she has a familiar face when she gets the news."

"You're automatically a suspect. I need you to stay in the vehicle." He opened his mouth to object, but she turned to Brian. "Want me to take the lead?"

Brian grimaced. "That would be my preference."

Reid reached for his door handle. "I want to go."

She whirled around. "If you make one move out of this vehicle, I'm arresting you and hauling you in for questioning."

His furious eyes glared back at her, but he held up his hands. "Fine. I haven't seen Gary since he was arrested, though."

She didn't answer and got out. She let Parker out the back and walked to the front door of the ranch home with the entourage behind her. The dog would be on his guard against a weapon being pulled, and Jane had no idea if the wife might be involved in this murder.

The yard was neat and nicely landscaped, but the navy shutters could use a fresh coat of paint, as could the front door. She pressed the doorbell and listened for the

94

sound of footsteps past the faint sound of a child calling for his mom from inside.

The door finally cracked open a bit to reveal a young woman. At least the half of the face Jane saw looked female with long blonde hair and blue eyes.

Jane held up her badge. "Pelican Harbor chief of police, ma'am. Could I speak with you a moment?" The door opened more fully, and the child's cry grew louder. "You need to tend to your little one? I can wait."

With the door fully opened, the reason for the woman's caution was in plain view — she sported a shiner that had nearly swollen her lid shut. Jane looked her over but didn't say anything.

The woman hesitated and glanced at Brian, who was behind Jane. "Come on in. He doesn't want to go to bed. I'll check on him." She left the door open and scurried to another room.

Jane stepped inside and followed her into a neat and tidy living room furnished with a brown tweed sofa and a turquoise armchair. Brian and Parker followed, and she motioned for the dog to lay down by her feet.

The woman went down the hall, and the child's calls subsided. She was gone for about five minutes before Jane heard the faint click of a door latch, and Mrs. Dawson came back down the hall.

"He's looking at a book," she said.

"How old?"

"Four. What'd you say your name was?"

"I didn't. It's Chief Hardy with Pelican Harbor. And you are?" Jane continued to stand.

"Fanny Dawson."

"Just you and your little boy live here?"

"And my husband, Gary." She reached up to touch her swollen eye.

Jane's palms curled into fists. "When did you see him last?"

"Um, Sunday?"

Three days ago. "You didn't see him on Monday at all?"

"I tried to call his phone, but it went straight to voice mail. H-He's been having some problems."

"He gave you that black eye?" Brian asked.

Fanny nodded. "But it wasn't his fault. I provoked him."

Was Gary's abuse the cause of his death? "No man should hit a woman. He vowed to love and cherish you, not beat you." Jane held up her hand when Fanny started to protest. "His abuse is not the issue here. Does your husband have any enemies?"

Fanny's lips trembled. "Not that I know of. Why would you ask something like that?

He's okay, isn't he?"

"I'm afraid not, Fanny. His body was found just off Pelican Harbor early yesterday morning."

Fanny's blue eyes widened and flooded with tears. "It can't be Gary. I want to see him."

The last thing Jane wanted to tell her was the body's condition. Maybe she wouldn't have to. At least not yet. "We made a positive ID with his DNA. He was recently arrested and was in the database. I'm afraid there's no mistake."

"H-He was murdered? You asked about enemies. He must have been murdered. Shot, stabbed?"

Jane would have to tell her. "The autopsy revealed he'd been beaten, and I'm afraid his head and limbs are missing."

Fanny's face blanched, and her eyelids fluttered as she sank back against the chair. Jane leapt toward her and pushed her head down between her legs. "Take deep breaths. You'll be okay."

Fanny obeyed, and Jane patted Fanny's back when she raised her head. "You have any family in the area?"

"My mother is in Washington, DC, right now, and my brother is a Blue Angel over in

Pensacola. My dad died a couple of years ago."

"Is there someone we could call for you?" Jane asked.

Fanny shook her head. "I'll call my mom. She'll be out of town a couple of days, but she'll want to know about this."

"Can I get your phone number in case I need to speak with you again? And I'm afraid we will need your computer and to search paperwork here your husband might have left. I can get a search warrant, but I'd rather take it now if you'll give permission."

Could this slight woman have killed her husband? It didn't seem likely, but Jane tried never to make snap decisions. She hesitated. "Did your husband have a gambling problem?"

Quiet tears tracked down Fanny's face. "That's been most of our problems."

"Did very many people know about it?"

"Some. And take whatever paperwork you need. I want the killer found."

Jane nodded to Brian, who headed down the hall in search of the office.

Fanny jotted down her phone number on a notepad she snatched from the coffee table. "And as far as people who knew — I'm part of a cooking club, and I think I talked about it with my friends a few times."

"Could you give me a list of those people as well?"

"They wouldn't have hurt Gary."

"I'm sure they wouldn't, but we need to perform a complete investigation."

Fanny nodded and wrote down some names, then passed the paper to Jane.

"What about Reid Dixon? We know he pressed charges against Gary for stealing from him. Have there been words or any kind of fight between the two of them?"

Fanny shook her head. "Reid sent me money — two thousand dollars — after Gary was arrested. He didn't want to turn him in, but he had no choice. Gary took a lot of money and expensive equipment from the company, but Reid is a good man and wanted to help me and my son. I'm sure he had nothing to do with this."

Jane wasn't so sure. "Do you know what your husband did with the money he stole?"

"I assume he used it on his gambling debts, but I don't think it was enough." Fanny reached for a tissue from the box on the end table and mopped her eyes.

"Do you have the name of his bookie?"

"No. I've never met any of his gambling friends. I'm sorry."

"Can you think of any reason your husband would have a Kennedy half-dollar on his person?"

Fanny clutched her hands together in her lap. "No, he didn't collect coins or anything."

"A note on his clothing read *Vow Breaker*. Did you kill your husband, Fanny?"

"Of course not! I loved him." Fanny's eyes flooded with tears again. "I want to call my mom. Can you go now, please? I need to be alone."

Jane nodded. "I'm so sorry for your loss, Fanny. We'll be in touch."

The holding room smelled of fear and cigarettes. Reid stared at the locked door. He should have called an attorney, but he had nothing to hide. Wasn't that always the way someone got railroaded, though?

The door opened, and Jane stepped inside accompanied by Detective Boulter. Both were somber.

Jane took the lead. "Mr. Dixon?"

His gut clenched when his gaze met her direct hazel eyes. "What happened to calling me Reid?" When she didn't answer, he wanted to strangle her. "Where's my boy?"

Jane sat in a chair across the table from him. "Having a Coke and a bag of chips in the break room." Jane pulled out a notepad. "You came here from New Orleans? What brought you to the area?"

"I already told you."

"I'd like to hear it again."

He pressed his lips together, then sighed. "The documentary I'm doing on you. My son and I got here a few days ago." *Careful. Never offer information.*

"I see," Boulter said. "With your job, you have the flexibility to live wherever you like?" A scent of cinnamon wafted from his mouth as he worked a piece of gum.

"What's that got to do with the murdered person?"

Jane lifted a brow. "Please answer Detective Boulter's question."

Reid pressed his lips together again and shrugged. "I travel all the time for my work. As long as I have an airport within driving distance, it's good. I can fly in and out of Mobile. I do this kind of thing all the time."

Jane fixed him with a hard stare. "Tell us about your relationship with Gary Dawson."

He didn't care for being on this side of an investigation. "He worked for me for ten years. He was basically my right-hand man, not just my videographer. I thought the world of him and trusted him. I was shocked when I realized he'd stolen equipment and money from me."

"He had access to your financials?" Jane

101

sounded skeptical.

Reid didn't blame her. "Looking back, it was stupid to have him drop off bank deposits and things like that, but like I said, I trusted him."

Jane's expression softened slightly. "How'd you discover the theft?"

"I decided to buy a new SUV and noticed there wasn't as much money in savings as there should be. I sent the files and receipts over to my accountant, and he found the discrepancy. I knew it only could have been Gary and confronted him about it. He didn't even try to lie. He promised to pay it back if I gave him some time, and I was going to do that, but then I discovered the missing equipment too. He admitted to a gambling problem and had the nerve to ask me for a hundred-thousand-dollar loan to pay his bookie before he got hurt."

"He was in trouble?"

Reid didn't like thinking about the fear in Gary's eyes. "He was panicked about it. I thought he'd be safe in jail, which was one of the reasons I turned him in. Why was he out?"

"He was released on bail. We identified the victim with fast DNA and uploaded it to the crimes database. Dawson's profile was in there because of his arrest for theft, and we got an immediate hit."

Reid felt completely disoriented by the continued suspicion in her face. "You think I had something to do with it?"

"You turned him in. I would assume there was animosity."

"There wasn't. I wanted him to get help for his addiction, and I didn't want to enable him."

"When was the last time you saw Mr. Dawson?"

"I called him to come over to the house and confronted him two weeks ago." The scene that day still bothered him. He'd trusted Gary, and he'd been floored when he found the source of the theft.

"Had you already moved to Pelican Harbor?"

"No, though I'd rented the house. We moved a couple of days later."

"I see," Boulter said. "Did you speak with his wife after he was arrested?"

"No." He hadn't known what to say to her, but he'd made sure he sent her a check for two thousand dollars in only her name. He'd hoped it would tide her over a bit.

Jane glanced at her notebook. "Dawson never contacted you after he made bail? Maybe tried to get you to drop the charges?"

"He tried to call me, but I didn't answer.

I had nothing to say."

"So you *were* angry," the detective said.

"Not angry. Disappointed, hurt, yes. But I know myself, and I would have been tempted to let him off. That wasn't the right thing to do, and I knew it. He'd been stealing from me for over two years, and he was in even deeper. He needed help."

"When did you find out he had a gambling problem?" Jane asked. "Did you know before he stole from you?"

"My IP guy found gambling sites in his work computer's search history. And of course he admitted it then too. When did he die?"

"The autopsy couldn't pinpoint it exactly because he'd been in the water, but nearest estimates put him murdered on Sunday. What were you doing on Sunday?"

Relief flooded through him. "I was in a phone meeting with my producer after church for about an hour, then Will and I went to Mobile to do some sightseeing. We took in the battleship and went to the carnival museum. If you check cameras, I'm sure you'll see us there."

Jane jotted down something else, then she and Detective Boulter rose. "What about your wife, Mr. Dixon?"

"Ex-wife." His hands curled into fists.

"What about her?"

"She's been missing for eight years. There's quite a detailed investigation in her disappearance. Did you kill her?"

He leapt to his feet. "I had nothing to do with her disappearance, and if you looked into it at all, you would see I hired an investigator three different times to try to locate her."

If he had to, he could tell them Lauren had resurfaced, but it might get back to Will, and he wanted to avoid that unless he had no choice.

Her expression remained skeptical. "I think we're done for now. You can collect Will from the break room. Until your alibis check out, I don't want you continuing with this documentary."

He knew better than to object. She was right. He followed her through the door and into the hallway. She directed him toward the break room, then walked the opposite way.

At least they hadn't questioned Will. He wasn't about to tell them that his son and Gary had been fishing buddies. Who knew what they'd make of that.

NINE

There she was, smiling with her arms open. Jane ran through the wildflowers toward her mother, who held an infant in her arms. The tiny violets enveloped her in their sweet scent. Joy sang through Jane's veins, a high-pitched strum that awakened every cell in her body. She couldn't wait to bury her face in her mother's neck and inhale the faint aroma of patchouli in her hair. Mom was in charge of worship, and she lit the incense in the sanctuary every night. That aroma would tell Jane she was safe in her mother's arms, right where she belonged. She couldn't wait to hold her son again, to smell the sweet scent of his newness and to touch his petal-soft skin.

She reached her mother and threw herself into an embrace. Now that she had Mom in her arms, she was never letting her go. Nothing could pull them apart now.

The spicy scent of patchouli made her smile, and she could feel her mother's hair tangling with her own. They were two peas in a pod, as alike as one blade of grass to another. They were meant to be together, to walk arm in arm through life. When her mother spoke, Jane was sure she could finish a sentence for her. It was supposed to be that way.

Her baby. She wanted her baby. She pulled back and reached for him even as he waved a wrinkled little hand toward her face. An acrid odor began to drift Jane's way.

"Mom, my baby!" She tried to take him from her mother, but Mom shook her head and stepped back.

A foul odor pushed away the scent of incense, and Jane saw flames dancing in the grass behind her mother. She tried to take her son again, but Mother turned and started to walk away.

"Mom, we have to run!" Jane tried to chase after her, but her feet were stuck in the grass as if encased in concrete. The fire raged into a suddenly dark sky, and fiery flickers raced toward where Jane stood rooted to the ground.

Her mother and baby disappeared into the billowing black smoke as the flames touched Jane's feet and burned the hem of her long dress. The dress flared as the fire raced up the length of the garment, and her hair caught fire.

"Mom! My baby!"

Jane opened her eyes at a worried huff and found Parker's cold nose pressed against her wet cheek. Her eyes burned, and a sob choked her throat. Still struggling to breathe, she sat up and swung her legs to the floor.

Would these nightmares ever end?

As usual she reached for the tattered and faded Polaroid picture of her tiny son. Tears blurred her vision, but she blinked them back and stared at his sweet face. If only she could go back fifteen years and hold on to him. Maybe he wouldn't have died if she'd been holding him.

She swallowed down the sobs still trying to build in her chest and grabbed her e-book reader. Pressing it to her chest, she unlocked the patio door and stepped out onto the balcony overlooking Oyster Street, with Parker close behind. At two in the morning the street was quiet except for the jazz music from a late-closing bar down the street. A few lights spilled illumination along the brick sidewalks and gleamed in the banks of shop windows.

Heading back inside, she took her sketch pad and drew as much of her mother's face as she could remember. After all these years, the memories of her were vague except during a vivid dream like this. Why was this all coming back in such a powerful way after all these years? Was she losing her mind?

Talking to her dad about it had always been forbidden, but she was tempted to try again. All he could do was clam up. Surely one of these days he would talk about it, wouldn't he?

Especially if he knew it was tearing her apart inside.

A sound from outside caught her attention, and for a split second she thought it was a car backfiring until the glass in her window shattered. Parker began to bark, and Jane leapt to her feet on the other side of the bed, then reached for her gun. "Parker, quiet."

Crouching down so she couldn't be seen, she scurried to the unbroken window and peeked out into the semi-dark street. No vehicles or people stood outside.

She grabbed her slippers before going around to examine the damage. Broken glass littered her hardwood floor, and she saw a paper taped to the unbroken mouth of the bottle that had come through her window. She went to the kitchen and grabbed a plastic grocery bag, then inserted her hand in it and went back to pick up the broken bottle. Gingerly she carried it into the kitchen and turned on the light to read the paper that was attached.

Retribution is sweet. Get ready.

Jane lowered the window of her patrol car and let in the scent of early morning dew. She punched in the code at the entrance to her father's compound, and the big iron gates moved more slowly than she would have liked. From the backseat Parker pushed his nose past her left ear to pant out the window. A low whine built in his throat. He loved the freedom of chasing squirrels at her dad's.

She was tired after her nightmare and the broken window. Brian had come as soon as she called and had retrieved the evidence, but she doubted they'd lift any prints or DNA from the glass. Brian had seemed worried, but she shrugged and hurried him off so she could go back to bed.

A police officer never knew when someone they'd arrested got his knickers in a knot. It came with the territory.

Had Dad heard about her appointment to

his position? If he had, he hadn't texted or called to congratulate her. Maybe it bothered him. And had he gotten any whiff of the events of the last two days?

She drove through the open gate toward her dad's residence and left it open since she wouldn't be here long. The roofs of the barns and house loomed in the distance, about a quarter of a mile from the road. There would be a barbed-wire fence and gate, then the privacy fence and its wooden door to get past before she would be able to park in front of her dad's house.

When she stopped her SUV, she saw her dad on the front porch. In his sixties, he was as fit as a Marine thanks to his state-of-the-art exercise equipment in one of the outbuildings. She opened her door and got out into the shade of the shagbark hickory trees lining the drive, then opened the back door to let Parker out. He ran off to sniff in the grass, then disappeared into the vegetation.

Dressed in camouflage, Dad lifted a hand in greeting to her as he set his rifle against the porch railing. "Jane."

She walked up the steps and hugged him, which was like hugging one of the porch columns. He always held himself erect and barely brushed his cheek against hers.

"Good morning, Dad. How's retirement going?" She'd tell him about the murders later.

He stepped back and lifted a bushy white eyebrow. "You're the new police chief."

"Only Victor Armstrong voted against me." She touched the badge on her uniform. "I hope I can do a good job like you have all these years."

Her dad looked as pleased as his granite face ever allowed. "Armstrong always hated me. I knew he'd never vote for my daughter to take my place. He was rooting for Paul Baker. The two of them are as thick as molasses."

The front door opened, and her father's longtime girlfriend, Elizabeth Spicer, exited with a searching glance Jane's way. She had a newspaper in her hand.

She tucked a blonde strand of her bobbed hair behind an ear. "Jane, what a nice surprise." She wore a T-shirt and jeans with a bit of mud on the knees, so she must have been gardening this morning. "I should have heard you sooner, but I was so mad about that trial."

Jane didn't want to ask which one. Elizabeth took what she called miscarriages of justice very personally after living with a police chief for so long. "Got any coffee?"

Dad merely inclined his head and moved

toward the door.

Elizabeth had always made Jane feel welcome, and she had never understood why her dad hadn't divorced Mom so he could marry her. But Elizabeth had never pushed him. They'd lived together for at least ten years, and Elizabeth seemed content enough with the state of the relationship. Maybe it was because of her horrendous first marriage to a man who used his fists against her.

Jane nodded. "I'd take some coffee if you've got it."

"Of course, come on in. I have warm cinnamon rolls too." Elizabeth hesitated. "Did you get the appointment?"

Jane followed her and Dad inside and told her about the vote. Did Dad ever think about Mom these days? She wished she could forget as easily.

The interior enveloped her with a shady welcome from the shimmering heat outside. The home reflected Elizabeth's taste and not Dad's. When Jane had lived here, the place hadn't been updated in decades. Now the rooms opened up into a space that flowed. Comfortable white furniture contrasted with hickory floors and gray walls. The space was both welcoming and soothing, but Jane seldom came or stayed long.

The more independent she'd gotten, the harder it was to be in her dad's demanding presence. He required perfection, and though she'd tried, she never felt she measured up to his expectations. Leaving here for college had brought as much relief as the air-conditioning now blowing out the vents.

Jane walked into the kitchen after Elizabeth and poured herself a cup of coffee as Elizabeth put a warm cinnamon roll onto a plate.

Her dad perched on a bar stool at the marble island. "Heard about the break-in at the grocery store. Any leads?"

She shook her head. "Nothing yet. We're checking video links."

Talking about her cases was the one place she connected with her dad. Before Mount Sinai, her dad had worked for the Mobile police department, and even at the compound, he'd been in charge of security as well as the treasurer. After they left, he'd worked here in Pelican Harbor until his retirement. He understood investigation and crime. It had been his life since he was twenty-one.

He lifted a brow. "You run it through the database looking for similar crimes?"

"Yep. Nothing." She should tell him about

the two deaths now. He'd be astonished something like that could happen here. But something bigger pressed against her after the recent spate of nightmares. She wet her lips. "Um, Dad, I've been dreaming a lot about Mom. Have you ever tried to find out where she is?"

He reached for his coffee. "Why would I want to do that? I don't ever want to see her — not after she chose Moses over you and me. You shouldn't waste your time thinking about her either."

Jane's rebuttal dried at his fierce reply. "You sound like you hate her. I can't hate her — she's my mother," she choked out, and her eyes filled with tears.

What was wrong with her lately? She'd long ago learned to wall off these emotional tsunamis. This outburst would make her seem weak in her father's eyes. She had too important a job to let this distract her. He wasn't looking at her, but she could tell by the tenseness in his manner that he was holding back what he wanted to say.

His granite face softened. "I know I don't say it much, but I'm very proud of you. Life hasn't always been easy for you, both at Mount Sinai and after we left, but you never complained, never disobeyed. I wish you could let it all go and forget about her. She doesn't deserve your love."

The silence stretched between them for a long moment before she exhaled. Maybe she should drop it.

A fist pounded on the door, and a gruff voice called out, "FBI."

Her dad raised a white brow and plodded back to the porch. Through the window Jane saw four men outside the door. Definitely FBI.

She darted past her dad and opened the wooden door but left the screen door shut. "What's going on?"

"We need to speak to Charles Hardy."

Dad moved her aside and opened the screen door. "I'm Charles Hardy. What's this all about?"

The man nearest the door thrust a paper in his hand. "You're under arrest for the theft of federal funds and money laundering. Come with us, please." He reached through the doorway and grasped her dad's forearm as the other men entered to search the house. "Take his phone and electronics as well as any paperwork you find."

Jane pulled out her ID to show them. "You've made a mistake. He's the former chief of police and has given his life to law enforcement."

Her dad didn't resist but allowed himself

to be propelled to one of the waiting black SUVs. "Call my lawyer, Elizabeth," he called over his shoulder as the agent hustled him into the back of the vehicle. "This is all a mistake. I've been following the man responsible, and they're on the wrong track."

Jane's chest compressed, and she felt short of breath as she ran after them. "Let me see the paperwork."

The agent in charge shook his head and got into the vehicle. Jane felt helpless as she watched the SUV's tires kick up dirt as it drove toward the gate. She couldn't watch the other agents search the property and ran for her vehicle.

TEN

Reid had texted Lauren two hours ago and told her he needed to see her. With the marina to his back, he sat with his feet dangling off the dock and listened to the sound of fish splashing in the water. A blue heron stood on the end of the pier and watched the water. The scents of lunch being prepared from the marina restaurant wafted toward him and mingled with the salty air, but he was too tense to enjoy it.

Lauren had said she'd be here in an hour, but he'd expected her to be late. She would want him to think she was in control.

After telling her he wasn't going to play her game, he would have to talk to Will. The truth would be hard for his boy to hear, but Reid didn't know how else to handle this. Lauren would want to extract her pound of flesh, and he had to do all he could to make sure that payment didn't come from Will.

Footsteps vibrated to his palms resting on

the gray weathered wood of the dock. He turned to see her silhouette. Showtime.

He rose and faced her. "I was beginning to think you weren't going to show."

And there she was — just as beautiful as ever — though she was thinner. Her blonde hair grazed her shoulders with that little flip she'd always hated but he'd loved. Her green eyes held a touch of pathos he didn't want to see. What kind of life had she led all these years? And why had she done it? So many questions crowded up into his throat, but he couldn't ask them. She'd see them for the weakness they were.

She stopped two feet away and tucked her hair behind her ears. "You got the money together faster than I expected. I wasn't in town, and it took me a while to get here."

Explanations from Lauren? Maybe she had a sixth sense about how this would go down. Her presence rattled him. Even now, he could feel the pull she'd always had over him, and he didn't like it. Not one bit.

"Let's get this over with." Her voice was low and husky. "I don't want to be around you any more than you want to be with me. I wanted cash, not a check. Where is it?"

He straightened and folded his arms across his chest. "I don't have it. I decided I'm not going to start down a path of blackmail, Lauren."

Her head jerked as if she'd been slapped. "You don't want to make an enemy of me."

"Aren't you already? You don't deserve anything from me. You chose your life, so go live it and leave me alone."

She took a step toward him and placed a hand on his arm. He shrugged her off. "Your wiles don't work on me anymore."

The raw pain caused by their skin-to-skin contact told him he'd lied, but he couldn't let her know she still affected him. He'd get past it, once he got over the shock of realizing she'd never cared about him except for his money.

Her perfume drifted toward him. "We could start over. Just you, me, and Will. This is a new place. No one has to know about our past."

"You're legally dead. How did you disappear so completely? Not even the private investigators could find a trace of you." He shouldn't have asked anything of her. She would see through to his heart.

Her slim shoulders hunched as if she didn't want to answer. A long pause followed before she spoke. "I had a friend who took care of that."

He flinched. "A male friend, I assume."

Her green eyes slid up to meet his gaze,

then bounced away. "Yes."

"And where is he now? Left you desti-tute?"

She shrugged. "Life goes on, Reid. You moved on, and I moved on. It doesn't mat-ter. All that matters is that I intend to have the money that's due me. I helped you get that business started."

"Oh? And how'd you do that? You were going to school, and I was working a second job to pay for your tuition. You thought journalism was a dead career."

"I did the books for you!"

"You did our taxes the first year. You think that entitles you to anything?"

Her chin rose, and she glared at him. "A judge would say yes."

"A judge would throw you in jail for at-tempted blackmail. You ever think about how *you* owe *me* money? You cleaned out the savings and checking accounts and left me with a child to raise on my own."

Her gaze faltered, and she looked away. "I had to have a start."

"And you didn't care about Will at all. What you did to me is nothing compared to what you did to our son." It pained him to say *our* when she had never bonded with Will.

"Yet you're willing to let him suffer even more."

He flinched again. "I have no choice. I know you. The requests for money would only intensify once you spent whatever I gave you. It's better for him to face the truth now. He's nearly fifteen — not a kid any longer."

"You can't do this. You *owe* me." Her husky voice held a note of desperation.

"I *am* doing it. You get nothing, Lauren. Not a penny."

"Why'd you have me come all this way for nothing?" she burst out.

Why indeed? Maybe he'd wanted to see her one last time. It had been important to him to test his own resolve. Though he'd felt her pull, he was strong enough to withstand it and to recognize it wasn't love. He wasn't crazy enough to get caught by her a second time.

He shoved his hands in the pockets of his Docker shorts. "I wanted to tell you in person."

"You're not going to like the consequences. I'll get an attorney." She spun on her heel and marched back toward the marina.

Sometimes life threw a curveball. They'd all have to learn to adapt.

■ ■ ■ ■

Jane entered the Pelican Harbor city limits with her siren blaring and her bubblegum lights flashing. How could the FBI think her father was a criminal? He lived and breathed law enforcement.

She parked in back of city hall and paused only long enough to let Parker do his business in the dog area. She swiped her card at the door, then headed for her office with her dog on her heels.

She dropped into the worn leather chair at her dad's desk — no, *her* desk. Feeling at home in the sunken spot left by her dad's bulky form was going to take some time. The office still smelled like him too — a mixture of Old Spice, donuts, and coffee. Though he'd rarely uttered a word of praise for her, she loved and respected him. He'd served his town for too many years to see it all crumble from false charges.

Jane turned on her computer and ran a search. Before the results came up, a tap sounded on her door. Elizabeth stood in the open doorway. She wore a strained expression. "Can I talk to you?"

Jane rose. "Shut the door behind you. I don't want this news to get out until it has to." Elizabeth must have jumped in the car right behind Jane to have gotten here so quickly.

Elizabeth closed the door, and Jane stepped around her desk. She wished she could hug Elizabeth, but Jane never liked being touched, a holdover from her other life. She gestured toward one of the chairs. "What's he charged with?"

Elizabeth perched on the edge of the chair. "They say he stole all kinds of things from the evidence room, then sold them and pocketed the money. There's another bank account where he's deposited the money in amounts under ten thousand dollars to evade detection. At least that's what the FBI claims."

"We both know that's not possible. Dad is the straightest shooter I know. He doesn't even know how to tell a lie."

A shadow flickered in Elizabeth's brown eyes, and she looked down at her hands. "Everyone has secrets, Jane. I don't know what to think."

"Don't you even dare consider the charges might be true! You know better."

Elizabeth clasped her hands together. "He's been acting funny. He's been gone a lot, and he's as tight as a new clam. It's hard to believe the FBI would arrest him without good reason."

Jane stalked around to drop back in her chair, and Parker trotted over to put his head on her knee. He whined at her obvious agitation, and she stroked his silky red fur until she regained her composure.

Elizabeth was right — the FBI wasn't likely to have arrested him without plenty of evidence. "Dad said he'd been following the real thief. Do you know who that might be?"

"No, he never discusses his work. He probably knows it upsets me to talk about criminals and jail."

"Did you call Scott?"

"Yes. He's on his way to post bail."

Scott Foster was the best criminal attorney in the south. He'd be able to figure this out.

She glanced at her computer and saw her search was finished. She pulled up the document and scanned the charges, then gave a low gasp. "They're saying he took five hundred thousand dollars' worth of diamonds, cash, guns, and drugs. I know he'd never do this. We've never even had that kind of property come through the county."

Elizabeth looked down. "You're the loyal sort, Jane. I've always loved that about you. But I-I think maybe he did these things."

Jane couldn't muster an argument without proof so she said nothing as Elizabeth rose and headed for the door. Once the older woman was out of the room, Jane groaned and buried her face in her hands.

Not only did she have to figure out how to get her dad out of this, she knew her own job would be in jeopardy. The city council might think she had something to do with this too.

She lifted her head and reached for her keyboard. First things first. She still had a job to do, and there was a murdered man who deserved justice, as well as Nicole Pearson's death to investigate. It was up to her to see that he got it. She'd work on her dad's case in her off-duty hours. Even though she wasn't sure she was qualified for this job, she had to give it everything she had.

She studied the detective's notes and examined the interviews they'd done so far. By the time she was finished, dusk was falling and hunger pangs rumbled in her stomach.

Her phone dinged with a message. Scott Foster wanted to meet her at his office.

On my way.

ELEVEN

Scott's French Quarter–style building was pale brick with elaborate wrought-iron balconies peering out under a Mansard black roof. It was the most photographed building in town, but Jane didn't have time to admire its beauty today. Dusk blurred the soft lines even more and hid the wide moldings under the eaves.

The door was unlocked, and she let herself in. Her boots clattered on the marble floors as she hurried through the main hall to Scott's office on the right. Light shone through the sidelights on the door, and she jerked it open at the sound of her dad's deep voice.

He and Scott sat in the waiting room's comfortable leather furniture. Her dad didn't look rumpled or upset by his arrest.

She rushed to her father's side. "What on earth is going on, Dad?"

Tears felt dangerously close, and she

blinked them back so she didn't disgrace herself in front of her father. A police chief didn't cry. An officer focused on facts and justice. They would get through this and prove her dad's innocence.

"Have a seat," Scott said.

He and her father had been friends for as long as she could remember. Scott and his family lived in a big compound next to Dad's, and he had enough stores to feed half the town for five years. He was the reason they'd ended up in Pelican Harbor. He'd sold the land next to his to her father for a song and had helped him find a job. His wife owned a candle shop in town, and people came from all over the area to shop her creations. Jane used to be friends with his daughter, but she'd moved away at eighteen and had never answered any of Jane's texts or calls.

Jane understood. Sometimes you wanted to walk away from the past and everyone in it. As far as she knew, Scott's daughter had never come back to town.

She sank onto the sofa beside her father. If only he would reach over and take her hand to comfort her, but that wasn't his way. He was not a demonstrative man.

Scott was about her father's age, but he was whip thin where her father was bulky.

She used to say he reminded her of a woodpecker, but his shock of bright-red hair had faded with age to a reddish brown. At least he still had hair.

Scott cleared his throat. "The charges are that your dad sold confiscated goods and money."

"That's preposterous!"

Her father still hadn't spoken, and Jane eyed him. Did he realize how serious all this was? He didn't seem upset or surprised by any of it. "Dad?"

He stirred as if he were awakening from sleep. "It's all lies, but the FBI seems to believe this without any real evidence." For the first time, anger rumbled in his voice.

Elizabeth's words came rushing back to Jane. "Why did you really retire? Did you know this was coming?"

He looked at her then, his hazel eyes hooded with fatigue. "Of course I did. I was chief of police. I heard every rumor swirling in the underworld. I didn't want to be arrested while I was an acting chief, and I didn't want to do anything that would hamper your being appointed in my place. I retired and laid low and was trying to figure out who was trying to frame me."

"I can't believe you didn't tell me."

"Just stay out of it. I don't want Lisa to

question her decision."

"You really think the mayor won't yank me right out? This will put her in an awkward position."

He shrugged. "My problem has nothing to do with you. You didn't even know about the looming charges."

"Someone had to have made an initial complaint." Frowning, she leaned forward. "And why didn't I hear anything about it? The FBI had to have been conducting interviews with department members. They would have talked to the evidence room and had all kinds of questions."

"I guess they didn't think you'd tell them the truth."

"That's why people have been clamming up when I come into a room. I thought it was because I was being considered for chief."

"Maybe not," her dad said. "These are all trumped-up charges."

"By whom? Who is the real culprit you mentioned?"

His gaze fell away from hers. "I don't want to point fingers until I have more evidence, and I want you to stay out of it. This is a frame-up, and I don't want you to be the next target."

"Who would want to frame you?"

"Who wouldn't? I've put plenty of criminals behind bars. I've had a lifelong law enforcement career. The list of my enemies is long."

An easy explanation for his comments to Elizabeth, but something still didn't feel right to Jane. "Who do you have evidence against?"

"I want you to do your job and don't worry about me. This is for me and Scott to figure out. When I get more evidence, I'll take care of it myself."

There was no way she would leave it at that. Her dad needed her help, and she wasn't about to walk away.

Reid's gut was in a knot when he entered the rental house to the sound of the TV in the living room. The house reeked of garlic and cheese, and he spied the remains of frozen lasagna on the table. Dad failure again. Was he repeating his father's errors? Reid shook his head. Tomorrow he would cook them a good meal, maybe a shrimp boil. They both loved that.

He stood in the doorway to the living room drinking in the sight of his son. Will wore a Saints T-shirt and shorts, and his bare feet looked like they'd grown. He was already in a size fourteen shoe, but new sneakers were probably on the horizon. His musculature was beginning to develop more, and Will would be every bit as tall as Reid when he reached his full height.

The two of them had come through a lot together, and their bond was one of the joys of his life. Will was a hard worker, responsible, affectionate, and more mature than his years warranted. People remarked about how much Will looked like him, but Reid caught glimmers of his mother in him, too, a fact that pained him.

All Reid could do was pray he could explain the circumstances in a way that didn't hurt his boy.

Will sat on the edge of the sofa as Tiger Woods eyed his putt. The comments droned on about the challenges Woods had to overcome the past years, but Reid tuned the announcer out and tried to decide how to bring up the subject. He watched Tiger sink the putt before the show went to a commercial.

Will glanced up and muted the television. "Hey, Dad, I didn't know you were back. Want some lasagna? And what do you think about going golfing this week? We haven't gone in a while."

"I'll eat later, but golf sounds like a great idea."

Will studied him. "Everything okay?"

Reid couldn't smile because it would be a lie. "Not exactly. I need to talk to you about something. A couple of things, actually. Since you're on spring break, want to be my videographer on this documentary? I can't seem to find someone on short notice."

"Cool. I'll do it." Will settled back and slung his arm across the top of the sofa. "You look serious. Did you change your mind about the move?"

"What? No, not at all." Reid settled in the recliner. "I've already contacted the real estate agent about buying this place, and I put in an offer. The seller accepted a few minutes ago, and this property will be ours soon."

"Awesome!" Will's smile fell away as he stared at his dad. "So what's up?"

He might as well plunge right in. "It's about your mother."

Will lowered his arm and leaned forward. "You found out what happened to her?"

"Not exactly. That phone call I got when we were shrimping? It was from her. She's alive."

Will's mouth sagged open. "Alive? You mean she has been hiding from us all these years? Where is she? Is she coming to see me?"

Though Will's voice raised a notch, his mouth flattened, and Reid glimpsed trepidation. Poor kid had never understood, and Reid had never been able to explain it to him. How could he when he didn't understand it himself?

Reid held up his hand. "Slow down, bud." He exhaled. "She called asking for money. She thinks she can get it by threatening to show up in your life and make you think she doesn't care about you."

Will's dark eyes widened. "Like that's a surprise? I always figured she left because she wanted to. When I was a kid, I thought maybe someone took her where she didn't want to go, but I figured it out. She never cared about me or she would have at least stayed in touch. It's one thing to leave your kid, but it's something else to never call, never send a birthday card, nothing."

The kid was way too astute. "It was never you, though, buddy. It was me. I was too tame, I guess. I'd come home tired from starting a new business, and she'd want to go out. I'd make excuses and she'd go by herself. I should have made more of an effort."

Will fisted his hands. "It's not your fault,

Dad. You've always been there for me. I'm sure you tried with Mom." He looked out the wall of windows to the sluggish Bon Secour River lit by the setting sun. "Did she say where she's been?"

Reid hesitated, then shrugged. "She wouldn't say exactly, but it sounded to me like her current boyfriend isn't paying anymore. She knows I've found some success as a journalist so she thought she could blackmail me by promising to stay away if I gave her money."

"By threatening to hurt me. She's some mother. I wish she'd stayed gone." He rose in a gangly movement and went toward the door. "Think I'll take a walk."

Reid wanted to go after him, but he restrained himself and watched Will cross the oyster shell driveway and head to the river. Will needed to process this on his own. The first hurdle was over, but what if Lauren followed through on her threat and showed up? She might even tell Will she'd adopted him. Reid didn't want to face the questions that would inevitably follow.

TWELVE

Jane parked on the street and took the black-iron staircase up to her apartment. Parker's nails clanged on the metal as he went up beside her. Every muscle in her body ached from being wound like a yo-yo. She had to figure out how to clear her dad, but with so much work on her plate from the homicides, she wasn't sure how she was going to do it.

And she still wasn't sure how to help Olivia. Her friend's illness weighed heavy on her shoulders.

Her foot kicked something, and she heard a *clink*. Looking down, she spotted a silver coin. She scooped it up and examined it. A Kennedy half-dollar. What was it doing on her doorstep? She glanced around and saw nothing else out of place. Struggling with the burden of her computer and bag, she unlocked her door and practically fell inside. She dropped her belongings on the counter and studied the coin more closely.

It was stamped 1964. She grabbed her phone and looked it up. That was the first year it was minted and was worth about ten dollars, just like the one found on Dawson's body. She'd already picked it up, so it was unlikely to yield any prints, but she'd turn it in to forensics anyway.

She put it and her phone down and headed to her bedroom to change. The last thing she felt like doing was going out to dinner, but Olivia needed her, and Jane wanted to assess how she was doing. Tonight they'd tell Megan what was going on as well.

Her head throbbed with the knowledge she was failing everyone.

Stepping into her apartment usually lifted her spirits, but it wasn't working tonight. Over the years she'd made the one-bedroom space into her sanctuary, and she loved every square foot of its light and airy open floor plan. Every feature was perfect, from the vaulted ceilings to the shiplap on one living room wall to the marble counters and gray cabinets in the kitchen.

When Parker nosed her hand, she shook her head and inhaled. Maybe routine would snap her out of her funk. She filled Parker's water bowl and fed him his dinner, then headed for the shower. Her light-brown hair wasn't dry but at least she was dressed when the doorbell rang. She scrunched the gel through her locks one last time, then raced for the door.

She opened it and stepped out of the way to let Olivia in. "I left it unlocked for you." Olivia wore jeans with sandals and a red top. "You must have gotten the memo to wear red."

Olivia shut the door behind her. "You're the chief — you should know better than to leave your door unlocked." She smiled and handed over a gift bag. "Happy early birthday."

"It's not for another week." Jane loved presents. "Can I open it now?"

Olivia stopped to pet Parker. "Sure."

Olivia seemed stronger today, and Jane hadn't seen her limping. She still hoped the first diagnosis was wrong.

Carrying the gift, Jane went to the sofa and settled on it before she dug into the bag. A large book was inside, and she squealed when she pulled it out. "The first book in the Masters of Rome series. I've wanted to get started on this series." After taking Latin in college, she loved reading books about Ancient Rome, and Olivia was one of the few people who knew it. Colleen

McCullough was one of her favorite authors.

"There's a code for an e-book in the bag too."

Jane dug back into the gift bag and pulled out a paper with a book cover and code. "*The Screwtape Letters.* I don't think I've heard of this one." And the cover didn't look like something she usually picked. "Have you read it? I've never heard of C. S. Lewis."

"You've never heard of C. S. Lewis? You know, he wrote *The Lion, the Witch and the Wardrobe.*"

"I've watched the movie." Why would Olivia get her a children's book? Though the cover didn't look childish. She laid the paper aside. "Thanks. I guess we'd better get going. Where's Megan? I thought we were going to tell her about your illness tonight. Did you change your mind? And what about seeking that second opinion?"

"She had play practice, so she's meeting us at the restaurant. I have an appointment with another neurologist next week."

Jane's phone rang and she answered it. "Chief Hardy."

Brian informed her that the video camera footage had cleared Reid of suspicion in Gary's death. He had an alibi for Sunday.

She'd hoped to keep him at arm's length longer.

When she ended the call, Olivia picked up her purse. "You're bailing on me, aren't you?"

"I wouldn't bail on you — not tonight of all nights."

It would be hard to tell Megan, and Jane wasn't about to let Olivia do it alone.

Olivia put her hand on her arm. "Don't try to put on a stiff upper lip for me. The whole department is buzzing with news of your dad's arrest."

"Had you heard anything about an investigation?"

Olivia shook her head. "The FBI must have really had it under wraps. No one I talked to knew what was happening." She made a face. "I ran into Paul at Petit Charms, and he was beaming about it."

"Of course he was. He hates my dad and me. I don't understand it. I have to find out who is behind this. Dad wants me to keep out of it while he investigates, but I have to help him." Jane looked out to the balcony where she'd settled after the nightmare. "I had another nightmare last night. I don't seem to get any respite from them. Maybe I'll try that therapy meeting you suggested."

Olivia's fingers tightened on Jane's forearm. "I wish you would." She released her and moved toward the door. "One of these days you're going to break free from your parents and your past. You're a strong, beautiful woman. I pray every day that you see yourself the way God sees you."

Olivia was the only one in town who knew about Jane's past, and that was the way she wanted to keep it, but she tuned out her friend's comment. God hadn't stopped the leaders of Mount Sinai from doing what they did, and she didn't trust him. Not one bit.

The metal stairs clanged as they went down them. They had reservations at Billy's Seafood just down the street. He grilled the best oysters in town.

In minutes they were seated at a table overlooking the setting sun over the bay. The aromas of various seafood wafting from the kitchen made Jane's mouth water.

Olivia gave her a searching smile. "What did you think about Reid Dixon?"

"What about him?"

"Honey, I know he did that documentary on cults, which put him on the map. I watched it with you, remember? Did seeing him bring back a lot of bad memories? You were already having some nightmares."

Jane frowned. "I've had them every night

since he came to town." She fiddled with her napkin. "I know it would help if I talked about it, but I'm so ashamed. I'm afraid there are still people trapped in it — people I recruited. I might have ruined their lives."

Olivia reached across the table and took her hand. "Jane, your parents took you there when you were five. You were a kid. You didn't choose to be there. I know you have a real fear of being thought of as gullible, but none of it was your fault."

"I didn't want to leave when Dad made me, though. I'd swallowed all the lies — hook, line, and sinker. That makes me just as stupid and gullible as my parents."

Ponytail bouncing, Megan came through the door, and her arrival stopped future conversation, which was just as well. Jane didn't like remembering that horrible night she escaped Mount Sinai.

Though Megan was fourteen, she was mature beyond her years. Olivia had raised her, so how could she be anything else than wonderful? Jane waited for a cue from Olivia. This wasn't her story to tell — only to support.

Olivia waited until they'd eaten their grilled oysters, garlic mashed potatoes, and asparagus. They were sharing a crème brûlée when she cleared her throat. "Megan, I have something I need to talk to you about."

Megan put down her dessert spoon and locked gazes with her mother. "You have MS, don't you? Look, Mom, I'm not stupid. I overheard you on the phone with the doctor. You think I haven't noticed the way you're stumbling. You slur your words sometimes too. It's okay. I'll take care of you."

Jane's eyes stung and watered at the love in Megan's voice. This news would devastate her, and it was like watching a train speeding toward them with no way to stop it. She clenched her hands together in her lap.

Olivia reached across the table to take her daughter's hand. "You're so wonderful, honey. I don't know what I ever did to deserve a daughter like you. I wish I could say I had MS. The news is worse, sweetheart. Much worse."

Megan's blue eyes widened. "Cancer?" she whispered. "Brain cancer?"

Olivia shook her head. "I have ALS."

Megan glanced at Jane, then back to her mother. "What's that?"

"Amyotrophic lateral sclerosis. It's also called Lou Gehrig's disease. It affects the nerve cells in the brain and spinal cord.

They basically degenerate, which is why I'm having trouble walking and why I sometimes slur my words."

"They can fix it, right?"

Olivia bit her lip, then shook her head. "It's usually fatal, Megan. I'm going to fight it — of course I'm going to do whatever I can, but I don't want to sugarcoat it. What we're facing isn't going to be easy."

"F-Fatal?" Tears pooled in Megan's eyes, and she shook her head. "They have to be wrong, Mom. You're still young! Let's get a second opinion."

"I'm doing that next week, but I'm not hopeful we'll find out it's something else. The doctor was very thorough."

Megan looked at Jane. "You'll help us, won't you? We have to find a cure for Mom."

Jane couldn't stop the tears from escaping her eyes, and she nodded. "I'll do everything I can, Meg. I'll be there for you and your mom no matter what happens."

"We have to find a cure! There has to be a cure."

Jane knew how she felt — she'd been scouring the internet for better answers as well — but this truth was something they'd all struggle to accept.

THIRTEEN

Fanny blinked her burning eyes and pulled into Harry's favorite roadside park by the water near Pelican Harbor. Palm trees lined the park, and blue herons vied with pelicans for fish in the blue water. Her poor son didn't understand what had happened to his daddy, of course, even though she'd tried to explain he'd gone away and they wouldn't see him again.

She wanted to say Gary was in heaven, but she found it hard to say something she didn't believe. He had often mocked her faith, and unless he'd made his peace with God in his final moments, she doubted she'd see him when she crossed those pearly gates someday.

She got Harry out of his booster seat and set him down. "I'll spread out the quilt so we can have a nice picnic. Then you can collect some shells. How's that sound?"

"Are we going to see Grandma today?"

She'd put it off as long as she could, but her mom had been generous enough to rent her a car. "We're going to her house after a while."

Her mother had gotten home late last night, and they'd been in touch constantly since the news about Gary's death. Her mom had never liked him, even though Fanny hadn't mentioned he'd started using his fists against her this past year. Fanny wished she'd been honest. She wished she'd left him long ago so Harry didn't have to see his father's rage. She hadn't wanted to admit to her mother that she'd been right, which was a really stupid reason to be someone's punching bag.

She spread out the quilt, then retrieved the breakfast from McDonald's she'd bought. Harry unwrapped his sandwich and started in on it, though his gaze drifted longingly to the shore. The small opening in the trees along Mobile Bay was great for seashells, and Harry's collection was overflowing. It felt safe and secluded here with the forest blocking the wind on the north and south sides.

A car pulled in behind hers, and a man got out. She smiled and waved before she returned her attention to Harry.

"I wonder if I could trouble you and bor-

146

row your phone a minute?" the man asked. "My car barely made it here, and I'm about out of gas. I left my phone at home, and I need to call for some help."

Fanny hopped up. "Sure thing. I left it in the car."

He seemed like a nice enough young man, probably in his twenties or early thirties. It was so hard to tell age these days. She opened her car door and leaned in to snatch her phone off the console. As she straightened to turn toward him, his arm grabbed her around the waist, and his other arm caught her neck in a choke hold. He dragged her toward his car, and she fought him with all her might.

Harry's eyes were wide and horrified as they locked with her gaze. "Run, Harry!" She fought harder as the man's trunk popped, and he propelled her into its recesses.

Was Harry running? What did this guy want with her? *Oh, Gary, what have you gotten us into?*

He trussed her up with duct tape, then slapped another piece across her mouth before he slammed the trunk lid, leaving her in darkness. The smell of oil and gasoline choked her, and she tried to break free of her bonds.

She had to get to her son and protect him.

"Harry," the man called. "Come here, and you can go with your mom."

Don't listen, Harry.

She'd taught him that if she ever told him to run, he wasn't to come back unless a family member called for him. But with a child, you were never sure if he knew enough to recognize danger. She held her breath and listened to the man calling for her son, but after several long minutes, she heard his footsteps crunching on the oyster shells lining the lot. His door slammed, and the car vibrated as he started the engine and pulled away.

Her boy was probably somewhere in the thick woods. Could he find his way to help? Tears poured down her cheeks, and she prayed God would direct and watch over him.

Harry was only four. Anything could happen to him out there. He could get lost or fall in the water. He could get bitten by a poisonous snake or attacked by a gator. She started to shake at the thought of everything that could harm him out there on his own.

She fought the bonds with every bit of strength in her body only to sag back, perspiring and faint from lack of air when she couldn't budge them. Her breath heaving, she rested long enough for the spots in her vision to clear, then searched for something, anything, in the trunk to use to cut the duct tape.

At 7:05 p.m. Jane slipped into a seat nearest the door. If things got uncomfortable, she could leave as easily as she'd arrived. She'd left Parker sleeping in his bed in the living room so she wouldn't draw too much attention. She'd had a little trouble finding the building on the east side of Mobile, and her tardiness had saved her having to endure small talk before the meeting started.

She scanned the group of eight people scattered among the circle of twenty folding chairs. She'd argued with herself all the way here. If she hadn't promised Olivia last night she'd come, Jane would have turned tail and headed back to her safe little home above the beignet shop. But if Olivia could face the horror of her future, surely Jane could face the past that couldn't reach out and hurt her any longer.

The woman across from Jane had given her name, but it hadn't managed to lodge in Jane's head. The woman seemed about forty with worry lines between her brown eyes. She wore jeans and a green T-shirt. Her brown hair curled wildly around her head and was only kept out of her face by a green stretchy headband. She had one of those motherly manners that tended to put people at ease, which was probably why she was leading this shindig.

The woman looked down at her notes in her lap. "Anyone want to share their experience in a cult? I know it's hard to talk about, but getting it out in the open is very healing. Please don't mention the cult's name. We'll keep it anonymous in case someone fears retribution."

Even hearing the word *cult* made Jane want to pull a blanket over her head so she couldn't be seen. Until the nightmares started three months ago, she would have insisted she'd healed from her experience without any repercussions. For weeks she'd hoped the nightmares were a fluke and maybe related to stress at the job, but when they continued without relenting, Olivia had noticed the dark circles under Jane's eyes and demanded a response.

Jane didn't think any psychobabble was the answer, but friendship had driven her here. Or maybe it was the lingering effects of the cult on her behavior. She tended to pay too much heed to what other people expected of her. It was a flaw she constantly battled.

A thin, pale woman who looked under thirty lifted her hand. "Um, I'll go. I've been out of t-the cult for about six months, but I can't seem to quit glancing over my shoulder. I have trouble making decisions, and I cry for no good reason. I-I miss my friends there, the camaraderie, the love they showered on me. I think I want to go back."

The older woman's expression didn't change. "Why did you leave?"

"They were shunning me for not being willing to marry who the leader told me to." The girl bit her thumbnail and didn't look at anyone. "I wanted to live my own life."

"And do you still want to live your own life? To date whomever you want and to pick your own friends?"

"I-I don't know. I don't really have any friends. It's hard to open up to new people. When they know I was in a cult, there's all this condemnation and eyebrow raising. So I usually say nothing, and how can you have friends without honesty?"

Jane could have said many of the same things about herself. Olivia was her only close friend, and she was more of a mother figure. How did someone get past all this? Her answer had been to avoid all religion and any talk or thoughts of God, but Olivia's influence had slowly been causing her to doubt that approach.

The nightmares scared her too. With her badge attached to her shirt and her gun on her hip, she felt invincible and strong. In the stillness of the night, she faced demons that didn't flee when she aimed her sidearm. They didn't run when she read them their rights. They lurked at the edges of sleep and consciousness and made her doubt who she was and what she could do with her life.

If she could go back to Mount Sinai, would she?

She wanted to say no, but if she got wind of the cult's new location, she feared she would head there right this minute. She longed to see her mother. The worst thing she dealt with was the way she'd failed her mother and her son.

She had failed those in the group she'd recruited too. She'd pulled them in and left them when things turned hard, when bullets were flying and people were dying. What kind of person did that make her? Maybe she was in law enforcement to prove something to herself. If that was true, she didn't think she'd proven anything other than she knew how to put up a good front.

The place felt impossibly hot, and perspiration gathered on her forehead and under her arms. With a muttered apology she leapt up and made her escape. This wasn't the right place for her. Maybe nowhere was.

She drove home and spent three hours on the computer looking up ALS information. Nothing she read gave her much hope.

FOURTEEN

Reid had been shocked at Jane's call this morning that he'd been cleared, but he'd grabbed Will and brought him along to city hall. He'd been directed down the hall to what they'd called the "war room," which turned out to be a conference room. A huge whiteboard covered one wall, and tables and chairs were occupied by four other people. He only recognized Detective Boulter and realized two were state troopers. He didn't know who the woman in the front row was. Jane must have asked for some help from the state.

Jane stood at the whiteboard with a marker in her hand. A flicker of her eyes told Reid she'd noted his and Will's arrival. They took a seat in the back, and Reid nodded for Will to begin recording.

She turned to the board and wrote *Gary Dawson* on it. "Let's go over what we have on his murder. You all saw the note about the hidden Kennedy half-dollar." She drew a circle around it and marked it with a 50. "What you don't know is that I found one of those same half-dollars on my doorstep night before last. It was a 1964 coin just like the one on Dawson's body." She drew another circle with a 50 as the men in the room gave a collective gasp.

Reid leaned forward and frowned. He didn't like the sound of that.

"I think the killer was taunting me, poking fun that we hadn't found him yet. I turned it in to Forensics, but I'd already handled it so we probably won't find any latent prints on it." Jane turned back to the board. "Dawson's head and limbs are still missing. I'm guessing the killer tossed them into the bay and we'll never find them, but we might get lucky. So far the media hasn't caught wind of the missing body parts, and I'd like to keep it that way. The sensationalism of what happened to the body is apt to increase the public's fear, so continue to keep it under wraps."

The woman in the front row raised her hand, and Jane pointed to her. "I ran the video you gave me from the bridal shop, and I wasn't able to get any real detail. We could release it to the news, though. Maybe the person's walk or movements would trigger something in a viewer."

"Good idea. Go ahead and do that," Jane said. "What about interviews with Dawson's friends and acquaintances? Any luck on finding his bookie?"

Boulter waved his hand. "I've got a lead to his bookie. I should know more in another day or two."

"Good work." She jotted down *bookie* on the board. "Anything else?"

The woman in the front spoke again. "I've been through his computer, but his phone still hasn't turned up. I tried pinging it, but it's nowhere to be found. Probably destroyed by the killer."

"Anything of interest on his computer?"

"Lots of gambling sites but no link to the bookie that I can find. Hopefully Brian has better luck."

Nothing they didn't know. "Anything else?"

"What about the note on the dress about him being a vow breaker?" Boulter asked. "I think that points to the vigilante. And I think Nicole may have also been killed accidentally by the vigilante. The ME thinks she was allergic to the feathers. Maybe our perp was punishing her for having an affair and didn't know about her feather allergy. It makes more sense than murder."

Jane nodded and wrote *Nicole* on the board. "We won't know for sure what killed her until we get the autopsy report. Nicole worked at the library. We need to talk to her coworkers and friends, then compare what we find out to the other vigilante victims. In all the cases the vigilante seemed to be punishing moral crimes, not necessarily illegal ones. Let's talk to the churches around and see if anyone has a wonky member people are unsure about."

Her voice changed when she talked about church, and Reid studied her face. A hint of animosity had crept into her eyes. She'd be unlikely to talk to him about it, but he longed to know what she felt.

"I'll do that," one of the troopers said. "My church is one of the largest in the area."

Jane glanced at the woman again. "What about monitoring comments on Facebook? Have you seen anything on Nicole's page?"

"Just one weird thing that was posted last night amid the condolences. There was a comment about sins finding you out. I tracked down the poster and gave it to Brian to check out."

Jane glanced at Brian, who nodded. "I'm going to talk to her. It was her boss, Carmencita Cook. She might know something."

"She left a message for me yesterday," Jane said. "I think I'll go with you to that interview. Anything else?"

Boulter consulted his notes. "Back to Dawson for a minute. I just remembered I found that cooler his body was in. He owned it, and it was missing from his storage shed."

"How do you know it was his?"

"There was a *D* carved into the bottom, and I showed a picture to his wife. She confirmed it."

"Another dead end." Jane grimaced. "What about Nicole's electronics and the search of her house?"

"Text messages with her lover," the woman said. "Paul Baker."

Jane showed no reaction. "Any kind of threat in the texts?"

"No."

Jane put down the marker. "Okay, that's it for now. Let me know if you turn up anything under a rock."

Reid waited until the team filed out of the room before he had Will stop the video. Jane walked back to join them, but her manner wasn't welcoming.

She stopped in front of them. "You're out on spring break, Will?" Her voice warmed, and a smile lifted her lips.

"Yes, ma'am. I hope you don't mind if I tag along to help Dad."

Her hazel eyes slid toward Reid. "I'd rather have you than your dad."

She clearly hadn't called him because she wanted him around, but that was okay. He'd get what he wanted and slip out of her life soon.

A few people wandered up and down the sidewalks and lounged on the balconies over the stores with books this Friday afternoon, the distant sound of jazz music lifting on the sultry breeze. In line at Pelican Brews, Jane inhaled the rich coffee aroma and looked out the window. Spring break had started, and she didn't have to jostle with high school kids waiting on their lattes. Not that she minded because she liked kids. She often looked at the teenagers and wondered what her life at that age would have been like if it hadn't been blighted by her past.

Her phone rang as the barista handed her the usual black coffee. She mouthed a *thank you* and answered it. "Chief Hardy."

"We've got a situation, Chief. This one is . . . strange," Olivia said.

"Strange how?"

"A jogger found an abandoned car by the Gulf."

Hardly a strange occurrence. "So?"

"There's evidence someone was having a breakfast picnic and left everything behind. There's blood at the scene as well. It's troubling. I told Brian to have the jogger wait for you."

"Shoot me the address. On my way." She hung up and her phone pinged with an address. She called for Parker, then raced for her SUV and drove two miles out of town to a roadside park.

She left her coffee in the cup holder and got out with Parker to join Brian at the scene. "What do we have?"

Brian swept a hand toward the water. "Take a look."

She considered the grassy park and palm tree–lined pavilion. Waves lapped at the shore, and a pelican scooped a fish from the water. A strong scent of salt and seaweed permeated the air this close to the water. It would have been an idyllic Friday-morning scene except for the signs of abandonment.

A newer Ford Taurus, baby blue, stood empty with the driver's door open. A quilt lay spread out on the sand with a bag from McDonald's at one end, and several egrets eyed the bag with interest. She peeked inside the bag without touching anything. There was a half-eaten egg sandwich, a bag of apple slices, and two juice boxes.

A glint of silver caught her eye on the driver's seat, and she stooped to squint at it. A Kennedy half-dollar. She automatically reached for it, then pulled her hand back. The evidence shouldn't be contaminated just because she was shocked to see the coin. Something disturbing was going on in her town, and she wasn't sure how to solve this puzzle.

"Person ate some of their food," she said. "And did you see the half-dollar?" She cleared her throat. "I can't tell what year this one is, and I don't want to touch it, so let's see if it's a 1964 coin like the one on Dawson's body."

"And the one on your doorstep." Brian gave her a quick look. "You have good locks, Boss?"

"I do." She smiled and set her hand on her gun. "And the best security right here." She peered inside the car. An array of crumpled fast-food bags littered the floor on the passenger side and in the back. A lip gloss was in the middle console, and a makeup bag had spilled its contents into the passenger seat.

Her gaze caught on a navy-blue booster seat in the back with the remains of a Mc-Donald's Happy Meal beside it. Unease stirred even more. What if there was a child walking around out here?

She turned toward Brian. "Any sign of a child? There's a booster seat in the back. Looks like maybe a boy's."

"I saw that. No sign of a kid, though. Appears the driver was a woman."

Unease rippled down her back, and she nodded. "I don't like the look of this scene."

"Me neither. Could have been an abduction."

Jane squared her shoulders and drew herself as tall as her five feet two inches would allow, then walked over to talk to the jogger with Parker on her heels. The woman had the lean, muscular physique of a runner and appeared to be in her forties. Her blonde hair was up in a ponytail, and moisture still beaded her forehead. She wore light-blue jogging shorts and a white T-shirt. Jane guessed her to be a tourist since she didn't recognize her.

Jane stopped two feet from her. "I'm Chief Hardy. You called in the abandoned car?"

The woman nodded. "I'm Linda Mason. I'm renting a house down the road for a week and have been jogging through here every morning. I came around the curve there and saw the car. I would have run on past, but the car door was standing open, and things just didn't look right."

"You have good instincts. Did you see anyone around? A woman or a child maybe?"

Linda shook her head. "Just the car and the items sitting around. I called out a few times, but no one answered. I almost went back to my jog, but I thought you guys should check it out. I would have worried all day if I'd done nothing."

"You did the right thing. Thanks for calling it in." Jane went back to join Brian. "Anything in the registration?"

"It's a rental car." He held up registration papers. "No rental agreement, though, and the plate on the car is missing. I'll contact the rental company and see if they sold it or if it's been stolen."

The whole scene smelled bad to Jane. "Let's get back to the office."

She supposed she'd have to call Reid and let him in on this incident. It wouldn't be a good idea to rile up the mayor any more than she was going to be when she heard about Dad's arrest.

FIFTEEN

The clock's red light shone out 12:02. Reid threw back the covers and climbed out of bed since sleep was impossible. He kept seeing the rage in Lauren's eyes when she promised he'd be sorry not to give her the money she demanded. He couldn't tell Will that Lauren wasn't his real mother — he just couldn't.

But would she tell him? She'd have more leverage over Will if he thought she was his birth mother.

Reid ran his hand over his shaved head and walked out to the kitchen to get a glass of orange juice. Tumbler in hand, he stepped out the door onto the back deck.

Stars twinkled in the velvet sky, and the roar of a bull gator shattered the serenity. He had a strange yen for a beignet with coffee and glanced at his watch. Petit Charms would be closed at this time of night, but they sold their leftover treats in the twenty-

164

four-hour convenience store in the middle of town. He could get there and back in fifteen minutes.

His running shorts would be fine for the quick trip to town. He gulped down his juice and grabbed his keys from the counter. In minutes he was parked outside the glaring neon signs. He ducked inside and bought half a dozen beignets and a cup of coffee, then munched two pastries while sitting on the bench in the courtyard next door.

An old codger ambled his direction and stopped for a moment. "You look as lost as a ball in high weeds, young man. Need help?"

"I'm just enjoying the night."

The scent of seafood wafted from the man's fish scale–encrusted shirt. "You been out shrimping?"

The man wiped his hand on his pants, then extended it. "Alfie Smith."

He recognized the name as the shrimper who had found Gary's body. Reid wiped the powdered sugar from his fingers on his shorts and shook Alfie's callused hand. "Reid Dixon."

"You're that photographer who has our chief's knickers in a knot. I hear you're planning to stay for a bit."

"You heard right."

"Well, you come on by my fishmonger shop and I'll give you a welcome gift of the biggest shrimp you've ever seen."

"I'll do that. Thanks, Alfie."

The old man grinned and walked on down the street before he entered a bar playing jazz music. Reid was beginning to feel more like a resident here and less like a tourist. The place had wrapped itself around his heartstrings faster than he'd expected.

Twinkling lights lit the silent streets, and shadows from the French Quarter buildings made interesting shapes in the side yards. Reid brushed powdered sugar from his fingers and leaned back on the bench. Faint music floated in the air, and he recognized Faith Hill's voice singing "Mississippi Girl."

Apartments were atop most of the quaint French-style buildings lining Main Street, and lights shone in a few residences. A patrol car slowly rolled along the street and eased to a stop by Reid, then pulled into a parking spot.

The window ran down, and Detective Boulter looked out. Recognition crinkled his eyes, and his gaze dropped to the box of beignets. "Hand over the beignets, and I won't arrest you for vagrancy."

Reid grinned and held up his box. "I don't

look good in orange. Help yourself." He opened the box and Boulter snagged two treats, littering powdered sugar down the side of his vehicle.

He liked the brash young detective. Brian might be a bit full of himself, but he seemed to care about his town and his job. "You're on patrol?"

"Nah. Just left a date and had a yearning for beignets. Looks like you did too."

Such honesty. Reid felt a compulsion to unload on him, but Gary's betrayal still stung. He would have trusted Gary with his life, and he still had trouble believing everything that had gone down.

Boulter turned off his engine and climbed out. At night he looked even more like Dwayne Johnson. "Something's bugging you. You have an idea who offed Gary, maybe?"

"Wish I did. Maybe his bookie had it done. You find out anything about who was fronting the money for him?" This morning Brian had thought he was close to finding out something.

The bench groaned as Brian lowered his muscular form onto it. "New Orleans PD has nothin'. He got out of jail on Saturday and never came home that night. We've been checking cameras at tollbooths and parking lots, but we haven't turned up anything. His car was found in the pier parking lot right here in Pelican Harbor. Would he have been coming to see you — maybe to ask you to drop the charges?"

Reid took the next to last beignet and handed the last one in the box to Brian, who inhaled it. "I made it clear that wasn't an option. I wish I'd handled it differently. I thought going to jail would get him away from his addiction and the loan sharks. I was wrong."

And maybe that was the crux of his low spirits. He'd made the wrong decision.

Boulter licked the powdered sugar off his fingers. "It's not your fault, man. Gary picked his own path."

"I guess." The Faith Hill music was still playing. "Someone likes Faith Hill."

"That's the boss lady." Brian nodded toward a second-floor residence above a coffee shop. "Jane has trouble sleeping. She's out there on her balcony listening to music and either reading or surfing her computer."

Reid raised a brow. "The chief seems to have it all together. I'm surprised she has trouble sleeping. How long has she lived here?" Maybe this was his chance to find out more about Jane.

"Fifteen years or so, from what I hear.

She's a little older than me, but she was fifteen when she and her dad rolled into town. He owns that big piece of property out north of town. I've always heard he and Jane escaped from some kind of cult, but no one ever talks about it. If you ask Jane about her past, she clams up. I think something happened there that traumatized her. I like her. She's a good boss and a caring person."

Reid wasn't so sure about that. He rose when Brian moved toward his car, but when the big detective was out of sight, Reid glanced at Jane's balcony. Maybe her guard would be down tonight. It was worth a try.

Sleep was often as elusive as a unicorn. Jane sat on her balcony looking out over the sleeping town with the bay reflecting the streetlights. Faith Hill sang softly through her computer speakers, and Parker sat beside her with his head on her knee. The briny scent of the bay usually soothed her churning thoughts, but she had so much on her mind.

Both of her birthday books were on her e-reader, and she could see well enough with the light in the living room to her back, but horror didn't appeal to her after the gory scene she'd seen this week. She tapped the strange little book *The Screwtape Letters*. It was a hard read to get into at first, because she couldn't figure out the speaker and the target of his advice. Then it clicked that the main character was a demon named Screwtape.

She nearly threw the book down in disgust when a statement stopped her. *"Jargon, not argument, is your best ally in keeping him from the Church."*

Moses at Mount Sinai was a pro at using jargon to keep the cult members tightly bound. Since she'd left, she hadn't darkened the door of a church. The thought of being deceived again made her shudder. She didn't want to be a gullible person, the kind who swallowed a lie in one gulp.

She returned to her e-reader. Maybe she'd read a little more of it. She became so wrapped up in the book that the first time Parker let out a low growl, she barely noticed. It was only when he did it again that she blinked and looked down into the street.

Looking handsome and casual in a Saints T-shirt and running shorts, Reid Dixon stood on the brick sidewalk. A quizzical smile lifted his lips. "You look engrossed in that book."

Without thinking she held up her device.

"*The Screwtape Letters.* Ever heard of it? It's a weird little book."

"Good one. I've read all of C. S. Lewis's books."

She shouldn't have shown him something personal like that. "What are you doing wandering the streets at this hour?"

"Beignets were calling my name."

"You should come back in the morning and get them fresh at Petit Charms." All too conscious of the jogging shorts and tank top she slept in, she rose and went to stand at the wrought-iron railing. "Did you need something from me?"

He spread out his hands. "Look, I could shout up to you from the street, but I'd like to come up and talk to you."

The lights were on next door. What could it hurt to have a private conversation? She wasn't afraid of him. She gestured to her left. "There are exterior stairs off the alley. I'll open the door for you."

He nodded and moved that direction, and she went inside to open the door in the kitchen. The iron stairs clanged as he ascended them, and for some reason, the sound made her pulse jump. Maybe this was a bad idea.

She stepped out of the way for him to enter, and his wide shoulders made her kitchen feel small. "The living room is through here."

He gave a nod of approval and followed her. "Nice digs." Parker thrust his nose against his hand and whined.

Traitor dog. "I like it." She led the way into the living room and sank onto the sofa. "It's late. What do you want?"

Parker was still dancing around Reid like they were long-lost friends. Reid settled on the floor and pulled the dog onto his lap. "I'd like to know why you hate me. This documentary is nothing personal. Is there something you don't want me to talk about on film? If so, just tell me. We can work around whatever you want."

Heat scorched her cheeks, and the last scene of the compound's buildings burning down blazed into her memory. "I don't know you well enough to hate you." She couldn't tell him about this. He wouldn't understand. No one did, not even Olivia really.

He cocked a brow. "Just tell me what's eating you."

With those dark eyes boring into her, she couldn't think, much less hold back the words bubbling up in her throat. "How did you know so much about cults?"

"It's a current state of affairs. People

searching for surety about the next life, people looking for a place to belong. Cults can provide that sense of community we seem to be losing day by day as social media takes over more and more of our lives."

He'd nailed it, and she gave a grudging nod. "It was disconcerting to watch."

"Why?" His gaze held her pinned in place. "It's just a documentary."

"Not for some of us." The whispered words startled her. She hadn't meant to tell him.

"You sound like you know more than most."

Something about the sympathy in his eyes opened the torrent of words. "M-My parents. They belonged to one for a while. Until my dad took me away. No one knows about it, though."

"I don't think your dad hides it, does he? That big compound is a sure giveaway that he's got a prepper bent to him."

"That doesn't mean anything. People can be preppers without being in a cult."

He shrugged. "People have guessed about it. Even your detective Brian thinks your dad was in a cult."

She bolted upright as the words seared her. "You're lying."

He crossed his arms over his chest. "Brian

told me just minutes ago."

"You *talked* to him about me being in a cult?" She could hardly choke out the horrible words.

"Of course not. I told him you seemed like a competent chief of police and asked how long he'd known you. He mentioned where your dad lived and the rumors about the cult."

She was going to chew Brian out tomorrow. He had no business discussing her. Not with this man and not with anyone.

"You look like you're about to explode. It bothers you that much that someone might know something that happened to you as a kid? Your parents took you there. You had no say in it."

While what he said was true, it didn't wash away the guilt she felt. "I don't want to talk about it. It was a painful time in my life, and I hate that anyone in town even suspects."

"So that's where your hostility toward me is coming from? The cult documentary I did?"

When he said it like that, it sounded ridiculous. He hadn't even interviewed her. "Don't ever bring it up to me again, and maybe we can get through the next couple of weeks."

"Done." He gave Parker a final pat and rose. "I'll get out of here and see you bright and early tomorrow."

She pressed her lips together and went to lock the door behind him. Somehow the conversation had left her feeling almost stripped bare of the protective layer she'd woven around herself over her past. How many people in town were looking at her and judging her because of her past?

She went back to the balcony, but instead of picking up her e-reader, she sketched Reid's face. She nearly sketched him with hair instead of a shaved head but put down her pencil at the strange impulse. He looked good the way he was.

SIXTEEN

Will's smile could light up a football stadium. The boy wore a Saints cap backward, and he slung two camera bags onto his shoulders as he exited Reid's SUV outside the police station. A tripod stuck up out his backpack.

A pelican fluttered down the strut on the grass by the road, and Will pointed it out. "Look at that!"

"No fish here in town." Reid locked his vehicle. "You don't look eager or anything. This will be hard work."

Will bounced a little on his flip-flops. "It's going to be great, Dad. I know I can do it. Thanks for giving me a chance."

The boy was obsessed with cameras and moviemaking. His phone was filled with movie shorts on various subjects, and he had an eye for composition and angle. "They'll be long days. There won't be time for goofing off."

"I'll stay focused." Will led the way toward the building.

Reid followed slowly. He wasn't sure about this. Being around Jane could be dangerous.

Jane was exiting the door as they approached. She held it open for Parker to exit behind her. "I saw your arrival through the window and thought I'd save you checking in." She shot a glance at Will. "You brought your son."

"He's my acting cameraman. Spring break started, and he's a good videographer." Not that he had to explain anything to her.

Will stooped and petted the animal. "Does the dog get to go with us?"

"I take him everywhere with me. He's a K-9 officer and a great asset. You mind driving? My vehicle is in for maintenance, which should have been okay, but I've been called to a meeting with the mayor."

"I don't mind," Reid said as they walked to his SUV. Her hazel eyes were shadowed this morning, and he suspected she didn't get much sleep after he left last night.

She stopped when she saw the pelican. "There's Pete."

"You know this bird?"

She nodded. "He's kind of a pet around here. I usually go out to the dock with minnows for him, but he must have gotten tired of my neglect." She squatted in front of the bird. "Sorry, Pete, no fish today. You'll have to catch your own."

The pelican eyed her with a beady stare, then flapped his wings and flew off toward the water.

Reid grinned and shook his head. "He acted like he knew what you were saying. So what's up with the meeting with Lisa?"

She made a face. "She sounded upset and wanted me to come to her house, maybe to lessen the chances of being overheard. She'll be pleased to see I haven't managed to ditch you. She lives just out of town."

"You worried she's heard about your dad?"

"I'm sure that's what this is about. News travels fast."

"Then what?"

"Then we'll see."

An evasive answer. What was she up to? Looking at her closed expression it was clear she wasn't about to discuss what was on her mind.

It was a perfect spring morning. The Alabama sun was hot through the windshield, and he turned on the air. Jane stared out the window and said nothing as he drove his big vehicle a few miles out of town. Parker was draped across Will's lap, and the boy was on his phone, so Reid filled the silence by turning on the radio. "Your Grace Finds Me" poured out the speakers, and he felt her tense at the music. He had no idea of her faith — or maybe lack of it — but he could see her jaw flex.

"What is that music? It sounds . . . different."

"Christian music."

"How is it different from other genres?"

He grinned. "The lyrics. Want me to turn it off?"

With the sun in her face, the eyes she turned his way were more gold. "I don't think I've ever met anyone who listens to Christian music."

"You like country. I noticed you listening to Faith Hill last night. I find Christian music helps keep me centered and focused on what's important in life."

"And what do you find important in life?" Her tone indicated she truly wanted to know.

He turned into the parking lot. "Micah 6:8 says God wants us to act justly, to love mercy, and to walk humbly with him. That kind of sums up what I strive for. I don't always succeed, though."

She made a small sound of disbelief. "If

only everyone did that. Instead injustice is everywhere and everyone pursues their own self-interest. Church seems to be a way to control people."

Her time in the cult had scarred her. "You've been in the wrong kind of church. In the right one we learn to be more like Jesus and to encourage each other to strive for eternal values."

"That sounds very foreign to my experience." She unbuckled her seat belt in front of a large brick mansion with pillars on the porch. "I guess we'd better get this over with."

Lisa Chapman sat behind her desk with her hands folded in front of her, and she didn't smile. She was always smiling.

Jane's smile faltered on her lips, and she shut the door behind her entourage. "Everything okay, Lisa?"

Lisa's gaze flitted to Will and Reid behind Jane, and she frowned as the boy lifted the camera to his shoulder to start recording. "There is no need to record this meeting."

"I thought you wanted the documentary to show all aspects of a small-town cop's life," Reid said.

"Not this one."

Ominous words. Jane's chest squeezed,

and she knew her initial trepidation was right. She waited until Will turned off the camera. "What's this all about?"

"Your father has been arrested."

"Yes, I was there when the FBI showed up."

"And you didn't see fit to call me?"

Uh-oh. She hadn't even thought about it. "I'm conducting two homicide investigations, and I didn't think."

Lisa rose and went to fiddle with her window blinds to shut out the sun's glare. "You realize how this looks now, don't you? His daughter in charge of the very department he swindled?"

Jane braced her hands on her hips. "You can't think he's guilty!" Parker came to press his nose against her leg.

Lisa returned to her desk. "The FBI wouldn't have arrested him without a great deal of evidence."

"I know my dad, and he would never do this." Jane hated the quiver in her voice. She tipped up her chin. "He says he's been pursuing evidence of who he thinks did this."

Lisa lifted a brow. "He have any proof yet?"

"Well, no, but over the years I'm sure he's made a lot of enemies." Aware she was grasping at straws, Jane shut up.

"Some of the town council members think we need to suspend you while this investigation is ongoing. The FBI will need help from the department, and we need assurance you'll cooperate with any requests."

Jane swallowed. "Of course I'll comply with anything they need."

"I expect you to put aside your belief in your dad's innocence and look at the evidence."

That might be harder to do. Jane gave a stiff nod. "I'll look at the evidence." *And try to find out who is framing my dad.*

"I'll let the FBI know they'll have your complete cooperation. Thanks for coming in. I'll let the council know there's nothing to worry about."

Jane nodded and forced her stiff limbs to move toward the door. She caught a glimpse of Will's head hanging down. This dressing down had probably been as embarrassing to witness as it was for her to endure.

She rushed for the exit and stepped out into the breeze. She kept her head high until Reid's hand fell on her shoulder and he whispered, "Hang in there."

Her cheeks went hot, and she couldn't look at him. "I'm fine." She walked quickly to the SUV.

He climbed behind the wheel and glanced at her. "Let's go get ice cream."

She finally looked into his warm, compassionate eyes. "Ice cream at nine in the morning? Where would we even find a place open?"

"Dairy Queen will do in a pinch, and I think this is definitely a pinch. I'd say a banana split is in order."

Will climbed in the back with Parker. "Or maybe a hot fudge sundae."

A smile took control of her lips. "I guess I could face-plant into a bowl of ice cream. There's a Dairy Queen in Foley. We can go there."

"I know where that is." He grinned and pulled out of the circular driveway. "Then where to?"

She wasn't sure when or how this new camaraderie had developed, but she wasn't entirely comfortable with it. "I need to check on Nicole Pearson's autopsy."

"Are we going to your office or to the morgue?" His lips twisted into a grimace, and he swallowed hard.

She grinned. "Big, tough guy afraid of a dead body?"

"I'd like to keep my banana split in my stomach. Is that so wrong?"

She huffed out a laugh. "Well put."

They fell into a companionable silence as he drove to Foley. She tried not to listen to the comforting lyrics of the Christian music playing. Wanting comfort and love was what got her parents into the cult situation in the first place.

Reid drove into the DQ lot and parked. He got out of his SUV and took Parker's leash from Will as they exited the backseat.

He held the restaurant door open for them, and she entered the cool wash of air-conditioning and the enticing aroma of sweet treats. The Peanut Buster Parfait was her favorite, and she licked the hot chocolate and caramel slowly from her spoon. What was she going to do about the FBI? First she needed to see what evidence they had on him. Was it someone's testimony or something more serious?

Reid threw away the empty boat from his banana split. "You're lost in thought."

"Just thinking about the trouble my dad is in."

"You seem pretty adamant he's innocent."

"If you'd ever met my dad, you'd be certain too."

He wiped his hands on a napkin. "I'm sure."

Her phone rang, and she glanced at the screen. "Chief Hardy."

"The autopsy on Nicole Pearson is done, Chief. I just emailed the results to you. Oops, sorry, gotta go. I have another call." The ME ended the call before Jane could ask any more questions.

"Let's head for my office. I want to see what killed Nicole for sure."

And if she was able to reinstate Paul Baker, her job might be in even more jeopardy. Lisa had made it clear Jane was on the rocks in heavy surf. One false move, and she'd be out and Paul would be in. While she wasn't sure she had the skills to do this job, she was sure he didn't.

Her head felt as big as a melon. Fanny blinked in the total darkness that was as smothering as a wool blanket and waited for her vision to clear enough to see where she was. It didn't happen. She reached out and felt a hard mattress beneath her. She sat up and set her hand down to touch the ground. The bed was just a mattress on a dirt floor.

Where was she and where was her son? Terror held her immobile for several seconds. She wet her lips. "Harry?" Her voice was barely above a hoarse whisper.

She eased up enough to stand on wobbly legs. "Harry!" The crushing weight in her chest grew. "Harry, come to Mommy. Follow my voice."

No matter how hard she strained, she couldn't hear anything but the wild pounding of her own heartbeat. She didn't sense anyone else with her. Had Harry managed to escape? She could only pray he'd made it to safety.

She smelled musty air and dirt like maybe she was in a basement. Hands in front of her, she shuffled across the uneven floor a few feet until she touched the cold wall. She worked her way around the room and counted her steps as she went. The space appeared to be about an eight-by-eight square with one door and no windows. No light penetrated the room from the door so she had to be underground somewhere. That realization made her shudder.

She took a calming breath and made her way back to the door. The doorknob wouldn't turn. Locked on the outside. Maybe she could find some way to pick the lock. She felt around in her hair for the bobby pin she'd used to hold back the bangs she was trying to grow out.

When she yanked it free, it fell to the floor. "No, no," she sobbed. She fell to the floor and felt around the cold dirt for it. Fanny finally found it in the crack between the floor and the wall.

On her knees, she felt for a hole in the lock to try to insert one end. There was nothing like that in the door, just a cold knob on a smooth metal plate. Tears burned her eyes, and she sat back on her haunches. She had to get out of here and find Harry. Her baby needed her. What if he was still wandering in the woods somewhere? What if he was hurt and crying for her?

The pain was almost more than she could bear. She got up and staggered around the room again. Maybe there was something in here to use. But no matter where she put her hands, the only item in the room was that bare mattress on the floor. With her bobby pin in her mouth, she went back to the door and felt for the hinges. Maybe they could be pried loose.

If only she had even a glimmer of light to see. She touched the hinges and tried to see with her fingers. There was a large pin holding the hinges, so she tried to pry it up with the bobby pin. It didn't budge, and she pressed hard until the pin bent. Nothing.

Terror for her son clawed at her chest, making it hard to draw air. The man could do what he wanted with her, but Harry had to be all right. She had to find him and breathe in his little-boy scent. She wanted to feel his small arms tight around her neck. "Harry," she said brokenly as she sank to the floor. "Oh, God, take care of Harry."

SEVENTEEN

Jane spotted Paul before Reid parked his SUV in the city hall parking lot. The detective wore a hangdog expression as he leaned against Jane's SUV as if waiting for her. It seemed odd to see him in shorts and a T-shirt instead of his uniform. They didn't socialize, so their contact had been mostly limited to here.

Her gaze went to the man next to him. Victor Armstrong looked smug and confident.

Reid turned off the engine. "Looks like trouble's waiting for you. Does this need to be a private conversation?"

"No. Maybe they'll make it fast if we're not alone." She shoved open her door and slammed it behind her before she strode over to join Paul and Victor. "Did you call Lisa and tell her about my dad?"

Paul straightened from his slouch against her vehicle. "Was it supposed to be a secret?

189

You should have called her yourself."

"So that's a yes. And I suppose you're here asking to be reinstated, but the whole time you're stabbing me in the back."

"Like I said, you should have called yourself. Lisa agreed with that as well."

"And I do too," Victor said. "You're not up to this job, Jane." Victor gave her a contemptuous sneer before walking away to cross the street to the coffee shop.

"I can tell I'm wasting my time." She turned toward the building.

"Wait, that's not why I'm here," Paul called after her.

She turned back around and stared at him. "Okay, let's have it."

His blue eyes blazed with hatred. "Try not to let your dislike of me cloud your judgment in the Dawson case, Jane. Take a look at the evidence."

It hadn't escaped her that he didn't call her Chief. "What are you talking about?"

"Your dad knows more about Dawson than you seem to realize. They're fishing buddies. We need to bring him in for an interrogation."

She'd never heard her dad mention Gary's name. "That's ludicrous."

He threw up his hands. "You're not worth my time. You're so sure you have all the answers so you figure it out." He stormed over to his truck and got in before he roared off with the engine revved at full blast.

Her hands shook as she walked off and headed for her office. Parker's toenails clicked on the hot concrete as he followed with Reid and Will.

She was almost too angry to speak. Paul was on suspension. He didn't get to tell her how to conduct this investigation, and he sure didn't have the right to try to betray her. She'd known the moment Lisa told her why she'd been called in that Paul had notified her. His jealousy and spite in the department were legendary. Even the cool touch of the air conditioner inside failed to dampen the heat in her face.

Reid closed her office door and dropped into a chair while Will sat on the floor and pulled the dog into his lap. "You were a little hard on him."

She whipped around and glared at him. "This is none of your business, Reid. You don't know how Paul operates. For years he's been behind every mean whisper and rumor. He's ousted multiple deputies with his innuendos and lies. And he's sneaky. He's gotten away with it because my dad liked him, but Dad hasn't been on the receiving end of his barbed tongue. Until now, that is. And I hate —" Her voice broke, and she cleared her throat. "I hate how much this will hurt Dad to know the man he's stood behind all these years has quickly turned to stab him in the back."

Reid's eyes filled with compassion. "He didn't seem to assume your dad was guilty. I think you're letting your dislike color what he said."

She opened her mouth, then closed it again. With every fiber of her being she wanted to deny his accusation. There had been bad blood between Paul and her ever since she came into the department as green as seaweed. It had started when Paul had gleefully pointed out an error she'd made in paperwork. He'd insinuated she was only hired because she was the chief's daughter, and there was enough truth in the accusation that she'd been defensive.

When she didn't answer, Reid glanced behind him to where Will sat with Parker. The boy looked uncomfortable at the heated exchange. "Will, how about getting us some Cokes from the vending machine in the cafeteria? I'll have a Pepsi." He glanced at Jane. "You want something?"

"I'll have a sweet tea, thanks." Her cheeks cooled a bit at his measured tone. She watched Will walk away with Parker. "You've raised a good kid." Better to steer the conversation into less controversial directions. "Is his mother still alive?"

A deep pain flickered in his eyes. "She hasn't seen him since he was seven. He's been in a private school in New Orleans. He likes it better here in the small public school, though. He wants to play football."

"Of course he does." Why did she care? She shouldn't find this topic as interesting as she did. She barely knew Reid and his son, but she was dying to know what happened between him and his wife. Her curious nature was hard to keep in check.

Before she spilled out the prying questions hovering on her lips, she turned toward her desk. "I want to take a look at the Pearson autopsy results."

"Why are you handling this anyway? You've got competent detectives."

"That's part of being a small-town chief. We all have to pull our weight and earn our keep."

Which was all true, but keeping her fingers in things went way deeper than that. She didn't intend to ever let herself be deceived and kept out of the loop. Not like at Mount Sinai.

Reid watched Jane as she leaned toward her

computer screen and studied the Pearson autopsy details. Will was in the corner with his video camera trained on her intent expression. This was going to make good viewing. Her passion for her job showed through, loud and clear.

She wore her hair loose today, and she tucked the light-brown strands behind her ear as she focused on her screen. The slatted blinds at the window behind her allowed filtered sunlight to highlight her hair. Did she bring this much attention to detail to everything in her life? He suspected she did.

When he got home, he'd take a look at the images they'd gotten so far. While the idea for this documentary had been a ruse to get close to her, he was enough of a reporter to recognize a compelling story unfolding in front of him. Viewers would eat up watching a female chief of police navigate the difficult job.

He adopted his professional manner and voice. "Chief, what's your next step in this investigation?"

She looked up but didn't glance at the camera. "According to the autopsy, Ms. Pearson died around five in the morning, and Paul has a clear alibi at that time with the ER visit. There were abrasions on her fingers where she tried to claw her way out of some kind of containment, most likely a car trunk, but the fibers haven't been matched yet. It appears that someone overpowered her and threw her into a trunk. There are no clues to where she might have been before she was taken. When we get the fibers back, we might know the type of car."

"Not much to go on."

"No." She leaned back in her chair. "Because of the time of death, it's doubtful my detective was involved — at least not directly."

"Will you be reinstating him?"

"I don't really have a choice. The town council will hear that he couldn't possibly have done it, and Paul's advocate on the council, Victor Armstrong, will demand I reinstate him. He's a good detective, and I'll assign him to the other homicide." She reached for her desk phone.

If she was dreading the phone call, her expression didn't show it. She punched in the number and waited several moments. "Detective, it's Chief Hardy. I'd like you to return to work soon, today if possible. You've been cleared as a possible suspect in the Pearson murder, and I'm assigning you to the Dawson case. All right, thank you." She punched the phone off. "He's across the street at the coffee shop and will be in shortly."

"Was he all right with not working the Pearson case?"

"Of course. He's a professional and knows how things work." She rose. "I want better coffee than this swill we have here. Let's go to Pelican Brews."

Will stopped the camera, and the three of them headed outside with Parker. He squinted up at the darkening clouds. "Storm coming in soon."

Jane glanced up. "Yep. That's Alabama spring for you."

Reid looked over her head at movement on the sidewalk across the street. His heart nearly stopped when he saw Lauren standing outside the coffee shop. Her green eyes were fixed on him. She teetered on high heels and wore tight-fitting jeans and a top that showed off her curves. False advertising. A cute figure was never a substitute for a beautiful spirit. His gaze settled on Jane as she moved across the street. Jane's spirit was much more compelling.

If he didn't go Lauren's way, she was sure to come after him. And Jane would wonder why he wasn't following. All he could do was act like nothing was wrong and she was no more than a casual acquaintance. Would Will recognize her from pictures? She was older, and her hair was blonder. Maybe Will wouldn't notice.

He forced a congenial smile to his face and went across the street with Will and Parker beside him. Should he just nod and keep on walking, or should he stop? At least Jane was already inside the coffee shop.

Lauren took the decision out of his hands. "Hello, Reid. And, Will, how big you've gotten. You're going to give the girls in school a heart attack."

"Um, hi." Will eyed her with an easy smile. He sidled past her with the dog. "I'll order our coffees, Dad. See you inside."

Whew, at least Will would be out of the way. When the door shut behind his son, Reid crossed his arms over his chest. "What do you want, Lauren? I said all I intend to about the situation already. This is finished."

Her fake smile faded, and she glared at him. "No, it isn't. I've retained an attorney. I want some alimony."

"And you seriously think any judge in the state would award you alimony after you abandoned us and let us think you were dead?"

She put her hand, tipped in pink fingernails, on his arm. "Look, I'm not giving up, Reid. You owe me. I could go right inside this minute and talk to Will."

"I already told him you've come back. He doesn't want to see you."

"I don't believe you."

He shrugged. "Go ask him yourself, but be prepared to be rejected." He could only pray his words deterred her. He didn't want to subject Will to this mess.

"You've turned him against me."

"You did that all by yourself. I'm not the one who left and never contacted him."

"Let's quit raking up the past and agree we want what's best for Will. I think you would prefer he didn't see me or talk to me. I'd rather not disrupt his life either. All I need is a little money, Reid. That's not too much to ask."

"The answer is still no." His heart hammered against his ribs as he turned and went into the coffee shop.

He could only pray she didn't follow him inside. If he gave her a piece, she'd take the whole pie and ruin Will's life. Maybe he was playing this wrong, but he couldn't stomach being blackmailed.

EIGHTEEN

The aromas of ground coffee beans and carrot cake muffins teased Reid's nose, and he dodged a couple exiting the shop before he joined Will and Jane in the line for pickup. "You ordered for me?" Parker pressed against his leg, and Reid rubbed his ears.

Will nodded. "Who was that woman, Dad? She smiled at me like she knew me."

Reid stopped a moment, unsure how to answer. "She's no one important." And she didn't know Will, not really.

Will shrugged. "Hey, Chief Hardy likes stuff about the Roman empire too. We were just talking about Pompeii. I told her I wanted you to do a documentary about it someday so I could go."

"We'll do that one of these days," Reid said.

Will's name was called, and he stepped forward to take the cardboard tray of three coffees.

"You might fool your son, but it's hard to trick a detective," Jane said under her breath. "Your body language gave you away. Old girlfriend?"

"Maybe." How did he allay her suspicions? He jerked his head toward Will, who was heading for an empty table by the window. "Not in front of the boy."

She nodded and followed Will to the table. Reid's mind raced with how he was going to handle Will's questions. His son wouldn't be satisfied with that lame response earlier. Maybe changing the subject would work.

Will handed the coffees around and leaned back in his chair. Before he could start in on the questions, Reid jumped in. "I took a look at the footage you shot, Will. Great job. I'll be able to use most of it."

Will's dark eyes gleamed. "Maybe I'll become your full-time videographer and travel with you when you go out of the country."

"You need to finish school first."

"You could hire a tutor."

"What about football? You wouldn't be able to play if you were being tutored instead of attending school."

"You're moving here for sure?" Jane asked. "I thought you were just thinking about it."

Will nodded. "Yeah, Dad's buying the

house we're living in. I like it here."

Jane's hazel eyes went greener, and she lifted her chin. Obviously she couldn't wait to see the back of him. Her reaction would be very different if she knew who he was.

A movement across the café caught his eye. "I think that's your reinstated detective coming to thank you."

Jane turned as the man approached. "Detective." Her voice was cool.

Paul had changed into his uniform, and he wore a confident smile. "Mind if I have a seat? I have something to talk to you about."

"Would this be better in my office?"

Paul glanced around and shook his head. "The place is nearly empty now. No one can overhear. I assume your reporter is privy to everything you're working on."

"Yes, he is. Have a seat." Jane took a sip of her coffee and set it back on the table.

"I've been poring over the information about the Dawson case. I mentioned Gary and your dad were fishing buddies. You didn't seem to know about it. I find that a little strange. Did you talk to your dad about the murder before he was arrested?"

"No." Jane's voice was clipped. "And I never heard Dad mention him."

"They've been friends about ten years, and I've got someone willing to testify that

Dawson was selling drugs. I think it might be the same drugs your dad stole from the evidence locker."

"You're assuming my dad is guilty, and I think we're going to find out that's not the case."

Paul's mouth twisted. "Spoken like a blindly trusting daughter. The FBI usually doesn't make mistakes like that. They have a boatload of evidence. Have you looked at it?"

"Not yet. I've got two homicides to investigate and there's been no time."

"All the things your dad has done will make your hair curl. I think he might have killed Dawson." Paul grinned as he delivered his opinion.

"And I think that's a crazy idea," Jane said.

Reid wished he'd had Will recording this. The conflict would make great footage, but it would be too intrusive for Will to unpack his camera.

Jane's hand trembled a bit as she picked up her coffee. "There are plenty of possible killers. His wife, his coworkers, and especially his bookie. This is way too early in the case to be jumping to conclusions."

Paul's grin morphed to something wolfish. "That's where I come in. I'm going to prove I'm right."

"You're to follow the evidence, Detective. If you can't objectively look under every corner, I'll reassign you."

"And I'll go to the council and tell them you're trying to hide your father's involvement."

Whoa, open warfare. Reid snapped his sagging mouth shut. The guy had a lot of guff to come back at her like that.

Jane stared him down. "You really hate having to report to me, don't you? Nothing you do or say can change what's happened. If you are insubordinate, I will put you on suspension again, and you won't get off so easily next time."

Paul gave an uneasy laugh, and his gaze skittered away from her steely expression. "I just want to follow the clues, Jane. That's not wrong."

"It's *Chief* Hardy. See that's what you do then. I want a daily report on my desk every evening. Interviews with everyone possibly involved. His wife, his boss, anyone who knew him. Check with Brian on leads to finding his bookie. I want this investigation to be perfect. If my father happens to be involved — which I highly doubt — I'll be able to see the evidence myself. I won't have him railroaded because you have a beef with me. Clear?"

Paul stood. "Crystal. I'm going to get to work." He stalked for the exit.

"You're going to have a lot of trouble with him," Reid said.

"I've had nothing but trouble with him for years." She stared through the window at the officer crossing the street. "I wonder if the person Dad suspects is Gary Dawson? If they're friends it would explain why he didn't want to tell me his suspicions yet."

"You might be right. Maybe you should flat out ask your dad."

"I think I will." Her gaze came back to him. "I doubt Baker will believe anything like that. He's after my dad, and he's got support on the council. It makes him feel invincible." She sighed and rubbed her forehead. "I probably shouldn't have taken the job. It might be more than I can handle."

"It's not. I've been immensely impressed by your capable handling of all this, Jane. You've got spunk and wisdom. Don't let a blowhard like Baker make you doubt yourself."

Her eyes brightened. "Thank you for that, Reid."

He watched her as they finished their coffee. She intrigued him more and more.

Jane glanced at her watch, though the

beautiful sunset out over the water confirmed it was close to six. Reid didn't seem rattled by being out here after quitting time. In fact, he looked pretty good in his khaki shorts and red shirt.

Parker lay at her feet on the pier and lifted his head to observe a gull tipping its head to study the pier for crumbs of bread.

Will leaned over the rail and aimed his camera down into the water. "There's a pelican."

"It's probably Pete again," she said without looking.

Reid smiled. "This is a new side of Chief Hardy. I didn't take you for someone who would name a pelican."

"Pete's not just any pelican. I raised him." She tried not to notice the way Will focused the camera back on her. It was getting easier.

"How did that come about?" Reid asked. "You didn't mention it earlier."

"A pelican had gotten caught in a fishing net and died. I heard squawking and saw her nest. There were several babies, and I tried to save them all, but only Pete survived."

Will's dark eyes, so like his father's, went wide. "How do you raise a pelican? What do they eat?"

"Small fish. Pete is a voracious eater. Once he was old enough, I brought him here and released him. He remembers me, though, and is always nearby when I stop. Townspeople like to feed him too. He's kind of the town mascot now. You should get a picture of him." It would feel stupid to admit she felt a strong connection to the brown pelican, almost like a child. She often came out here in the evenings to talk to him too. Silly, really, but she could bare her soul to the bird.

"Good idea." Reid directed Will to get some footage of the pelican. "So what are we waiting on?"

"I called Carmencita Cook. She posted a Facebook message on Nicole's page about her sins finding her out. I think she likely knows something."

"How does she know Nicole?"

"She's got her fingers in most everything that goes on in town. If anyone knows who Dawson's bookie is, she will. And she might have some information about Nicole's death."

Reid jerked his head toward the shore where a lone figure hurried their way. "That her?"

Jane squinted. "It is." She rose from the bench and waved.

Carmencita Cook had been the head of the library board for ten years. In her fifties, her flashing dark eyes and curly dark hair made her appear younger. She never seemed to meet a stranger and was a frequent patron at the coffee shop, so Jane knew her fairly well. And her gentle demeanor hid the steely backbone everyone in town depended on.

Jane stepped forward and smiled. "Thanks so much for agreeing to meet me."

Carmencita wore a red flowery dress that swirled around her brown calves. "It's a terrible thing, Jane. Of course I want to help all I can, but I didn't want to be overheard. I abhor gossip."

The statement sounded promising even though Jane knew the woman thrived on gossip. If she didn't, she wouldn't have posted that comment on Nicole's Facebook page.

Jane got out her little notebook. "Let's talk first about Nicole. What can you tell me?"

"It's a small town. I often saw her with her friends out and about. She went bar-hopping most Friday nights up in Mobile, and I picked her up one night when her car broke down on her way home. I didn't care much for her associates. Her brother was not a good influence on her."

Jane looked up. "Her brother?"

"Marshall Thomas."

That name struck a chord with Jane. "He's been arrested several times for dealing drugs. They don't have the same last name."

Carmencita nodded. "Half siblings. His associates seemed even worse than him. Nicole often had someone sleeping on her sofa. She was a sweet girl but had no discernment. I suspect one of her brother's associates killed her."

"But why the weird punishment? That doesn't seem like something a drug dealer would do. They tend to take care of problems with a bullet," Reid said.

Carmencita pressed her full lips together, then shook her head. "I don't trust her brother and his friends, but I could be wrong." She hesitated. "She was seeing a married man. Maybe he killed her."

"Paul Baker?"

"Oh good, you already know."

"Is that affair why you posted the comment on Facebook?"

Carmencita's face went pink. "I shouldn't have said anything, but her morals were questionable. I think Detective Baker should be interrogated."

"Paul has an alibi for when she was killed."

Carmencita shrugged. "So perhaps it's the vigilante in town."

It was looking more and more like the vigilante. "Anything else?"

"No." She glanced at her watch. "I must go soon. You want to hear about Gary?"

"Yes, please."

"I knew him well. His wife is my cousin."

Whoa, Jane hadn't been expecting that. "Small world. Did you know he gambled?"

"I did." Carmencita's gaze cut to Reid and Will, and she frowned. "You are taping this?"

"This is Reid Dixon. He's doing a documentary about small-town police departments." She shook her head at Will. "Turn off the camera, please." She waited until Will complied. "About Gary's gambling."

Carmencita's frown eased. "He was in trouble. I saw him grow more and more stressed, and my sweet cousin too." Her eyes narrowed, and she clenched her fists. "He hit her."

"I saw the bruise."

"Perhaps I shouldn't say this, but I told him if he touched her again, I would kill him. And I meant it. Scum of the earth to strike the mother of his child in that way!" She muttered something in Spanish, and her dark eyes flashed.

Jane believed her, but she also knew Carmencita hadn't killed him. It would have taken a large man — or even more than one — to bludgeon someone Dawson's size. "What did he say?"

"He tried to borrow money from me. Me! The one person who knew he would never pay it back."

"Do you know who he owed? And how much?"

The other woman's frown returned. "I do. He lives in Mobile, so you're unlikely to know him. He's not someone to mess with, Jane."

"His name, please."

"Joseph Davies."

The name sounded vaguely familiar. "He's got ties to organized crime?"

"Of course. He's got this area totally covered for some big boss in Atlanta. When Joe says jump, everyone asks how high. The rumors about him are bad — extortion, torture, murder. He's evil clear to the bone. Ask your dad."

"Dad's had run-ins with this Davies?"

Carmencita looked confused. "I meant you should talk to your dad about Gary. Gary owed him money too."

Coldness snaked down Jane's spine.

"You're saying my dad knew Gary well enough to loan him money?"

"Honey, the two went fishing the last Sunday of every month. Surely you knew that."

Jane shook her head. "I only heard they were fishing buddies recently. I've never heard Dad mention Gary, and I never met him."

She didn't go out to the house that much since she saw Dad every day at work. They talked about law enforcement, and she'd been happy to keep her head buried in the sand.

Carmencita's dark eyes went soft. "Your dad will be able to tell you more, but the two have been friends awhile."

"How do you know he owed my dad money?"

"Gary wanted to pay your dad back first. That's why he asked to borrow money from me. I hated to say no because it would benefit your father, but I had to."

Jane forced speech past her numb lips. "Of course you did."

She didn't like the way this was looking for her father. Could Paul be right? She didn't want to believe it. She thanked Carmencita before she headed back to the vehicle.

"Now what?" Reid asked.

She appreciated the way he didn't look at her. "I'm going to examine Paul's evidence before talking to my dad."

NINETEEN

Jane reined in her anger and pushed open Paul's office without knocking only to find it empty. She went to his desk and glanced at his computer screen. The Dawson file was up, and she scanned through the evidence again, though she knew it well except for Paul's focus on her father.

There were pictures of her dad and Dawson aboard her dad's boat. She scrolled through them and noted the various dates. Paul was right. They'd been friends awhile, and as she thought again about her relationship with her dad, she realized he'd never talked much about himself. If they mentioned anything personal, it was about what she was doing. On the rare occasions she tried to talk to him about his personal life, he changed the subject.

There were pictures of her dad and Elizabeth out to dinner with Dawson and his wife as well. She recognized the backdrop of one of the restaurants in Mobile. There were also statements from a couple of fishermen who mentioned they'd overheard an argument about a loan between Dawson and her father that got heated.

Was this what Elizabeth meant when she implied her dad had secrets? Jane glanced at Reid and Will, who stood in the doorway. "I don't really know my dad at all. How is that possible?"

"Some people wrap themselves in a steel wall that's impossible to penetrate," Reid said.

Parker brushed past the guys and went to stand by the closet to the left of the desk. Jane started to call him back, but he whined and pawed at the doorknob, then looked back at her and barked. Frowning, she went to his side and opened the door.

A small boy, his face streaked with dirt, stared up at her with pleading eyes. He whimpered but didn't speak as she took an automatic step back.

Reid must have seen her involuntary reaction, and he stepped across the room to her side, then knelt in front of the little boy. "Hello, buddy, what are you doing in there?"

The child didn't speak, but tears pooled in his big brown eyes. Jane recovered herself and knelt in front of him too. "What's your name, honey?" She wanted to touch his soft brown hair, but she didn't want to scare him.

His lips trembled. "Harry."

"How old are you, Harry?"

"Four. I'm four."

Jane wanted to scoop him up and hold him close. Poor little guy was terrified of something. "Where's your mommy or daddy?"

The tears left tracks in his face, and he swiped at them, smearing them through the dirt. "I don't know. Mommy and I were in the park, and a man took her to his car. She told me to run and hide so I did." His gaze darted to Will, and the pleading expression intensified.

Will stepped closer and leaned down with his arms out. The little boy scuttled into Will's embrace, and the older boy stood with Harry in his arms. The child put his head on Will's shoulder and sighed as he relaxed against the teenager. Jane exchanged a long look with Reid. Maybe Harry had an older brother who cared for him.

She touched his dirty hand. "When were you in the park, Harry?"

His forehead wrinkled. "A long time. Before it got dark. I slept on a bench, but Mommy never came to get me."

Overnight then. Jane shuddered at what could have happened. She needed to call Child Protective Services, but she hated to turn this fearful little guy over to someone else. She caught the combative look in Reid's eye. He was thinking the same thing. She had some discretion here as chief.

She motioned for Reid to follow her to the other side of the office. "I don't want to turn him over to CPS. He might be an eyewitness to a crime from what he's saying. We don't know what's going on here, and he could be in danger."

"Let me and Will take him. Will is a kid magnet."

"We can't haul a little guy like that around searching for answers."

"I'll hire a nanny, and I'll have Will stay with him."

"What about your video camera?"

"I'll hire a temp."

He had all the answers, but they were answers she'd hoped he'd come up with. "Okay. Let's see if he remembers anything that might help us. I'll check the missing persons database too. Someone has to be looking for him and his mother."

She started for the door, then stopped so quickly Reid almost ran into her. "Wait a minute. Yesterday we found an abandoned car with the door standing open. There was a booster seat in the backseat, and the situation seemed like it could have been an abduction. Maybe Harry was there."

"Did you get a gander at his clothes? He's wearing Nike shoes and a Calvin Klein jogging suit."

"You know designer brands?"

He shrugged. "Part of my job. I only mention it to say he's well dressed. His mom is probably in serious danger if she hasn't been frantically pounding on your door to find him."

"Good point."

They rejoined the two boys and Parker, but she couldn't ask Harry any more questions because his dark lashes fanned out on his cheeks, and he hung limply against Will. "He's asleep."

Will nodded. "Poor little guy is tuckered out, probably from being so scared. You're not going to give him to CPS, are you?"

"No, we're taking him home with us if you're game," Reid said.

The worry in Will's face ebbed, and he smiled. "I'll help take care of him."

"That's what I told Jane."

She glanced toward the window. "We need to get out of here without being seen. Get your SUV and bring it to the side door. I've got a throw on the love seat in my office. We'll toss it over him and scoot out the side door. It's lunchtime, and we're short-staffed. Hopefully no one will see us."

"What was he doing in that closet?" Will asked.

"Good question. Maybe he can tell us more after he wakes up."

"What about a car seat?" Reid asked.

She frowned. "I don't have one."

"Anything in the evidence room or somewhere on the premises?"

She shook her head. "Not to my knowledge."

"At least the house isn't far. I'll drive slowly."

She liked Reid's take-charge attitude and the way he'd quickly wanted to help this little guy. He wasn't just a pretty face.

He couldn't believe his eyes. Chief Hardy and her nosy journalist had just hustled Harry out the back of city hall. If he hadn't been driving by at that moment, he never would have seen her. He'd been looking all over for that kid.

How had Harry escaped him and found his way here? Was someone helping him — someone who suspected what was going on? But no, he didn't believe that. The kid had probably been told to go to the police for help and had managed to do it without detection.

Sometimes the universe worked in weird ways, but he wasn't going to let this stop him. He turned around to try to follow them, but they'd vanished. Maybe they'd gone to the journalist's place. He drove as fast as he could out to where the journalist lived, then motored slowly past the driveway. He grimaced when he saw the SUV in the drive.

He couldn't snatch the kid with so many people there. Hardy would have her gun, and Reid seemed to be the type to carry a gun given all his exotic travel. Plus, there was his large son. It would be difficult to get in and out without being seen.

He'd bide his time. At least he knew where the kid was. The right circumstances would show themselves, and he'd be ready.

He rolled around a Kennedy half-dollar in his fingers. No one would understand the significance, and he liked knowing something they'd never figure out.

Jane was beginning to be a problem. She was tenacious and way too smart. He'd enjoyed taunting her, but he might have to take her out of the picture. He didn't want to do that until he'd extracted the full measure of his revenge, but he'd do whatever was necessary.

Harry slept on the leather sofa in the living room while Will stayed close in case the boy woke up frightened. Reid sat in his office with Jane while she logged on to her laptop and into the system at the office. He watched her intent expression as she looked for information about the lad. Parker slept at her feet.

The sun shone through the window and turned her brown hair to a fierier color. She was a tiny thing, but her personality and drive were giant sized. He liked her more than he'd expected.

She looked up and caught him staring. He fiddled with his mouse to cover his embarrassment. "Finding anything?"

"No missing child's been reported. No missing mother either. When he wakes up, we'll see if he knows his last name or his address. That will give us a lot more to go on."

"What about the abandoned car? Any information on the owner?"

"Not yet. Brian is trying to run down the rental agreement. I just shot him a text to tell him I might have found the occupant of the car's booster seat."

She closed her laptop and stood, stretching out her back. "I need coffee. I'll make it if you don't mind me poking around in your kitchen."

"I'll show you where the stuff is, and I'll warm up some gumbo."

"Gumbo sounds good. I'm hungry, and the boy might want something."

He likely wouldn't want gumbo. At that age all Will wanted was a peanut butter and jelly sandwich, but he had the ingredients for that in the kitchen. He showed her the coffee and filters, then put the soup in a pan and turned on a burner.

The coffeepot began to gurgle, and Jane went to stand by the big windows that looked out on a tributary of the Bon Secour River. "Beautiful setting here. Gators I bet, though."

"We've seen a few, and I've warned Will to keep an eye out for copperheads and water moccasins too. I'm sure there are snakes around, though we haven't seen any."

The scent of coffee mingled with that of the bubbling soup. He turned off the stove and transferred the soup to three bowls, then handed her one. "Spoons are in that drawer." He pointed to the drawer under the coffeepot.

She nodded, and he carried the other two

bowls to the dining room table, a trestle design with cushioned seats. He motioned to Will, who eased off the sofa away from the sleeping child to join them.

Jane ate a spoonful. "I see you've discovered Tin Top Restaurant. They make the best seafood gumbo around."

"Dad found them the first day we got here," Will said. "What about Harry? How are we going to find his family?"

Reid loved his son's tender heart, but it would be best not to allow him to get too close to the boy. Once they found his parents, they'd be unlikely to see him again. "I'm sure Jane will find them soon."

Will bolted down his soup before going over to look at Harry again. "Why isn't he waking up? He's been asleep for two hours."

"He had a rough night," Reid said. "Just let him rest for a little while. We don't want to traumatize him more."

Will frowned. "I think I'll go watch TV in my room. Call me when he wakes up. He'll want me." He glanced back at the sleeping child as the boy's eyelids fluttered open.

Harry sat up and yawned. "I'm thirsty."

Will whipped back around and picked him up. "Juice? We've got apple and orange juice."

"Apple juice." Harry looped his left arm

around Will's neck.

Reid turned for the kitchen. "I'll get it." While he was there, he made a PB and J sandwich and hurried back to the living room, where he found Harry on Will's lap watching a cartoon on TV.

Harry accepted the juice and sandwich. "Did you find my mommy?"

"Not yet, little man."

Jane squatted in front of Harry and Will. "Do you know your last name, Harry? Or your address? It will help us find your mommy."

His large brown eyes were somber, and he nodded. "I'm Steven Harry Dawson, but Mommy calls me Harry after the prince. He's way far across the sea."

Jane blinked and shot a glance Reid's way. Reid saw the confusion in her hazel eyes. Gary had a four-year-old boy, but Reid hadn't seen him since he was a newborn. This had to be Gary's boy. Which meant something had happened to Fanny.

"Your mommy is Fanny?"

Harry nodded at Reid. "Something bad happened to Daddy. Mommy said he went far away, and I won't see him anymore." His eyes filled with tears. "I want my mommy." He turned his head and buried his face in Will's shirt. His shoulders shook with the ferocity of his sobs.

Reid's heart squeezed. Poor little guy. They had to find out what happened to Fanny.

Jane rose from in front of Harry and was on her phone. He heard her putting out a BOLO for Fanny Dawson with a description. Why had Fanny rented a car? Had someone been following her?

A worry line crouched between Jane's forehead. "I left a message for Brian about Fanny being missing. I thought she planned to go to her mom's. Do you know her name? I'll call her and see if she's heard from Fanny."

He hated to add to her worry, but there was no choice. "You probably have better access to her number than I do. Her mother is one of our US senators. Senator Fox."

She gaped at him. "Her mother is Senator Jessica Fox?"

"One and the same."

Jane pulled out her phone again. "This is going to blow up in the media. I'd better call the senator right now. I can't believe this is a coincidence — it has to be related to Gary's death. What was he involved with that could reach out like this and envelop his entire family?"

Good question, but Reid had no answers.

Twenty

Jane waited for what felt like an eternity to be connected to Senator Fox. She'd told the assistant she urgently needed to speak to the senator about her daughter, but she must have been hard to track down with the length of time Jane was forced to listen to Debussy playing.

"One moment please. I have the senator."

There was a click, and the senator's signature husky voice came over the line. "You have Fanny with you?"

Jane swallowed. "No, Senator, but I have Harry." She told Senator Fox the little that Harry had told her.

The senator uttered a soft moan. "Fanny should have been here yesterday morning. She called to tell me about Gary's murder and said she and Harry would join me when I returned from the fund-raiser in Washington, DC. I offered to cancel and come home immediately, but she wanted some alone time to process it all and talk to Harry."

"Do you know if she took her own car or rented a car?"

"Her car was in the garage getting a new transmission, so I told her to rent one and I'd pay for it. I called the rental place and arranged for them to pick her up."

"What time was this?"

"Wednesday evening, about seven I think."

Right after Jane left Fanny. So had Harry been on his own since yesterday morning? Jane's heart squeezed at the thought. "Did you talk to your daughter after that?"

"I spoke to her several times on Thursday. She seemed to be doing all right. When she didn't arrive on Friday, I tried calling multiple times, but I never reached her."

"Did you report her missing?" Jane kept her tone non-accusing.

"No. Fanny is a grown woman, and I thought maybe she'd decided to go to a friend's. I've received no ransom calls or anything like that, so I didn't know she was in danger. She and I have a . . . difficult relationship."

That statement was fraught with implications, and Jane had to tread carefully. "So it's not uncommon for her to say she was coming and not show up?"

"Uncommon? What's more uncommon

was for her to ask me for help of any kind. What happened to Gary?"

"We don't know yet." Jane told the senator all she knew about Gary's death and his gambling. "We now know the name of the bookie. It's Joseph Davies. Does that ring a bell at all?"

"No, I've never heard the name."

"Did you know Gary was hitting Fanny?"

The senator's gasp was loud in Jane's ear. "He laid his hands on my daughter?"

"She had a black eye, ma'am. She blamed herself." Jane hated telling her about Fanny's words and behavior. "She seemed devastated by his death."

"He was a gambler. That much I knew because he asked me for money about a month ago. I refused, of course. I don't believe in enabling that kind of behavior."

"Can you think of any other misgivings you had about Gary? Fanny's abduction has to be related to his death."

"Just the gambling. I didn't know he was hitting Fanny. The gall of that man. If I'd known, he'd have been in jail."

"Did Fanny know he asked you for money?"

"I doubt it. We never spoke of it. How is Harry?"

Jane winced, knowing how much it would

likely upset the senator to hear Harry had been on his own. "He was scared, hungry, and dirty when I found him. He's slept and been fed, but I still need to get him cleaned up."

"Hungry? Just how long was he on his own, Chief Hardy?"

"We think since yesterday morning. Over twenty-four hours."

"Good heavens. That poor child. I'm going to come get him. You're in Pelican Harbor?"

"Yes."

"I'll be there within two hours." The senator hesitated. "I'd like to speak to Harry."

"Of course." Jane stepped nearer to Will and Harry and held out the phone. "Harry, your grandma wants to talk to you."

Harry's brown eyes widened. "Grammy Jessica?"

"Yes, she's coming to get you."

Tears flooded his eyes, and he reached for the phone. It barely touched his ear before he broke into sobs. "Grammy, a bad man took Mommy. You have to find her."

Would Harry be able to tell her what the man looked like? She hadn't had a chance to ask him yet. He was only four — probably too young to give a description, but she had to try. She touched the boy's soft

228

brown hair as his sobs subsided. He kept nodding into the phone as his grandmother obviously tried to soothe him.

He finally handed the phone back to Jane. "Grammy wants to talk to you."

Jane took the phone. "I'm here, Senator Fox."

"I want the tightest security possible on Harry. Are you at the station?"

"No, I'm at a friend's home." She explained how Harry had taken a liking to Will. "I wasn't sure who he was and what had happened, but I sensed he might be in danger and got him out of sight before anyone saw him."

"Can you assign an officer to watch him?"

"I'll watch him myself, Senator Fox. I won't let him out of my sight."

"Thank you. You're armed?"

Jane touched the butt of her gun. "Yes."

"I'll be there as soon as I can. Text me the address."

She gave Jane her personal phone number, and Jane put it in her contacts. "I'll do that now, Senator."

The senator ended the call, and Jane texted her Reid's address. "She's coming here."

Reid's expression was grave as Jane told him about Fanny's call and her failure to show up. He glanced at Harry, then knelt in front of him. "Harry, do you remember what the man looked like who took your mom?"

Harry's brow wrinkled. "He wore a Texas Rangers cap. I have one just like it. My grammy went to school in Texas, and she bought me a cap." He chewed on his thumbnail. "His eyes were scary." He demonstrated a mean, squinty-eyed glare.

So he wouldn't have seen his hair. The Texas Rangers cap wasn't much of a clue since half the men in town were Rangers fans. "Did your mommy say his name?" Jane asked.

Harry shook his head. "He parked behind our car and asked to use Mommy's phone."

That was a new detail. "What color was his car?"

"Blue, I think? Dark blue."

"What was he wearing?" Jane asked. "Did you notice anything except his hat?"

"Jeans?" Harry's voice was uncertain. "And a red shirt."

She was pushing him too much. Jane touched his hair. "You're so smart, Harry. How about Will gives you a bath?"

"I'll go buy him some clothes," Reid said. "You'll be okay here by yourself?"

Jane scowled at him. "Of course." Where'd

he get off thinking she was not competent to protect a little boy?

He raised his hand. "Sorry. I'll be right back."

Reid listened to the distant sound of the boys playing Uno on Will's bed. Parker was with them. The tags had been cut out of Harry's new clothing, but Reid had guessed right on the size. Harry had been thrilled with the Ninja Turtles pajamas. Reid had gotten jeans and a T-shirt as well, but the boy had quickly climbed into the pj's.

Jane glanced at her watch. "The senator should be here any time. It's been two hours, and I thought she'd be here by now."

Her phone buzzed, and she answered it. "Brian, we've got trouble." She pulled it away from her ear and put it on speaker-phone before she launched into all she'd learned about Fanny's disappearance and finding Harry. "Did you talk to Joseph Davies yet? Maybe he took Fanny to try to squeeze the senator for the money Gary owed him."

"I talked to him, and he has a good alibi. He's been in jail in Pensacola for the past two weeks. I don't think he's our guy, unless he hired the hit. Which he could have done. He's one mean dude."

Jane scowled. "I think Gary's killer took Fanny, and it's not likely to have been Davies. He has no motive. So if he's not our killer, what could have gotten Gary killed and Fanny abducted? Did you find any other evidence in the car or at the scene that might indicate Fanny escaped from him?"

"No, but we found where the little guy ran into the brush. He left a red sweatshirt behind in some thick briars. Looks like he slept there. We found some Little Debbie wrappers and an apple core."

At least he'd had a little bit to eat while he was hiding. Reid had been worried about that. He'd been poking as much food down the boy as he could.

"Okay, keep me posted."

As she put her phone away, someone tapped at the back door. Why would the senator be knocking on the back of the house? Maybe it wasn't Fox at all.

She exchanged glances with Reid and pulled her gun before creeping toward the back of the house. He followed her, though everything in him wanted to take the lead. Dusk cast long shadows into the yard, and it was hard to see. In a crouch she sidled to a back window and glanced out into the yard. He peeked over her shoulder. The driveway held a small blue car. It couldn't be the senator.

The door rattled with another knock, and a woman's voice echoed through the door. "Reid, I know you're in there. I want to talk to you."

His gut clenched. Lauren. Jane would be sure to recognize her as the woman they'd seen in town.

He put his hand on Jane's shoulder. "I'll get rid of her." He moved past her, opened the door, and stepped onto the back deck before she could push past him into the house. "What do you want?"

Her pink lips twisted in a derisive smirk. "You know what I want, Reid. I'm not going away without it. Either give me the money right now or I'm going inside to speak to Will."

"Go ahead." He didn't know whether he'd managed to convey enough boredom with his shrug until her smirk faded and uncertainty took its place.

She fidgeted with the bow on her pink blouse. "You told him already that I'm back?"

"Did you expect me not to tell him? I already told you he knows. He doesn't want to see you."

She bit a trembling lower lip. "I really

need that money, Reid. I have to have it."

"You'll have to look elsewhere, Lauren. We've been over this way too many times already. I'm not giving you one penny."

Tears glimmered in her eyes. "You're a hard man."

"You created this mess, not me."

"My lawyer will make you change your tune."

He skewered her with a hard gaze. "I'll let my attorney know to expect his call."

She spun on her heel and stalked back to her vehicle. The door slammed and tires spit oyster-shell gravel as she pulled away.

He needed to go back inside, but he didn't want to face Jane's questions. Inhaling the pine-scented air a few times, he waited until his knees quit shaking. The door squeaked behind him, and he knew it was Jane before she touched his arm.

There was no way she hadn't overheard the conversation. He turned to face her. "I'm sure you have a lot of questions after hearing all that."

The salt-laden breeze spun her curls around her head, and her hazel eyes were soft. "I think she might be more than an old girlfriend. She's your missing wife, isn't she? I heard you call her Lauren."

"She is." He dropped into a deck chair

and rubbed his shaved head. "She deserted me and Will when he was seven. I hired detectives several times over the years to try to find her, but she had just vanished. I never found where she'd gone or what had happened to her. I had her declared dead finally and tried to move on with my life. I never expected her to show back up demanding money."

"You don't want Will to know she's turned up?"

"He knows that much." How much should he tell her? Everything in him wanted to spill all of it, but he wasn't ready. She wasn't ready, and neither was Will. Too many people could be hurt by the truth, and he wasn't about to risk his son. "It was hard enough for Will when she disappeared. Deep down, he's always thought something happened to her and that's why she never came back to see him. For him to know she just walked away without a second thought was very painful."

Sometimes Reid thought he'd chosen his profession so he didn't have to sit in any one place for long and think about the people who should have stuck around and didn't.

She held his gaze. "The truth is easier to handle than most people think. A lie is a betrayal that hits you where you really live. I'm glad he took it well. He's a remarkable boy."

The truth hovered on his lips, but he bit them back. "Could you find out where she's been all these years?"

"Do you really want to know? What good will it do?"

"It might be ammunition to keep her away from Will."

"Maybe Will would want to have a relationship with his mother. I'd give anything —" She broke the contact of their locked gazes and glanced down at her hands.

"You'd give anything if what?"

"If I could talk to my mother one last time."

His stomach plunged. "She's dead?" He'd lost track of Kim many years ago, but she'd been the survivor sort. The last time he saw her, she'd been in charge of the women.

She raised her eyes to meet his again. "I don't know, and that's the worst part of it all. Does she miss me like I miss her or has she completely forgotten me? I could handle it if she doesn't think about me, but it's the *not knowing* that destroys me."

Jane only thought she could handle it. He kept seeing the wounded expression in his boy's eyes after Lauren left. It had lasted for months and resurrected every now and then. Death was better than rejection. He knew all too well the cost of betrayal and the way lies could destroy a life.

He would do anything to keep Will happy and safe. So much of this was Reid's fault, and he wanted to fix it for his son, but maybe the whole sins of the father thing was real.

During his documentary on the cult, he'd located the last known location of Liberty's Children, but he hadn't gone there to interview anyone. "You know I did that documentary. I know where some of the cults in the country are located."

"My father said the remnants of Mount Sinai joined up with Liberty's Children. Do you know where to find their compound?"

He nodded. "It's about two hours away, outside Coffeeville."

She clasped her hands together. "So close? She's been so close all this time? W-Would you take me there?"

He knew it cost her to ask. "Just tell me when."

"Let me think about it. Soon, though."

He could see the trepidation whirling in her hazel eyes, but he hoped the reality wasn't the disappointment he predicted.

TWENTY-ONE

The rumble of vehicles brought Jane to the window and out of her churning thoughts about her mother's location. A line of black vehicles pulled into Reid's driveway. Two state police cars flanked the senator's black SUV. The senator stepped from the backseat of the middle one and hurried toward the front door.

In her fifties, Senator Fox seemed to always be dressed in navy suits and sensible pumps. Gray streaked her short dark hair after seven years in the senate, but she was still as energetic and driven as the first time Jane had met her, the year she went to work for the Pelican Harbor police department.

The senator paused and spoke to the officers climbing out of their cars, and they all got back in their vehicles.

Jane opened the door before the senator reached the porch. "Senator Fox, I'm Police Chief Jane Hardy. We met a few years ago."

The senator barely touched her fingers to the hand Jane extended. "Where's my grandson?"

"Inside playing a game with Will and Reid. Come in." Jane stepped out of the way, and Senator Fox brushed past her.

In spite of the woman's brusque manner, Jane warmed to her obvious concern for her grandson. She'd often heard others talk about their grandparents, and for the umpteenth time she wondered about her own. Were they still alive? Did they even know about her? She'd tried to probe her father about remaining relatives, but he always changed the subject. Over the years she'd thought about trying to track them down on her own — after all, she had all kinds of resources at her fingertips — but what if they didn't want to see her?

After her mother's rejection, she wasn't sure she could face more. Maybe she'd muster the courage soon.

"Harry," Jane called. "Your grandmother is here."

Footsteps rushed down the stairs, and a small Harry tornado burst into the entry with Parker on his heels. He flung himself at the senator, who scooped him up and held him close. The way he nestled his head against her shoulder told Jane that Senator

Fox was a safe haven for the boy. Whatever his mother felt about Harry's grandmother, the little guy hadn't been tainted by it.

Senator Fox's eyes were wet as she looked at Jane. "Is there somewhere we can talk?" She set Harry back on the floor. "You want to finish your game before I take you home with me?"

"Yay!" Harry darted away and ran up the stairs shouting for Will. Parker followed him.

"We can speak in private in the living room." Jane led her into the spacious open living room and indicated she should sit on the leather sofa. "Coffee or something else to drink?"

The senator sat and clasped her knees as she leaned forward. "No thank you. Any word on my daughter?"

"I'm sorry, but no. We verified the abandoned car was the one you rented for her. Harry says the abductor asked to use her phone as a ruse, then he grabbed her and put her in his trunk."

"So he must have her, just like he said," the senator murmured.

"You've had contact from the kidnapper?"

The senator's dark eyes held desperation. "A man called my personal cell and said he had Fanny."

"Ransom?"

"Not yet. He is supposed to call with his demands at nine o'clock tonight."

"Did he mention Harry?"

Senator Fox shook her head. "I didn't either. The last thing I want is for him to try to snatch my grandson too."

"Harry said his mother told him to run. The man was looking for him too. Harry said he hid."

"I suspect the ransom won't be a request for money."

Jane raised a brow. "No? What do you think he wants?"

"I've been threatened by supporters and haters of Ray Stone. Some want him executed and others want his sentence commuted to life. One of them might have taken Fanny to try to get me to talk to the governor to commute his sentence."

Jane knew the case. Ray Stone had been stopped in a routine traffic stop. High on drugs, he'd killed two cops in a horrific shootout several years ago. The media coverage had been on every station in the country for weeks. Some said the cops were harassing him because of his skin color, and others railed against his quick propensity to pull his gun. He'd been convicted for armed robbery fifteen years ago and hadn't been out of prison long.

"You look dubious," the senator said.

"Taking your daughter seems an extreme reaction to the case. And it has to play into Gary's death somehow. This can't be co-incidence."

"Maybe so, but if the kidnapper wanted money, why not lay out the demands when the call first came in? It feels like he wants me to worry and fret so I'll do whatever he says."

Jane nodded. Did the senator expect her to continue the case? The state police would be working on it too. There weren't many good options for finding Fanny. Blind luck maybe.

Jane rose. "I'll get Harry for you. Reid bought him some clothes."

"How nice of him. I'll be happy to re-imburse him for the expense."

"He and his son already love Harry. I'm sure he won't want your money." It would do no good to try to tell the senator how to handle the ransom demand. "Would you let me know what the kidnapper demands tonight? It might help me find Fanny."

"Of course. I want as much attention on finding my daughter as possible."

Jane heard the finality in the senator's voice and went to get Harry. The state boys would think her tiny police department

242

couldn't offer much help, but they were here on the scene. And she had great detectives. She'd continue to dig until Fanny came home.

After the senator left, Jane's phone dinged with a message. Seeing her dad's face on the screen made her pulse blip.

I'm home. I need to see you.

Fanny sucked the blood from her fingers and choked back a gag at the taste of iron. Her fingertips throbbed from the effort to try to dismantle the door hinges. No matter how hard she tried, nothing had budged them.

A sound came by the door, and she jumped to her feet with her heart trying to pound out of her chest. "Please help me!"

There was a scraping sound, and before she could reach the door, it opened and quickly closed again. Waving her hands in front of the darkness before her, Fanny made it to the door and stumbled over a tray on the floor.

"There's some food." The disembodied voice sounded as though it was coming through a distorter. It was impossible to tell if it was male or female.

"Please let me out." Ignoring the tray of

food, Fanny yanked on the door. "My baby needs me. Do you have Harry?"

"If your mother complies with our request, we'll let you out. We'll have Harry soon too. In the meantime, you're not going anywhere."

Fanny pressed her ear to the door and heard retreating footsteps. "Harry, I want Harry!"

A door slammed from somewhere, and she collapsed onto the floor and covered her face with her hands as sobs tore from her throat. Her poor baby. He had to be so confused and scared.

TWENTY-TWO

Why had she let Will and Reid come with her? Jane parked her vehicle and stared at her dad's house. Something about Reid bolstered her courage and made her feel she could do whatever she had to. Facing her father's charges wouldn't be easy, but Reid might have an idea of where to look. At least that's what she told herself about his presence.

She unbuckled her seat belt. "My dad can be a little brusque. Don't take it personally." She opened the back door to let Parker out, and he barked happily before he ran off to the woods.

"I won't. This is some place he's got here. Must have cost a lot."

"He got the land for a song from his best friend, but yeah, the other stuff cost a lot of money. He brought a nest egg with him when we came." She'd often wondered if he'd taken the money from Mount Sinai.

He was the treasurer, and the whole place was burning up when they fled. He might have thought it was better to take it than to see it all destroyed.

Not that it was right.

Reid nodded and got out with her into the looming twilight with the cicadas sounding off. The wind brought the scent of pine, and the woods were coming alive for the night.

Will trotted along behind her with his camera. He was such a good kid. She liked him a lot. After mounting the porch, she went to the door, but it opened before she could twist the knob.

Her father frowned when he saw Will and Reid with her, but he stepped out of the way. "Mr. Dixon, I didn't expect to see you."

Reid shifted and looked down. "Hello, Mr. Hardy."

Jane glanced at Reid's guilty expression over to her father's impassive one. "Y-You two have met?"

"Mr. Dixon paid me a visit a few days ago."

"Why?"

"For my documentary. Questions about patrolling a small town."

It sounded routine, but why did Reid look so defensive? Jane glanced around as she entered and didn't see Elizabeth.

Her dad answered before she could ask. "Elizabeth left me. She's embarrassed, and I think she believes I'm guilty." His hazel eyes blazed with fury. "After all I've done for her over the years. The minute her parole is over, she deserts me. Typical woman."

Jane recoiled at the venom in his words. Did he really hold women with such contempt? Was that the real reason he kept her at arm's length?

She stalked to the kitchen with the men following behind her and began to make coffee. "I saw pictures of you with my murder vic, Gary Dawson. You seem to be friends, but I've just now heard about it."

Her dad pressed his lips together. "We've been fishing buddies for some years now."

She took a step back. "And you're just now telling me?"

He lifted a brow. "I've been a little occupied, Jane. When would I have had a chance to tell you? It's not like I know anything about the murder. If I had any evidence, I would have mentioned it to you, but you're the chief now. It's your job to nail the killer, not mine."

"You could have told me when I saw you and Scott. It's clearly not a surprise to you that he's dead."

Reid touched her arm. "Give your dad the benefit of the doubt."

She jerked her arm away. "I feel like I'm surrounded by people keeping secrets. You made not a single mention of knowing my dad. And now this news."

Her dad heaved a sigh. "Something is going on in town. Something deeper than what we see. I don't know what it is yet, but you're going to have to figure it out. It feels like a personal vendetta."

This was all too much for her. What made her think she could unravel something this complex? She turned her back on the men and poured coffee to try to regain her composure.

It felt like the waves were crashing over her head nonstop, and she couldn't catch her breath. Why did she even take this job — who did she think she was that she could handle something this big? She couldn't even come to grips with her childhood, so how could she deal with this much pressure?

She could feel Reid's gaze on her like a physical touch. Did he have as many doubts about her ability as she did? She dared a quick look at him, then, unable to absorb the kindness in his eyes, she diverted her attention to the coffee.

248

"There's more than you know. Gary's wife, Fanny, has been abducted." She told him about finding Harry and how the bookie was a dead end. "Paul is convinced you killed Gary. He'll be sure to think you have Fanny too."

"Someone is building a case against me. This charge by the FBI is false, and I suspect it's related too. I told you I was following some leads about it — the theft has to have been done by someone in the department. Someone had to have access to the evidence room. I think Paul might be behind it."

Paul *had* seemed obsessed with taking down her dad. More than just her detectives had access to the evidence room. There were several part-time employees who manned that desk, her two forensic techs, and Olivia. She trusted Olivia implicitly, but she didn't know the others all that well. Could any of them have a vendetta against her dad? It was entirely possible in their small town that someone had simply broken into the evidence room during the night when only one employee worked.

"Who would have the most to gain by taking you down, Dad?"

"It's a long list." He reached for a tablet on the island. "I wrote down everyone I could think of — people I've busted and sent to jail as well as personal enemies I've made along the way."

She took the paper he offered and scanned it until a familiar name caught her attention. "Daryl Green. He's out of jail?"

She knew him well — he was another Paul in the flesh. Arrogant and bent on his own way. That attitude had led him into providing "security" for a whole host of drug dealers in the area. He raked in so much money he bought a big boat that ended up being his downfall. Dad noticed he was living above his means and investigated. Daryl was sent to jail for five years for extortion.

Her dad took a sip of coffee. "He got out about two months ago. He'd have the connections to frame me."

"Maybe. I'll go talk to him."

"He lives out on the peninsula. I tried to go see him earlier today, but his truck wasn't there and no one answered the door."

"I'll see what I can find out."

"But work on finding Fanny first."

"That's out of my hands. The state boys are working on it."

"You could still be involved."

"I could, but they have better resources. And I've got two other homicides to solve. If I focus on Gary's death, it might lead to whoever is behind Fanny's abduction."

If her dad was right about it all leading back to his trouble, Gary might be the key there too.

Reid sat across the table from Jane at Jesse's Restaurant at Magnolia Springs amid the clink of silverware. She'd left Parker sleeping in the shade in the SUV with several windows halfway open. The white tablecloth was already marred by crumbs from the bread Will had wolfed down. Though Will had eaten all the bread, Reid had no doubt the boy could eat every bite of the filet he'd ordered. That kid had a bottomless pit.

Reid watched her study the list of possible suspects again. "Anything jump out at you?"

Even with the dark circles under her eyes, she looked beautiful. A lock of light-brown hair had come loose from its side barrette, and the wisps grazed her cheek. He needed to feed her and insist she get home to bed. The whole town seemed to be blowing up around her, and he wished he could take some of the burden from her.

She took a sip of water. "My dad had a lot of enemies. I still think Green looks good for it."

"Want me to take a look?"

She glanced at his outstretched hand.

"The names probably won't mean much to you, but have at it."

He glanced at the list, but the only thing that jumped out at him was Liberty's Children. "Why would your dad list a cult as a possible suspect?"

She shrugged. "He hasn't had any contact with them in nearly fifteen years. I think it's more of his paranoia. Did you interview anyone from Liberty's Children for your documentary?"

How did he even talk about this with her? Every time the subject came up, he wanted to sink into the floor. He valued honesty and transparency above everything, and keeping such important truths from her felt as much like a lie as a blatant falsehood.

His gaze slid to his son. But Will meant more to him than life itself. All he could do was walk this tightrope and hope not to fall.

"No, I had plenty of other people to talk to." Not to mention he hadn't wanted to see any of them. He knew where they were, but he hadn't wanted any contact.

He glanced at the list again. "That cop he sent up seems a likely suspect. He was in line for a promotion when he was accused of providing protection for a drug runner. He'd know the right people to give as witnesses against your dad."

The frown between her brows flattened, and she nodded. "I wonder if he's already skipped town. Dad couldn't find him. I'd like to run out to the peninsula after dinner and see if we can find out anything." She glanced at Will. "You haven't had much of a spring break."

"It's been fun so far." Will's gaze went over his dad's shoulder. "That woman you spoke to in the street earlier is staring at you, Dad."

Reid dropped his napkin as he whipped around to look out the plate-glass window onto the covered patio seating. Sure enough, Lauren was staring through the glass. She appeared to be looking right at them, but could she even see him in the dim light? He half rose to try to get rid of her, then sank back into his seat when she turned and walked toward the parking lot.

Will looked thoughtful, and a frown crouched between his brows. "She sure has been turning up a lot. I feel like I should know her."

Reid curled his fingers into his palms. How did he get to this place of subterfuge and lies? He didn't even recognize himself any longer. Even more importantly, he was letting God down. He'd wanted to be the kind of man who stood for truth and what's right, not a man who did what was convenient to make things easy. He'd always thought he could stand up to any temptation, but this one had felled him in one blow.

He wasn't the man he thought he was.

The truth sat like a rock in his throat, blocking his airway and choking his clear thinking. He had to tell Will the truth. Lauren wouldn't let this go — she just wouldn't. And Will already knew his mother had been in contact by phone.

He opened his mouth just as the server brought their food. The sizzle and aroma of the steaks turned the mood at the table instantly, and he could suddenly breathe again. This conversation shouldn't be in front of Jane anyway. When they got home tonight, he'd spill it all and ask Will to forgive him.

He glanced across the table at Jane, who wore a contemplative expression as she stared back. Would she look up Lauren like he'd asked? There had to be some way to combat the woman. His biggest fear was losing Will. While it was unlikely Lauren would try to take his boy, Will might be tempted to ask to visit her, and if he didn't give her the money, Reid could see her deciding to disappear with him.

The sizzle of garlic and butter on the steak

suddenly didn't smell very appetizing, and he wasn't sure he was going to be able to eat. If he didn't, though, it would be a sure sign to Will that something was wrong. Reid forced himself to cut a bite of steak and chew it. The steak almost lodged in his throat, but he took a sip of water and swallowed it down.

He'd get through tonight and see what tomorrow held after he was obedient to what God clearly was telling him to do.

Jane put down her fork. "Tomorrow's Sunday. I-I'm going to church with a friend, but I have the rest of the day off. Would you want to take me to the Liberty's Children compound?"

He nearly choked on his bite of food. He nodded. "I have all afternoon free too. We'll get back late. Is that okay?"

"I don't sleep much anyway. Maybe after the visit I'll find I can."

Or it would bring her nightmares. He shut his mouth and took a sip of water.

The blooming magnolia trees outlined in the setting sun made for a pleasant drive out to the peninsula after dinner. Jane's thoughts churned too much to make conversation as she directed Reid to Daryl Green's house. He lived in a small community

255

known as The Rookery off Fort Morgan Road. A porch fronted Green's small cottage, and a light was on inside.

Reid parked in front of the house. "Looks like someone is here."

She nodded and shoved open her door. "Will, you stay here. I'm not sure how safe it is."

Reid was close on her heels when she went to the door and pressed the doorbell. The sound of footsteps came toward the door. When it opened, she found herself face-to-face with Daryl Green.

Prison hadn't enhanced his appearance. His jowls sagged, and his hair was more gray than brown now.

His brown eyes narrowed. "Jane Hardy, as I live and breathe. I wondered how long it would be before someone from the department showed up to harass me. I thought it would likely be your dad, but I heard the old coot retired. What do you want?"

"I wanted to ask you a few questions."

"Which I don't have to answer unless you are charging me with something. And even then, I don't have to answer."

He started to shut the door, but she put her foot between it and the jamb. "Do you know Gary Dawson?"

His muddy eyes widened. "You're trying

to tie me to a murder? Typical. This conversation is over. Move your foot or have it smashed in the door."

She could tell he meant it, so she pulled her foot out of the way. The finality of the door's slam made her turn back to the SUV. "Well, that went well."

Reid fell into step beside her. "Do you think he knows anything?"

"He used to know everything that was going on in the criminal community. I wouldn't trust him at all, but he's right. I have no evidence he knew Gary or has any knowledge about the murder."

She shot Boulter a text to have him see if he could find out about Daryl's activities since his release, though. She suspected he might have his fingers in this.

TWENTY-THREE

A big frog croaked from the Bon Secour River to his left as Reid and Will waved good-bye to Jane and walked to the front porch. Mosquitoes and no-see-ums descended in a cloud, and Reid swatted at them as they ran the last few feet and reached the safety of the foyer.

Will started for the stairs, and Reid almost let him go since the boy's lids were dropping, but that was the easy way out.

Reid touched his arm and stopped him. "I need to talk to you, son. It shouldn't take too long."

Will gave him a curious look and nodded. "It's about that woman, isn't it?"

Smart kid. Reid often didn't give him enough credit. "Yes. Let's go to the kitchen for a snack."

Will followed him into the kitchen. Reid said nothing as he poured milk and got out the container of oatmeal cookies he'd bought from the bakery. He put the cookies in front of Will before he settled on a bar stool beside his son.

Will picked up a cookie. "Is she my mom? Is that why she seems familiar?"

Reid caught his breath at Will's matter-of-fact tone. His boy was always full of surprises. "Yes, that's Lauren."

"If I'd known for sure, I would have told her to leave us alone. I'm not going to help her extort money from you. That sucks."

Reid's heart warmed. Will was solid gold, through and through. He cleared his throat. "It's a little more complicated than I've told you, son. I-I'm afraid I have to ask you to forgive me."

Will's head came up, and his dark eyes sharpened with interest. "What is it?"

Reid wanted to look away, but he forced himself to let Will in — to let him see the anguish and remorse he was feeling. "Lauren's biggest sword over my head is that s-she adopted you, Will. When we met, you were two. After we were married, I pushed her to adopt you. Unless I pay her, she plans to tell you the truth because she knew I hadn't."

The color receded from Will's face. "Not my mother? You were married before her? Who's my mother?"

Reid cringed at the barrage of questions. This was precisely why he hadn't told Will. How did he even tell him all of it? And *should* he? Truth was important, but so was Will's mental state. While logically he knew he couldn't keep hurts from his boy, he hated being the one to inflict the wound.

"We were never legally married, and s-she left us when you were a newborn."

Will's shoulders slumped. "I must have been some kid to have two mothers desert me."

Reid winced and he put his hand on his boy's shoulder. "I was afraid you'd take it like that, which is why I didn't want to tell you. Your real mother loved you, but there were circumstances that happened after you were born. It wasn't your fault. It was mine."

He'd bought into all the lies, all the deception. True faith didn't live the way he'd been taught back then. He'd learned so much, but it was too late. Much too late.

Will shoved back from the island bar. "Nice try, Dad. I can't believe you lied to me like this. How can I ever believe anything you say now? I should have known about this from the start."

"You're right. I have no excuse other than wanting to protect you. I was wrong. I hope you can forgive me." Reid reached toward his son, but Will knocked his hand away.

"Don't touch me. Not now. I don't know how to feel."

Will rushed to the stairs. Moments later his bedroom door slammed. It was several minutes before the strains of "Hotel California" floated down. Will loved classic rock, and the Eagles was his band of choice when he was upset.

It wouldn't be long before Will returned with more questions. He would want to know his mother's name and if Reid had ever found her. He'd want to see pictures and know why she left. He'd demand the truth — all of it.

And Reid didn't know what to say. Did he refuse to speak of it? If he clammed up and didn't tell Will everything, their home would turn into an armed camp. And how could that be the right thing to do?

Reid groaned and slapped his forehead. If only he'd told Will the truth from the time he was young. He'd have gotten over any curiosity long ago, and Reid wouldn't be facing this tiger right now.

He plodded back into the living room and sank onto the sofa. His Bible was on the stand, and he picked it up. Running his fingers over the buttery leather, he prayed for wisdom and for his son's heart. This could destroy Will. Reid had been so very stupid and shortsighted.

He riffled through the pages, and his Bible fell open at Ephesians 4. A highlighted verse jumped out at him.

"Therefore each of you must put off falsehood and speak truthfully to your neighbor, for we are all members of one body."

So if he lied to Will, he was basically lying to himself. If the situation were reversed, he'd want the unvarnished truth, but it had the ability to blow up their lives in ways Reid couldn't even foresee.

Yet the apostles had gone to their deaths with the truth. He wasn't being asked to put his head on a chopping block. How did he refuse when faced with that?

The back of his neck radiated pain up his head, and he rubbed the sore spots. He didn't have to spill it all yet — not until Will asked. It was a reprieve, but it wouldn't last long. A few days, a week. In the meantime, he had to figure out how to soften the blow.

I shouldn't be here.

The blended voices singing a peppy praise tune of some kind felt like a blow against Jane's heart. If it wasn't for Olivia standing beside her, Jane would have already bolted for the door. But Olivia needed her. While her condition hadn't deteriorated, Jane knew it was coming.

The church was fairly new with modern seating instead of pews. Discreet can lights illuminated the room from the cathedral ceiling. The church was full this morning, and she caught a glimpse of Reid and Will on the other side toward the back. She hadn't realized he attended here.

Megan craned her neck. "It's usually packed on Easter."

The girl looked pale and drawn. She'd probably researched ALS, too, and discovered the severity of the diagnosis.

Easter Sunday. Jane hadn't even thought about what day it was. She followed Olivia's cues and sank back into her seat as the pastor took the podium for the message. She tensed as she waited for him to harangue the congregation on their sins. Instead, he began to talk about love, God's love, loving others, patience, and long-suffering. She blinked at his lack of condemnation.

The words were a soothing balm on an emotional wound she'd carried for years, but it would take a long time to truly heal her deep lacerations. Still, this church was very different from what she'd experienced.

Maybe it was all a front. She would reserve judgment.

After shaking what felt like thousands of hands, Jane escaped with Olivia and Megan into the sunshine. "I'm going with Reid after church. Could you check on Parker this afternoon and see if he needs to go out?"

"Megan and I will take him for a walk. I wish you wouldn't do this," Olivia said. "No good can come from trying to confront them."

"I don't plan to confront them — I just want to see if my mother is there."

"And what if she is? What will you do? March up and demand she come with you? That's a recipe for disaster."

"I'll try not to make a scene. Just . . . pray for me." She pressed her fingers on Olivia's arm when she saw Reid's SUV pulling up in front of the church. "I-I think I might come back to church with you, Olivia. No promises, but it was . . . nice."

Olivia's blue eyes brightened. "I thought you might like it. I'll see you tomorrow at work. Good luck, and hang on to your temper."

"I will." Jane hurried out to the SUV but didn't see the boy. "Will isn't going?"

"He went home with a friend to play

basketball in their driveway."

Reid looked handsome today in khaki pants and a red polo shirt that accented his dark eyes and tan. She smoothed the skirt of her blue dress and wished she'd brought a change of clothes.

She pulled her small laptop from her bag. "I thought I might research on the drive. I've got my hotspot on. Honestly, I don't want to dwell on what's about to happen."

He shot her a glance. "I'm sure you're tense about it."

"Beyond tense." She flipped the laptop open and called up her browser. "Do you know much about ALS?"

"Just that Stephen Hawking lived over fifty years with it."

"What? Seriously?" She'd seen pictures of the famous physicist in a wheelchair but had assumed he'd been born with a disability.

"He was diagnosed at a young age. You're concerned about Olivia, aren't you?"

"You know about her diagnosis?"

"She's on the prayer list."

Jane hadn't realized Olivia would be so open about it, but of course she would want her church to know. "It seems like such an awful disease."

"I've been wondering if she's been tested for Lyme. It's often misdiagnosed as ALS."

"I hadn't heard that. I doubt she has either. I'm going to look it up." She plunged into research, and what she learned gave her a ray of hope.

When she emerged from her research, they were on the outskirts of Coffeeville.

A few minutes later Reid slowed the SUV. "There it is."

Every fiber of Jane's being knew this was a wild-goose chase, but she couldn't help herself. Though the air-conditioning blew full blast out of the vents, her forehead still beaded with perspiration. She drew in several shaky breaths.

A heavy chain and padlock secured the metal gate, and beyond the barrier she saw a small encampment of cabins and tents, very similar to the compound she'd fled with her father. Had it really been almost fifteen years since that icy, terrifying flight into the dark night?

The heavy humidity pressed in on Jane like a suffocating wool blanket when she got out to look at the lock. "I'll need bolt cutters."

"I brought some. I called the landowner and asked for permission to go onto his land. The group has been squatting here, and he's started the eviction process, but it takes a while. He was glad to let us in."

He got out and popped the back hatch, then carried the cutters to the chain.

She held out her hand. "Let me do it."

He gave her a quick look, then handed them over. The bolt cutters were heavy and hard to maneuver, but she managed to snap the thick chain, and it jangled as it fell against the metal gate. She pulled it free and opened the gate.

"Let's do this." She got back in the SUV and stared at the compound as Reid got in.

It felt as though every cell in her body was trembling and vibrating as he drove through the gates toward the rough-hewn building squatting in the center of the clearing ahead. The meetinghouse would be the first stop. At this time of day the group would likely be there.

She ran her window down and flipped off the air so she could hear better. Mount Sinai had more guns than most armies, and she didn't want to risk Reid's life in a surprise attack.

The vehicle barely idled forward as she scrutinized the little colony. Though only two hours away, this place felt otherworldly in a way that made the hair rise on the back of her neck. The metal buildings would hold the community's arsenal, and she held her breath, listening for the chambering of a shell into a shotgun barrel. The only noise that floated through the window was the cawing of a grackle from a stand of trees.

Reid slowed the SUV to a stop in front of the meetinghouse and threw it into Park, then opened his door. "Stay here."

She opened her door. "Not on your life. I don't like the feel of this place, but I don't want you to go alone. It's not safe."

Hand on the grip of her gun, Jane stalked toward the meetinghouse and mounted the rough wooden steps. The door opened with ease, and she peered into the gloom of the windowless building. Dust motes swirled in the shaft of sunlight slanting into the interior from the open door.

It held only empty benches. She frowned and turned back toward Reid. "No one's inside."

And now that she was looking closer, she realized no clothes flapped from the clotheslines and no food smells wafted in the air, though the women should have been preparing dinner.

"We're too late. They're gone."

The rock in her stomach hardened, and for the first time she realized maybe Olivia was right. Her search for her mother had turned into an obsession, but she wasn't sure what to do about it. "Let's go. There's nothing here for us."

She needed to let it go. Her mother and the life they'd shared were both part of her past, and if she wanted to heal, she had to close the curtain on that part of her life.

She was strong enough to do this, and she would.

TWENTY-FOUR

Three o'clock. Reid's stomach rumbled since they had driven straight to the compound without stopping for a meal. He'd brought a few Kind bars and some jerky, but it wasn't much.

Jane liked Mexican so he'd found this place in Jackson. He eyed Jane over the top of the menu. She hadn't spoken two words since they left the empty compound, but he knew it had hit her hard.

He closed his menu and snagged a tortilla chip the server had brought a few minutes ago. "I think I'll have chicken enchiladas."

"I'll have arroz con pollo." She laid her menu on top of his. "I want to thank you for bringing me all this way, Reid. It was above and beyond the call of duty. I'll see what I can find out about Lauren to show my gratitude."

His neck heated at the mention of her name. "I appreciate it. I'd already told Will

270

she was alive and asking for money, but last night I told him she was the woman who'd been staring at us. He's a little upset I hadn't told him sooner."

And a whole lot upset about even more, but he wasn't ready to tell her that yet.

She took a sip of her sweet tea. "Is that the real reason he didn't come today?"

"Yeah. I wish buying him a stuffed animal would soothe things like they used to. He's a little big for that."

"You've done an amazing job raising him. I haven't seen many teenagers like him. He's so respectful and hardworking."

Her words were a balm to his hurting heart. "I've made plenty of mistakes."

"Nothing fatal."

She looked so beautiful with the sun through the window lighting her hair. Her eyes seemed more green than hazel, and he reached across the table to grasp her hand. "You doing okay with the disappointment, or would you rather not talk about it?"

Her fingers closed around his, and she gave a gentle squeeze. "It's funny. I'm not as upset as I thought I'd be. It was almost a relief, you know? What was I really going to stay to her? Why didn't you love me more than Moses? Why haven't you even sent me a birthday card?" She wrinkled her nose.

271

"Wednesday is my thirtieth birthday, and I think it's time I grew up and put childish things behind me. People have had much worse childhoods than I did."

He supposed she'd seen horrific home situations over the years. "What was it like for you?" His own experience wasn't the same as the other children in camp. His dad had power, and he got away with more than the others.

But in spite of all that, he realized his childhood had hardly been a normal one. His father had been more like a taskmaster than a dad, and there hadn't been any real play time in his memory. Only work and rules and punishment. Once his mother disappeared, all that had gotten even worse. Reid couldn't remember a single time his father had ever said he loved him.

She hadn't released his hand. "I have no memory of my life ever being lighthearted. No playing on a swing set or climbing trees or fishing. One of my main duties was the garden, and it felt like I spent hours and hours pulling weeds and hauling buckets of water. I was doing the laundry by the time I was eight. But it wasn't the work — that's good for a kid. It was the constant disapproval, the imminent feeling of punishment coming my way."

He squeezed her hand tighter. Her memories mirrored his. "Your parents were harsh?"

"Harsh, distracted, yes. But it wasn't just them. The group believed all adults were charged with the job of disciplining the children. I might have been Harry's age or even younger when I came home with blood streaming down my legs from a switching the neighbor gave me. I'd been peeking at the horses and had opened a gate. One of the ponies got out. I avoided that man, but he was always glaring at me."

"What did your parents do?"

"They told me it was my own fault for opening the gate, of course."

"I don't believe in punishing childhood mistakes. Will has only been punished for direct disobedience. Accidents, childish behavior — those go with the territory. You have to teach a kid obedience and manners. Character and kindness."

Her smile came then. "Which is why you've got such a good kid." Her gaze wandered to the plate-glass window beside them where two teenagers stood looking at their phones. "I don't think I ever had more than two minutes to myself. Every moment was scripted and planned. The thing I hated the worst was how we overwhelmed initiates or prospective members with our so-called love. Total approval and love were supposed to reel them in. Once they were hooked, it all changed."

"Some people in a cult believe that work gives them a purpose and makes them feel they are working for something greater than themselves."

Her attention snapped back to him. "I keep forgetting you know so much about it. And that's true, it does feel like you have a goal that's big and important. I think they try to keep you so busy, you don't see the contradictions between what they teach and what they live. And the contradictions between what they preach and what the Bible says. I kind of saw that clearly today in church. I don't think I'd ever heard that verse the pastor quoted. It was in 1 Corinthians."

He smiled. "Chapter 13. It's called the love chapter. It lists what true love looks like."

"And I haven't seen much behavior like it in my whole life. Well, except maybe through Olivia. She's pretty great. She's always taking in street kids, and I've never heard her say a bad word about anyone."

"What's next for you?"

She finally pulled her hand away from his.

"I'm going to let it all go. I'm going to go to counseling and try to get rid of this weight of guilt I feel all the time. I'm going to be the best police chief and the best person I can be."

He wanted to tell her that she didn't have to change her life on her own — God would do it for her — but he could see she wasn't ready to hear it yet. The door had only opened a tiny crack. He'd let God kick it open wider.

And with Reid's growing feelings for her, he prayed it was soon.

The morning sun slanted through the blinds in Jane's office, and she glanced at Reid, who was pouring coffee into a mug from a carafe. "It's pretty abominable this morning. Way too weak."

He'd been quiet ever since he and Will had arrived, and there was a noticeable tension between them. They obviously hadn't made up. She hadn't slept well, so she'd been out on her balcony with Parker until nearly two, listening to music and trying to figure all this out. She'd dipped into *The Screwtape Letters* for a few more chapters, then reached for her drawing pad to sketch. She had meant to draw Harry, but her fingers had a mind of their own, and a succession of Reid's expressions marched through four pages of sketches.

She needed to rein in this interest she had in him, no matter what it took. There was no room in her life for a relationship. She'd seen too many officers with failed marriages. Her work demanded everything she had to give.

Reid dropped into a chair. "Even weak coffee has caffeine." His eyes were shadowed with fatigue as if he'd been up all night too.

He shot a glance at Will, who stood with his arms crossed in front of the window. The boy's stiff posture and flattened lips spoke volumes of his displeasure with either his dad or the situation here this morning. Had he objected to coming to video this morning? If so, she could let him off for the day. It had to be boring for a teenager.

She looked over the reports on her desk. "Brian checked out Nicole's brother, Marshall Thomas. He moved to Chicago four days before her murder."

Reid took a sip of coffee and grimaced. "Anything new this morning on Fanny?"

Before she could answer, someone tapped on her closed door. "Come in," she called.

Paul stuck his head through the doorway. "Got a minute, Chief?"

She didn't care for the gleam in his eyes

or his jaunty walk as he approached her desk. "What's up?"

"I'm requesting a search warrant for your dad's house on suspicion of murder, and I need your approval."

She stiffened at his elation and the pungent odor wafting from him. He ate roasted garlic like nuts and almost always had a bag on his desk that made his office uninhabitable. "What evidence?"

He held up a sheaf of papers and waggled them her direction. "Witnesses who saw Charles fishing with Dawson the day of his death. He never told you that, did he?"

His gleeful tone made her want to throw the paperweight on her desk at his head, but she held it together. "Who are the witnesses?"

"A man and a woman fishing from the town pier saw them go out on your dad's boat. I have their statements here." He handed her the paperwork. "And a picture of the boat passing." He dropped a glossy photo that had a date and time stamp in the top right corner.

Nausea clutched her stomach in its grip, but she still held it together and took the documentation. She scanned the papers. He was right — the witness statements provided probable cause. "I want to be there when you go through his place."

Paul scowled. "That's a conflict of interest."

"I don't plan to participate in the search, and it's not your call, Paul." She stood, planting both palms on her desk, and glared at him. "I want to make sure the search is by the book."

Paul's dark-blue eyes were steely, and he shrugged. "Suit yourself. It's your hide if the mayor gets wind of it."

"Going to call Lisa again?"

His jaw flexed. "I won't have to. She'll hear about it on her own."

He was probably right about that. "I don't want you or Brian searching anything alone. You'll handle the search together as a team."

His lips curled in a sneer. "Don't trust us?"

"I don't trust *you*." She held the papers out to him. "Get the order, and we'll see what we find."

He snatched them out of her hand, retreated, and shut the door harder than necessary when he exited. He didn't want her there, but she didn't trust him not to plant evidence.

The compassion in Reid's eyes brought moisture to her eyes, and she sank into her desk chair. "I know the couple who saw them go out together. I don't think they would lie. I'll talk to them myself, of course."

"I'm sorry. This has to be hard."

She leaned back in her chair and rubbed her aching neck. "Dad hadn't said a word about being with Dawson the day he was murdered. He could have told me last night, but he didn't say anything beyond admitting he knew him."

"Any chance someone else took your dad's boat out? Did the witnesses actually identify him?"

His dark eyes held hers with a gentleness that made her hackles calm. "Actually, they both said they saw his boat going out with two men, but they didn't specifically say they saw Dad. Maybe you're right. He could have loaned out his boat."

It was her dad's only hope of not being arrested for murder. "It won't take long for the search warrant to be approved." She glanced at Will. "Would you record the entire search? I want to make sure there's no planted evidence. It's easy to miss something."

He unfolded his arms and shot a stiff glance at his father. "Sure. That's gotta be hard to see your dad facing something like this."

"It is." She saw the yearning expression Reid wore. Something was clearly wrong between the two of them, and it felt bigger than a teenage temper tantrum over not telling Will his mom was in town. Maybe she'd get a chance to talk to Will or Reid alone and find out what was going on.

It was none of her business, but that didn't mean she didn't care. These two were special.

TWENTY-FIVE

Jane inhaled a calming breath of pine and new spring flowers. She stood on her dad's porch with Parker and waited for Brian and Paul to appear. A plume of dust on the dirt drive indicated their arrival was imminent.

Reid squinted in the sunlight as he moved across the yard with Will in tow. "Your dad's not home?"

She shook her head. "And I can't text him. I have to do my job no matter how painful." Parker pressed against her leg, and she rubbed his ears. He always sensed her emotions.

The SUV doors opened, and her detectives spilled out. Brian shot her an apologetic glance, but Paul's head was high and his step held a spring of triumph. She nodded to Will, who shouldered the video camera and began to record.

Paul saw the movement and stopped. "You're not taping this."

She stepped away from the door. "I *am* taping this. I already used my key to unlock the door. You can all go on in."

Paul scowled as he pulled on Nitrile gloves. He pressed his lips together and brushed past her without a word. A wave of fatigue swept over her. Conflict sapped her energy and drained her focus. Being around Paul was like a star circling a black hole.

"Sorry," Brian whispered as he stepped through the doorway into her dad's house.

She beckoned to Reid and Will without answering, and they stepped into the entry to watch the detectives sweep the house. She trailed behind them as they opened every cabinet, drawer, and closet in the place. They yanked out the contents of end tables and poked through boxes on the closet shelves in the bedrooms. Will's video catalogued every move.

They found nothing in the house, and she should have felt relief, but her gut tightened as they moved out of the house and toward the barn where her dad stored the boat. She let her gaze roam past the barn to the concrete bunker where her dad stored guns, food, and other supplies. Without her father here, they wouldn't be able to get into it. It had enough barricades and locks to keep out an army.

She stepped to the barn and unlocked the padlock with a small key on her key ring, then stepped aside. Paul wrestled the lock from the door and gave a shove. The light filtered into the darkened space, and she waited until Will had gone inside and boarded the boat with the detectives.

Reid stopped to touch her arm. "Hang in there, Jane. Truth always comes out eventually."

She lifted her gaze and searched his warm brown eyes. "Do you really believe that?"

He gave a jerky nod. "Today more than ever. I'll tell you about it some time."

She wanted to ask him what he meant, but the crunch of tires on gravel caused her to spin her around. Her father's big dually truck slid to a stop, and he jumped out almost before it had quit rolling.

He moved fast for such a big man. "What's going on here?"

She passed the search warrant over to him. "We're searching the premises."

His jaw flexed as he scanned the warrant. "I see. Find anything?"

"Not in the house. It's a mess in there. Sorry."

He blinked as he continued to read the warrant. "I'm under suspicion for Gary's death? You've got to be kidding. On what evidence?"

"Witnesses who saw Gary on your boat the day he died. They saw two men."

"Well, neither one was me. Gary has a key, and I told him he could take the boat out whenever he wanted."

She wanted to ask him where he'd been and if he had an alibi, but she had to stay out of the interrogation. Her dad had to know it too.

"Got something!" Brian called from inside the boat cabin.

Jane moved into the barn and sneezed at the dust kicked up by the men milling around. She squinted up at the boat on its trailer and tried to see what Brian had in his hands. Maybe a cloth of some kind. A T-shirt?

She moved closer. "What is it?"

Paul stepped into view. "Blood. Splatter on the starboard side and bloody clothes."

Her dad made a noise of disgust. "Most likely fish blood. What do you expect on a fishing boat?"

"We're taking pictures and collecting evidence. Don't go anywhere, Charles."

Paul's terse command made her wonder. Could her dad be guilty? She shoved away the stray thought.

Reid stepped close enough for her to catch

his cologne, a spicy, appealing scent. "Your dad is smarter than this. If he'd actually killed Gary, he would have cleaned that boat top to bottom. He would have discarded any bloody clothing. Someone is pushing this narrative. I'm beginning to think you're right and he's being framed."

Warmth surged up her neck. "Maybe I'm not crazy?"

"I didn't say that. Anyone who lounges on her balcony half the night instead of sleeping might not have it all together."

A soft explosion of laughter escaped, and she put her hand over her lips. She tended to laugh at the most inappropriate times, mostly when she was stressed like now. But her dad would think she didn't care what he was going through.

She collected herself and glanced back at her father. He was keeping things from her, but she couldn't question him without being accused of impropriety. It had to come from Brian and Paul.

Carrying evidence bags, the men climbed down from the boat and Will followed. Jane stared at Will, who gave her a quick nod. Good — he'd gotten everything. She'd check it out later.

Paul strode toward her dad. "Charles, I'm arresting you for the murder of Gary Dawson. Put your hands behind your back."

Jane sprang forward. "What? Until we get the DNA back on the blood, you can't arrest him without proof."

Paul shook the evidence bag at her. "This is Gary's shirt. It has his name on the back, and it's covered with blood!"

"But you don't know if it's even human blood, let alone if it's Gary's."

"I've got probable cause," Paul said.

And he did. She chewed her lip before she turned to her father. "You need to come down to the station and answer questions, Dad."

He skewered her with a glare that told her he wasn't happy with her handling of the situation. She wasn't either. "I'll ride with you, but not him."

His stiff back was all she saw as he stalked to her vehicle and got into the backseat. *Great, just great.*

Since he wouldn't be able to be in on the interrogation, Reid left the police station and drove home with Will. His boy sat in the passenger seat with his face turned toward the window. He hadn't said a word to Reid all day.

The estrangement hurt worse than an open wound. "Want to go shrimping? We've

286

got all afternoon."

Will looked at Reid. "I want to talk about my mother. My real mother."

Reid felt sick. It had come sooner than he'd expected, but he'd promised God he wouldn't turn away from doing the right thing, even if it hurt.

He pulled into the drive of their house and turned off the engine. "Okay. Let's talk over lunch."

Reid's feet felt like lead as he walked to the front door. A flash of red caught his eye, and he saw Lauren rise from a rocker on the porch. She wore a red sundress and gold heels that nearly matched her hair. Another slash of red painted the lips she parted in a smile directed at Will.

"Hello, son." She shot Reid a triumphant look. "It's been a while since I saw you. You know who I am, don't you?" With outstretched arms she started for the steps, but Will backed away into the yard. Her smile faltered. "I'm your mother, Will."

He folded his arms across his chest. "I know who you are. Dad told me all about you. You're not even my real mother, just someone who signed her name to a paper saying she'd love me. But you took off right after that, didn't you? Couldn't stand me, could you?"

"Is that what he told you? He didn't tell you he asked me to leave and that he never wanted to see me again?"

Will shot a startled glance at Reid. "Dad?"

"You know better than that, Will."

Will rushed for the kayak swaying at the dock. "Leave me alone! I don't know what you want from me." The kayak bobbed as he stepped into it.

Reid sprang after him. "Wait a minute, Will."

Will grappled with the rope tethering the kayak to the dock, then grabbed an oar and pushed off into the slow-flowing river.

"Watch for gators," Reid called after him.

Doing the right thing wasn't easy, but Reid had to believe it would turn out in the end. Will was a smart boy — he'd see the truth.

He walked back to the porch and stood on the brick sidewalk staring at Lauren, who was reapplying her red lipstick. "What did you hope to accomplish here today?"

"Revenge. You're sorry now you didn't give me the money, aren't you?"

"No, I'm not. I'm sorry I didn't tell him the truth earlier. He knows it now, though, Lauren. All of it."

She slanted a skeptical glance up at him. "Even I don't know all of it. Like who his real mother is. You would never talk about it. He's going to ask, you know."

"He already has."

"I'm suing for visitation rights."

His chest squeezed. "And you think a judge will award you any rights after what you did? Plus an attorney costs money. You said you were broke."

"I'm going to make you pay attorney fees."

He gave a wry laugh. "You are dreaming. No judge in the country would make me pay for what you've done."

For all his bravado, he wasn't sure it was true. If Will wanted to see Lauren, Reid might be forced to agree. And he knew Lauren — she had a way with men. If the judge had any testosterone left in his body, she might get her way.

But it all boiled down to trust and obedience. He either did what he knew God was telling him or he let more lies take him down.

"I guess I'll see you in court, Lauren."

She narrowed her eyes. "You've changed. You sound so sure of yourself. What's happened to you?"

He'd managed to throw off the guilt and shame he saw Jane still dealing with. And he'd managed to cling to the true source of strength. If Lauren only realized what her abandonment had done to him and Will. But she'd never understand it. She was like a turtle laying eggs in the sand, then going back to the sea with no attachment to its offspring.

"You've never even thought of Will in all these years, have you?"

She shrugged. "He's not really mine. Have you ever thought about *why* I left? There was an unspoken wall between us, and it was *her.*"

"Her? I never looked at another woman while we were married."

"Don't be obtuse. Will's mother. She was always there because you'd never talk about her. If you'd even once brought her out into the light of day, we might have gotten past whatever was binding your heart to hers."

"I-It's not what you think. There was no real bond to her. It was always about Will."

She lifted a perfect brow. "I don't believe you. I lived with her ghost between us the whole time we were together."

She made it sound like an eternity. "It was your imagination. It wasn't any kind of real marriage."

"You weren't married to her?" Lauren shook her head. "You'd never live with someone outside of marriage. I tried everything I knew to get you to move in with me, and you wouldn't have it. I should have run right then. You're a cold fish, Reid."

She dropped her lipstick back in her purse. "See you around."

Was it true what she'd said? It might explain the pull he felt toward Jane even now.

TWENTY-SIX

Jane would give anything to sense Reid's steadfast presence beside her behind the viewing mirror. She reached out to put her hand on Parker's neck. She could watch this play out. She had to.

Her dad sat at the same small table where he'd interrogated countless suspects. He seemed smaller somehow. It wasn't so much his lack of uniform as it was the way he looked deflated. Diminished.

Brian sat across from him, and Paul was in the chair at the end of the table. Paul had seniority — and the most animosity — so he would take the lead and be the most unpleasant to deal with. He'd barely kept his contempt for Dad in check throughout the last year he'd worked for her father.

Paul put his palms flat on the table. "Let's start by talking about your relationship with Gary Dawson. How long have you known him and how did you meet?"

Her father's eyes were rimmed in dark circles. "We met at a sporting goods store up in Mobile. I was getting a new fishing rig."

"How long ago?"

Her father shrugged. "Time slips by, and it's easy to forget, but I'd guess three years ago. Could have been a little longer or shorter. I was taking down the rod I wanted, and a whole bunch of them came crashing down on my head. Gary was at the end of the aisle, and he ran to untangle me. He had a rod just like I was buying in his cart, and we started talking. He told me about his job and that he likes to fish to get away from the stress."

Dad turned and looked directly at the glass. Even though he couldn't see her, Jane knew he had no doubt she was there watching the interview. And why wouldn't he? He'd spent years in this small room observing other interrogations.

"I didn't kill Gary," he said quietly. "If someone saw my boat out, it wasn't me in it. Gary often took friends out."

Paul tapped his fingers on the table. "Where were you Sunday, Charles?"

Her dad looked away from the glass to face Paul. "Elizabeth and I were shopping in Mobile. She wanted to buy a new rug for the living room. We were at Lowe's and a couple of carpet stores." He listed off a couple of familiar names.

"That's not what she says."

Jane barely noticed her nails biting into her palms. Was her dad lying — or was Elizabeth? This made no sense.

Dad lifted a brow. "She might have the day confused or something. That's where we were."

"Did you buy a rug and have a receipt?" Brian ignored the glare from Paul.

"We bought one at Lowe's. Elizabeth should have a receipt."

"She says you took the boat out and told her you were meeting Gary."

"That's a lie." Her dad's tone was even, but his eyes were narrowed.

Jane gasped and leaned toward the glass. What was going on and who was telling the truth? She grabbed a notepad and jotted down a reminder to check store cameras in Mobile.

"Tell us more about your relationship with Gary," Brian said with a swift glance at Paul.

Dad shrugged. "Not much more to tell. We had a lot of the same likes and dislikes. I care about the bay and our environment, and so did Gary. I love to catch flounder, and so did he."

294

"Did you ever go gambling with him?" Paul asked.

Her dad paused. "I don't like gambling. Gary never mentioned he liked gambling. You mean at casinos or what?"

"Looked like he was more into betting on races and that kind of thing. Some online stuff too. He was in hock for a lot of money. You guys were best buds, yet you knew nothing about it?"

"Nothing. He knew I thought gamblers were stupid sheep. Maybe he was ashamed to tell me. I wish he had. Maybe I could have helped him."

"We already know he owed you money — a lot of money. Didn't you wonder why he needed to borrow it?"

"He told me it was for repairs on his house. His basement flooded, and he didn't have insurance to cover it."

Paul's face showed his disbelief. "Let's get back to Sunday. We have a witness telling us you took your boat out, yet you claim you were shopping with that same witness. I'm not sure how we are going to reconcile those two stories. Did Gary ask to take out the boat?"

"No. I tried to call him that morning to let him know I couldn't go out, but he didn't answer. I left a message telling him

295

to take the boat if he wanted. You should be able to call it up when you retrieve his cell information."

Jane did a fist pump. Yes! Her dad knew how all this worked, and he'd know Paul had nothing. The pings should show where Gary's phone had been when the call came in from Dad and if they were together. The biggest questions were why Elizabeth would lie — and why she'd moved out of the house.

They'd been together for years, and Jane had thought Elizabeth really loved Dad. So what was happening here?

Paul leaned his chair onto the two back legs. "You have any idea how that blood got on your boat?"

"Nope. You don't even know what kind of blood it is yet."

"I've got probable cause to throw you in a cell, so don't play games, Charles. You're telling me that boat sat out in the barn all week and you didn't so much as look at it and see that blood?"

Her dad gave him a level stare. "You have a boat, Paul. How often do you look at yours unless you're taking it out? The answer is not at all, just like me. I have better things to do than to examine my boat for no good reason. I don't even do the maintenance on it. I take it out and fish from it. It's not like it's a prized race car."

He rose and rotated his neck. "I'm done talking without an attorney. Unless you're arresting me, I'm going home to get something to eat."

Paul's face reddened, and Jane didn't think he'd capitulate, but he jerked his thumb at Brian. "Let him go. But it won't be for long. The blood is going to be your ticket to jail."

Her dad gave him a long look but said nothing as he exited the room. Jane sagged into the chair and put her head in her hands. She had to have some help on this, but who?

The sun had set just over the trees by the time Reid heard the swish of Will's paddle. As he waited on the back deck, he'd rolled around how to address all of this, and he still hadn't come up with a good plan of action or even where to start.

Bees buzzed through the flowers, and he heard the distant chug of a fishing trawler making its way to Mobile Bay as he rose to face his son.

Will had his head down as he strode up the hill from the river. He was pale, and Reid thought his eyes were red. Poor kid.

This should not be happening. He hadn't seen Reid yet, and he took a moment to let his gaze linger on his son. He was a handsome young man, but even more attractive on the inside. His care for kids and other people had always brought Reid pride and joy. He should have known better than to keep the truth from the boy.

He'd been so wrong.

"Will."

Will looked up at the sound of Reid's voice, and his steps slowed. His gaze darted past Reid. "She still here?"

"No, she's gone."

"Good. I don't want to talk to her."

"She claims she's contacted an attorney to sue for custody."

Will's chin jutted up. "I'm not going with her, and no one can make me."

"I don't think the court will even try, not with what she did."

"Why'd she come back now? She's ruined everything. I was happy. I'm going to play football, and everything was great. Then she had to come along."

Reid wanted to hug his boy, but Will wasn't ready for that. He swept his hand toward a lawn chair. "Have a seat, and we can talk. Want something to eat or drink?"

"I'm not hungry." Will dropped into a

chair and crossed his ankles.

"We'll get through this, son. I hope you can forgive me."

Will looked up, and his Adam's apple bobbed as he gulped back the tears in his eyes. "Why, Dad? Why would you keep something like this from me? I'm almost fifteen! For fifteen years you've lied to me."

"I'm sorry." He'd been so wrong to hide all this.

"Why would she leave a baby? Was she like M— I mean, Lauren? Just didn't want a screaming kid around her?"

"It wasn't like that at all." He inhaled and prayed for guidance and strength. "She was very young, Will, about your age now. Her father forced her to go with him right after you were born."

Will's brows rose. "You robbed the cradle, Dad?"

"I wasn't much older, son. There were . . . circumstances beyond our control."

"Where is she now? Does she keep up with me at all?"

Dread churned in Reid's stomach. "She thinks you died, Will."

Will gaped. "You never told her I was alive?"

"I didn't know where she was for a long time. This was fifteen years ago, and it wasn't that easy to track someone down. I was mad, too, and didn't think she deserved to know anything. I didn't trust her either."

"You sound like you hate her."

"I did for a while."

"You know where she is now?"

Reid nodded. "And she's a better person than I thought she was."

"Have you told her about me?"

"No. I wanted to make sure it wasn't a mistake to allow her into our lives. I think it's okay to do it, but I don't want to hurt her."

"I want to meet her and make up my own mind."

Reid moved restlessly. "Think about what a shock that will be, son. I need to handle this carefully. Can you trust me just a little? Give me some time to figure out how to break this news? I don't want you hurt either."

Will chewed on his lip. "What's her name?"

Reid forced a grin. "I'm not going to tell you yet because you'll google her. Can you give me a week? That's not too much to ask. Let me figure out how to tell her."

Will held his gaze. "I know I've been mad at you, Dad, but I forgive you." He exhaled. "I don't like how I've been feeling. So yeah,

I'll try to give you a week. Are there any pictures of her or anything?"

"I've got a couple of faded, blurry ones." Reid rose. "Come inside. I'll get them, and we can have some dinner after."

Knowing Will would ask, he'd gotten out the pictures to be ready. He led Will to the master bedroom and picked up his Bible. There were four pictures inside the front cover, and he handed them to Will. "You can't see much."

The first one was of Will and his mother in the bed right after Will's birth. His hair was still matted, and a bit of blood smeared his face. Her hair fell over her face, and only the curve of her cheek could be seen. The second was of her outside in the trees. She wore a dress that went to her ankles with long sleeves. She was squinting up into the sun, and her long light-brown hair tumbled around her face. It wasn't a clear shot either.

Will frowned. "You can't really even see her. This is all you've got of her? And who's the dude in the other two pictures?"

"Those other two are me. I'm sorry, but those are all I have of her."

"Whoa, Dad, you look totally different. All that beard, and your hair is clear down your back. You can't even see your face. And you're pretty chunky."

"You can say fat." Reid grinned. "I wasn't very happy and ate a lot. I think I wanted to hide behind all the hair too."

Will stared at the first picture again. "I think she loved me."

"I'm sure she did." Reid turned toward the door. "Let's get some dinner. You can have the pictures."

He didn't want to explain the circumstances of Will's birth, but he would have to eventually. Just not today.

TWENTY-SEVEN

When Reid left his house after dinner, Will was watching TV with the pictures on his lap. Reid had an irresistible compulsion to talk to Jane and see how it had gone with her dad. He grabbed the last few beignets he'd bought and took them with him.

Strains of jazz music played softly from Moreau's Seafood down the street, and the wind brought the aroma of their famous grilled oysters to his nose. He stood with the beignet box under his arm and looked up at the wrought-iron railing on Jane's balcony. She wasn't outside tonight, but he thought he saw a shadow pass in front of the window, so she was likely home.

He dug out his phone to call her, then put it away. No, he'd just show up at her door. He had a sense that she needed to talk, but she was so reserved she might not realize it. He didn't want to take the chance of her turning him away.

The iron stairs clanged and wobbled under his feet as he went up to the second floor. He pressed the ornate doorbell and waited. Parker woofed, and he heard light footsteps coming.

"Who's there?"

"It's Reid, Jane. I hope it's not too late, but just in case, I brought beignets so you'll forgive me."

The dead bolt scraped, and the door opened. Parker thrust his head out and huffed. Reid rubbed his ears. "It's okay, boy, it's just me."

The door opened wider. She was in yoga shorts and a T with her light-brown hair up in a ponytail that made her look about twenty. Perspiration dotted her forehead and chest, and her cheeks were red.

She stepped aside and reached for a paper towel that she dragged over her face and chest. "I'm a sight."

He wanted to tell her she looked beautiful, but he could sense how skittish she was by the way she avoided his gaze. The last thing he wanted was to be tossed out. "I tried yoga once, and I kept falling over in the triangle pose."

She shut the door behind him and slanted a grin up at him. "That's why it's called yoga *practice*. One time isn't enough to prove to yourself that you can do it."

He set the box of beignets on the kitchen island. "I suppose beignets are out of the question since you were doing yoga."

"I'm famished. Yoga destresses me, and so do the carbs." She lifted the lid and grabbed one of the raspberry-filled ones. "Yum." She devoured it in three bites, then licked the powdered sugar from her fingers. "What's up?"

He selected a beignet and glanced at the coffeepot. "Coffee fresh?"

"I made it before I started yoga. I'll get it while you tell me why you're here." She grabbed two mugs and the coffeepot, then returned to the island.

"Nothing like making a guy feel welcome." He polished off his beignet and grabbed a paper towel. "Did your dad get arrested?"

"No, but it's only a matter of time. I talked Paul into waiting until we have the DNA back, but I'm not hopeful." She poured coffee in the mugs and handed one to him. "Elizabeth is contradicting his alibi. I can't believe she'd do that."

He listened while she went through what the interrogation had revealed. "Store video should tell the truth of all that."

"I'm going to contact the Mobile police tomorrow to see about looking at the video.

But it's weird. I tried to call Elizabeth, but I got her voice mail. She hasn't called me back yet either. I don't think she wants to talk to me."

"You think she's trying to punish your dad for something?"

"Seems that way."

He didn't want to point out that her dad could be lying. It wasn't like he had never told her a lie — but she didn't know about that yet.

"Mind if I sit down?" Without waiting for an answer he went into the living room and settled on the sofa. Parker pressed against his leg, and he rubbed his head. "Sorry, buddy, my beignet is gone."

There was a file of papers in the armchair across from the sofa so she sat beside him. He caught the coconut scent on her hair and wished he could lean in for a sniff.

She pulled her legs onto the sofa under her. "What's up with you and Will?"

"He found out the truth about his mother." Reid looked up to catch the surprise in her eyes. "Lauren isn't his real mother, and I never told him. I think we have it all worked out now. But it's shattered his trust of me a little bit, I think."

"I'm sorry. So he's lost two mothers. Poor kid. I hate that he's hurting."

306

"You could see the tension between us?"

She nodded. "Hard to miss."

"I suppose so."

Was she going to ask about Will's mother too? He rushed into a different topic. "Lauren says she's contacted an attorney to sue for custody, but Will says he'll refuse to go with her. You think a judge would make him?"

She shook her head. "Doubtful at his age, especially given the circumstances. Though she's legally his mother and has rights, she deserted him. You have any proof she tried to blackmail you?"

"My phone automatically records conversations. I put an app on it some time back to help me keep track of research calls. Is that admissible?"

"Yeah, we're a one-party state, meaning as long as one party — in this case you — is aware it's being recorded, it's legal."

"Then I have proof. That's a load off my mind."

If she kept looking at him like that, he was going to have a hard time resisting her. The silence between them stretched out until it felt like they were saying something without words. And maybe they were. The next thing he knew he was leaning toward her, and she wasn't moving away.

He slipped his arm around her, and she turned her face up to his. Her lashes fluttered closed and fanned across her cheeks. He stared, mesmerized, into her face before he lowered his head to brush her lips with his.

It was like coming home, like they'd been together all these years. The sweet scent of her breath mingled with his, and her lips were as soft as peaches under his. He closed his eyes and deepened the kiss. Nothing mattered in this moment but the feel of her in his arms.

She gave a little gasp and pulled away. When he lifted his head, she was staring at him with her fingers on her lips.

"Should I apologize?" he whispered.

"N-No, just a silly flashback of some kind."

Had she felt what he did with that kiss? He didn't dare ask if she had recognized him. Surely she would have said so if that were the case. Even his own son hadn't recognized him in the pictures. A lot had changed in fifteen years.

He scrambled to his feet. "I-I'd better get back to Will. We'll come by tomorrow to go with you on the next phase of the investigation."

She was blinking like she'd just awakened,

and he rushed for the door before it happened.

Jane's hands shook as she locked the door behind Reid. She touched her fingers to her lips again. What a crazy moment of déjà vu. It took her back to a time she didn't like to think about, to a young man as green as she was.

There was no way she could sleep, not now. She grabbed her keys and her gun and unlocked the door again, then told Parker to stay. Olivia wouldn't mind a visit. She was a night owl and would welcome a little company. Jane clanged down the stairs and went along the alley beside her building.

Normally the darkness didn't bother her, but the hair rose on the back of her neck as she walked through the darkened streets. Several times she whirled with her hand on her gun and her heart pounding.

Olivia lived on Dauphin Street, two blocks from the water. Jane was practically running as she reached Olivia's house and pounded on the door.

"Hold your horses," Olivia called from inside. The lock scraped and she opened the door. "Jane, goodness me, you're as white as oyster shells. What's wrong?" She stepped aside and shut the door behind Jane.

"N-Nothing's really *wrong.* Well, that's not true. Nearly everything is wrong." Jane was mortified to feel her eyes start to burn and well with tears.

Olivia embraced her. "I'm glad you ran straight to me, dear girl. Tell me what's the matter. Megan's sleeping, and you can talk about anything."

A flood of emotions and tears erupted as Jane wept on her friend's shoulder. "Someone's framing Dad, and I can't stop it. The town is falling apart, and it's more than I can handle. I'm not up to this job, Olivia. I don't know how I thought I could do this."

Olivia took Jane's shoulders and nudged her back to stare into her face. "You listen to me, Chief Hardy. If anyone can figure out what's happening, it's you. You've solved more cases in this town than all the other detectives put together. And as for Paul — his heart's a thumpin' gizzard. You pay him no mind."

Jane managed a watery smile. "Okay."

"And this isn't worthy of tears. What else has happened? The Jane I know wouldn't be ready to run away over a few hard challenges. Tell me."

Jane rubbed her forehead. "I have to sit

down. My legs are wobbly."

"So are mine."

Jane gave her a sharp look. "The ALS?"

"Probably. I've been a little shaky, but maybe it's nerves from the worry about Megan."

Olivia's strong faith usually helped her weather any storm. "I should have been here more. And Reid told me something really encouraging. The famous physicist Stephen Hawking lived over fifty years with ALS."

"Really? I hadn't heard that."

"Plus, he said Lyme disease is often misdiagnosed as ALS. Have you been tested for Lyme? We have so many ticks down here."

"I haven't."

"I looked up the symptoms, and he's right. What I read said you needed to be tested properly. I have a list of Lyme-literate doctors I'm going to send you."

"I'll take a look." Olivia grabbed her arm and steered her toward the living room of the French Quarter home.

It had three bedrooms, two bathrooms, a minuscule kitchen, and a slightly more expansive living room. It was the homiest place Jane had ever stepped foot in. The place breathed welcome and warmth. She found her favorite chair, a rocker by the dining table.

Olivia sat in the big armchair and picked up the baby blanket she was crocheting. She made baby blankets for all the new arrivals in town. The one in her hands was pink.

Her crochet needle moved through the loops. "Tell me what's riled you up. I know it's more than your dad's problem. This feels personal."

Jane held her gaze. "How on earth do you do that without looking at the yarn?"

"Practice, honey. Quit changing the subject."

"You know about the nightmares." Jane sighed. "But tonight I had a flashback."

"From the cult? I did some reading on recovery from one of those places, and that's pretty typical." Olivia pulled out more yarn from the skein. "Any idea what's causing these thoughts?"

Heat washed up Jane's chest and neck. "Um, Reid kissed me tonight."

"Yes!" Olivia did a fist pump with the crochet needle in her hand, and the sight made Jane laugh. It was so out of character.

"But it made me remember Moose and the baby. I almost imagined I was kissing Moose and not Reid. Isn't that weird?"

"How many guys have you kissed besides Moose?"

Jane didn't have to think about it. "None. That sounds weird, I know. In college I was still too broken to date. I've dated a few men in town, but when they've taken me home, I couldn't wait to get in the door before they could put the moves on me. I've been scared."

"You've been as lost as last year's Easter egg, honey. I've prayed and prayed for you to get past all this. So it's no wonder you thought of Moose."

"You think that's all it is? Something about Reid reminds me of Moose. It was almost like he *was* Moose. He smelled like him and tasted like him."

Olivia put down her needles. "What are you trying to say — that Reid is Moose? Surely you'd know your own husband if you saw him again."

"I-I'm not sure I would. He was only eighteen, but he was one of the few teens with a full beard. And his long hair and hat covered up most of his face. We were only t-together like-like that a few times, and candles don't give much light. They worked us hard, and most of the time I only saw him from a distance in the day. Everything from that time is so blurry and distorted."

She couldn't believe she was saying all this. The words had spilled out before she could stop them. She still shuddered to remember. She didn't *want* to remember, but the kiss had opened the floodgates.

"Did you love Moose?"

She bit her lip, then shook her head. "I didn't even know what love was. Every bit of life was regulated — who we were to marry, my duty to bear children." Her voice broke on the last word. Her dear little baby. She could still smell the scent of his head and remember the softness of his skin.

Sudden tears blurred her vision again. "I think I could have come to care for Moose if we'd been together more. He was kind and gentle. And I think he was just as confused as I was. All we knew was to do what we were told."

"Come to church with me again on Sunday. I need you with me."

Olivia had never asked her to come support her, and Jane found herself nodding. "Okay. I'll pick you up."

"I'm going to pray for clarity for you, Jane. Come talk to me about this more, and maybe that will ease some of these fears and flashbacks."

"Maybe you're right. This strange sense of déjà vu will pass. It's probably all the stress." She rose and went to hug Olivia. "Sleep well. Thank you for always being there for me. I'll lock the door on my way out."

Jane stepped back out into the humid night and walked home at a slower pace. The moon lit her way, and she wished she had an internal light to figure all this out.

TWENTY-EIGHT

Reid sat cross-legged on his dock and
watched the moon glimmer on the river's
turgid water. It was a cool night for spring
in the south, and the mosquitoes weren't as
troublesome as usual. A big splash to his
right indicated the gators were active, but
he wasn't concerned about them.

He should have told Jane who he was
tonight. Instead, he'd made a fool of himself
and kissed her. What had he been thinking?
That was the problem — he hadn't been
thinking. He'd wanted to kiss her since the
first time he'd seen her again. Being so close
to her had worn down his defenses.

Once she found out the truth, she was going to hate him. He hated himself. Why was
it so hard to open up and tell the whole
truth? Pure and simple, he was afraid.
Afraid of being rejected, afraid of hurting
his son, afraid of failing God. It was all a
whirlpool of fear sucking him under. He'd

thought he left all that behind as he'd healed from the experiences of his childhood.

The pier groaned and shifted, and he looked back toward the shore. Will, dressed in the basketball shorts and T-shirt he usually slept in, headed his way. His black hair stuck up, and as he neared, Reid could tell he'd just awakened.

"Dad, it's after one. What's going on?"

Reid grinned at the plaintive note in his voice. He patted the dock beside him. "How'd you even know I was out here?"

Will dropped beside him. "I woke up to go to the bathroom and saw the downstairs light still on. You weren't anywhere so I looked out here and saw you."

Reid gazed across the water to Plash Island where a few lights still glimmered this time of night. A shrimping trawler moved past its mooring on the island, and he caught the strong scent of sea life from the boat. Maybe this was the time to be honest with Will, to tell him everything except Jane's name.

"There's more to the story about me and your mom, Will. It's an ugly story, and one I haven't wanted to talk about — not with anyone. You were too young to hear it until now, but you're nearly a man."

Will shifted. "Okay." He sounded cautious and eager all at the same time.

Reid had thought about this moment a thousand times over the years. How did someone convey that time without coming across like someone too stupid to live? It had taken him a long time to come to grips with his passivity and acceptance of something he now knew was ridiculous.

"You were only a year old when I escaped."

"Escaped? From where?"

"My dad was a rigid man. He believed he was second only to God and that every person should accept his word as law. I think I was about five when he started Mount Sinai up in Michigan."

"What was that? A town?"

"A cult." The word was bitter on Reid's tongue. "He was sure the end of the world was coming soon, and when it did, he wanted to be ready to lead us all. It was a small community of maybe twenty cabins or so. When my mom objected to him having more than one wife, she went missing. I think he probably killed her, though I don't know for certain. I've tried to find her in case he simply ejected her from the camp, but I've never found a trace of her."

Will made a slight sound that could have

been a gasp or maybe a sigh. Reid didn't look at him. He couldn't — not if he wanted to get through this.

It all sounded so ugly and sordid, and there was more to come. Much more. Nausea roiled in Reid's belly, but he had to tell it all.

"It was a hard, cold place. During the day I worked in the fields or stocked supplies. We practiced shooting constantly."

"No wonder you're a crack shot."

Reid nodded. "With a gun and a crossbow both. I can use most any weapon. When the guys turned eighteen, we were expected to marry whomever my father designated for us. A fourteen-year-old girl was picked for me. Everyone called her Button because she was a preemie when she was born and stayed small. At fourteen she was about five two, I guess. They called me Moose. You could tell why by the picture you saw of me. We didn't look like we went together. My father married us, if you can call it that. There was never a marriage license, and after I left, my attorney told me the cere-mony wasn't legal."

"Did you love her?"

Reid tossed a small stick in the water and watched the ripples in the moonlight. "I didn't know her very well. Relationships

319

were discouraged. We were supposed to procreate for the good of the group. I didn't live with her or anything like that. We were only alone a few times."

"Wow. I wasn't expecting anything like this." Will's voice was shaky.

Reid dared a quick peek at his son and saw Will staring out over the water with a stunned expression. This had to be a bomb to Will's sense of right and wrong.

"What happened?"

"You were born on Button's birthday, and it was the day Mount Sinai imploded. The state police swarmed the place and rescued a woman my dad had kidnapped. Fires broke out all over the camp. Everyone was screaming and running. It was total chaos."

"Which is why my mom thought I was dead?"

"Yes. Her mother brought you to me to see. I was holding you when the first shots rang out. I wanted to protect you so I ran for the forest. I had a four-wheeler out there, and I got us out of the melee as quickly as I could. When I went back to the camp, it was in ruins, burned to the ground. A few people were left, but only a handful. My dad was dead.

"An offshoot group, Liberty's Children, wasn't far so I took my four-wheeler to find help and tell them what had happened. Button's mother was there too. She told me her husband had told Button you died in order to get her to leave with him. She was spitting mad about it and wanted to take you from me, but I wouldn't let her."

"Where is my grandmother now? And your grandparents?"

"Your grandmother is still with Liberty's Children, and I've never found my grandparents on either side. The past is something I've tried to bury. For your sake I'll see if I can find any of them. You deserve more family than just me."

Will clasped Reid's hand. "You're enough, Dad. You've always been enough."

Reid's fingers tightened around his son's. "I stayed with Liberty's Children for about a year, then slipped away one night with you. I changed my name and tried to become someone else. Someone you could be proud of — someone I could be proud of."

"You were nineteen then and a single dad? How'd you make it?"

"It's a long story, and I don't think I can tell it tonight." Reid yawned and rubbed his gritty eyes.

"Wow, a cult. That's nuts."

"More than you know. It took a long time to find healing. And to find my way. You were the one thing that kept me sane."

Will reached over and gave him a fierce hug. "I want to hear all of it tomorrow, Dad. Thank you for what you did for me. You left because of me, didn't you?"

Reid's eyes burned, and he clutched his boy back. "Yes. Everything I've done has been for you. You're the best thing that ever happened to me."

It had gone better than he'd expected, but there were still treacherous roads to navigate ahead.

Reid's eyes were shadowed when he and Will entered Jane's office. She shot a glance his way before going to the coffeepot. She probably looked as bad as Reid did. She'd tossed and turned a long time before finally falling asleep sometime after three. Will was quiet as well, but the strain between father and son was noticeably missing, which relieved her.

She'd relived that kiss for hours. Had it meant anything at all to Reid?

Footsteps came running down the hall, and Paul burst through her doorway. He held up a paper. "Results from the blood. Same blood type as Gary Dawson. He was killed on your dad's boat. We have to issue an arrest warrant."

"Did you check out his alibi?" Jane put her hand on Parker's head and told him to stay.

"Elizabeth already destroyed it."

"I meant with the stores he mentioned. Yes, Gary was killed on the boat, but that doesn't mean my dad did it."

Paul gaped and shook his head. "Listen to you, Jane. If this were any other suspect, you'd haul him in here fast enough to leave a grease mark. You're too close to this."

She tried to hang on to her objectivity. Was he right? She shook her head. "Paul, you know I always try to consider every single possible variant in a case. We haven't checked out Dad's alibi. Right now it's his word against Elizabeth's. That's not good police work, and you know it."

"You're really not going to arrest him?"

"Not until we are sure of our facts. I'll go up to Mobile today and see what I can find out about any corroborating evidence. Impartial evidence." And she planned to talk to Elizabeth herself.

"I can't believe this!" Paul slammed his fist against the doorjamb, then turned and stomped out.

"Trouble," Reid said. "He won't let it drop there."

"I just need a little time to see if Dad's

alibi checks out. He's wrong about me being too close to it. If this were anyone else with the same evidence, I would still check the alibi first."

She wasn't sure Reid believed her, but he didn't know how careful she'd always been with evidence. When a prosecutor got a case from her, she wanted to make sure every T was crossed. The prosecutor had thanked her more than once. Paul's cases weren't always so clean.

She grabbed her keys. "Let's head to Mobile."

Her phone rang before she'd taken two steps, and her gut clenched when Lisa's name appeared on the screen. "Good morning, Mayor."

"I just spoke to Paul. Is it true you're refusing to arrest your father?"

Jane swallowed at the hard note in Lisa's voice. "We haven't checked out his alibi, Lisa. This is not how I conduct a case. We don't have all the evidence in."

"I'm suspending you, Jane. I'm sorry, but we can't have the public perception be that we are shielding your father because he was the former police chief. And get rid of Reid Dixon as quickly as you can. This documentary is done as well. Clean out your office and vacate the premises as quickly as possible."

"But —" She was speaking to dead air. Lisa had hung up.

Will and Reid were both wide-eyed. "She suspended me." She jerked open the lap drawer on her desk. "I've got to get my stuff and get out."

"That snake in the grass," Reid ground out. He turned toward the door.

"Don't. It won't help." She went to the closet and rummaged until she found a box she'd used to transfer her things when she moved in. It was probably the shortest police chief stint in history. She dumped her belongings back into the box.

"What are you going to do?" Reid asked.

"Find out who killed Dawson. It might be my dad, and I have to be ready to accept it. But it might be someone else, and I won't rest until I find out. Fanny's life might be depending on it."

"Any news from the senator? Wasn't she supposed to get a ransom demand on Saturday night? That was three days ago."

"I've heard nothing. The case belongs to the state boys." She went back to her desk and pulled out a USB drive from the drawer to insert into her computer. "I'll take the files with me and any other cases Dad had investigated. There might be something in them."

"How will you do that without resources?"

"Brian won't shut me out of the investigation, and I can still ask questions." She stared at him and felt a pang that he'd likely walk away without a documentary to work on. "Lisa wants you gone too."

He lifted a brow. "Lisa isn't my boss. I'm not going anywhere. I have some contacts with the state police from a documentary I did a couple of years ago. I'll help you."

He held her gaze for a long moment, and her traitorous heart did a quick blip. Was he remembering last night too? She could still taste him on her lips.

She finally looked away before he could read the yearning in her face. "That will help. I want to talk to Elizabeth first. I can't believe she'd throw Dad under the bus."

Reid didn't answer, and she knew he was wondering if her dad was the one who'd lied. Only finding a tape from Sunday with them on it would prove whether or not he'd told them the truth.

She had her work cut out for her. Warmth ran up her neck at Reid's offer of help. This wasn't his fight, and he could walk away if he wanted. The fact he didn't meant more than he'd ever know. At least she wasn't facing this mountain alone.

She could do this. On Easter Sunday she'd realized she was stronger than she thought. Nothing would make her go back on the promise to herself.

TWENTY-NINE

Reid squinted in the sunlight as they emerged from the police department and walked across the parking lot to his SUV. Jane wouldn't have a vehicle here since she'd been suspended. He slanted a glance her way and saw her set, determined expression. This wouldn't deter her from finding out the truth. Parker walked close beside her as if he sensed her churning emotions.

A big man in a suit and tie got out of a Mercedes. He shook his head when he saw Jane. "I knew you weren't up to the job. Now that Paul is in charge, we might see some results on these murders."

Jane's chin rose. "Nice to hear your vote of confidence, Victor."

She strode away, and Reid jogged to catch up with her. "Who was that rude guy?"

"Victor Armstrong. He voted against me on the council. He predicted a small woman like me could never manage the job."

Reid curled his hands into fists. "What a jerk."

"He's not worth my time."

A male voice spoke behind him. "Reid Dixon?"

Reid turned to see a man in his early twenties rushing to catch him. "Yes?"

The man slapped an envelope in his hand. "You've been served, sir." He pivoted and walked away.

Reid's gut clenched as he looked at the official return address. He ripped open the envelope and pulled out the papers. It was all he could do not to crumple the sheets and toss them to the street.

Will stepped to his side. "What is it, Dad?"

"Lauren is suing for custody just like she threatened." He glanced at Jane, who stopped beside them. "Is there anything I can do to avoid having to go to court?"

Jane held out her hand. "Can I see?"

He handed the papers to her, and she perused the order. "You'll get a summons in a few days that will tell you when you have to appear. You should definitely hire an attorney. I know some good family law attorneys in town. This won't be resolved overnight, though."

"If it's going to take time, I'm surprised she's doing this."

"She might not stay in town the whole time. She'll find out when she has to appear as well. You'll have time to gather your facts, and so will she."

This wasn't something he wanted to deal with — especially not when Jane needed him.

Will folded his arms over his chest. "I'm not going with her, and they can't make me."

"The judge actually can." Jane handed the papers back to Reid. "But you're old enough that the court will most likely listen to your desires. You don't know her and don't seem to want to know her, so this might be more of a nuisance than anything." She looked at Reid. "Plus, you have the proof that she was trying to blackmail you. You could press charges for that."

He straightened. "That's a great idea! I could tell her she has twenty-four hours to withdraw her complaint, or I'll file criminal charges."

"I think you should just file the charges," Jane said. "She doesn't seem the type to listen to anything but what she wants. It's usually better to just do what you know you need to and get on with it. Talking to someone with a vendetta shows them they've gotten your goat. If she's after power, you'll play into her hand."

Reid hated the thought of filing charges and spending more time in court, but maybe Jane was right. He needed to do whatever he could to protect Will.

He examined the papers. "I've probably got a couple of weeks before the hearing at least?" He waited until Jane nodded. "Who would you suggest?"

"Scott Foster is a longtime friend, and he'll be at the jail when they bring in my dad. You could talk to him after that. And I suppose he might even say you should talk to her and try to come to an agreement, but that wouldn't be my choice if I were in your shoes. It's your call, though."

He could sense her impatience to get on the road to talk to Elizabeth, and he was just as eager. This couldn't have come at a worse time.

"Thanks, I'll do that." He squinted in the sun. "I think that's Lauren across the street. You think it's a sign I should talk to her?"

"I'm not into signs," Jane said.

"Do it, Dad. I just want this over."

"Maybe I can get her to see sense." He started for the street and paused to let traffic pass.

Will came after him. "I'm going with you. I'll tell her I'm not going."

Not that Lauren would listen to Will. She wanted what she wanted, and she wasn't the kind to be easily deterred.

Lauren's gaze locked with Reid's, and her triumphant smile needled him. She waited for them under the coffee shop awning. Her gaze dropped to the paper in his hand. "I see you got your papers. I warned you."

He stopped in front of her. "And I'm warning you. I've got evidence you were trying to blackmail me, and I'm going to file charges. You brought this on yourself."

Her smile faltered. "You have no proof." She tossed her head, and her golden hair rippled. "Our conversation was private."

"It doesn't matter what you do, I'm not going anywhere with you," Will said.

She narrowed her eyes at Will. "Then tell your dad to pay up, or you won't like the outcome either."

What a piece of work. Talking to her son like that. What kind of person did that?

Reid pulled out his phone and clicked on the recording. Her voice came through the speakers, and Lauren's face paled.

"You can't use that. I didn't know I was being recorded."

"Wrong. This is a one-party state, which means since I was part of the conversation, I can legally record it and use it."

"You should have told me you had it." She took a step forward on her impossibly high red heels and snatched the phone from his hands.

He grabbed at it, but she took a step back, then slammed it to the ground where it shattered. "There's your evidence." Her sneer turned to a predatory grin.

"It's backed up on the cloud. You did nothing except open yourself up to another charge of vandalism."

Her green eyes widened, and she turned to stalk away. The next move was hers.

Any contact with her dad could play against him in court. Since Jane couldn't ask him where to find Elizabeth, she asked Brian. After stopping to buy a new phone and download his backup file, Reid drove her around to Plash Island, where she found Elizabeth working in the yard of a small waterfront cottage near a shrimping operation that sent its briny odor out onto the wind.

Dressed in a long-sleeve shirt and pants, Elizabeth looked up from under the brim of her straw hat when they pulled into the drive. Her face was expressionless, and she swatted the small flies swarming her.

Jane got out and forced a smile. "Flies are

bad this morning." Reid got out, too, but Will stayed in the backseat with the dog.

"I hope you have on repellant."

Jane shrugged away the fake concern. "They're arresting Dad today."

Elizabeth gazed back at her with a calm, still manner. "Is that why you're here?"

"Why'd you leave, Elizabeth? You guys have been together a long time. I thought we were close, and you never even called."

"I didn't want to harm your relationship with your dad."

"He says he was with you the Sunday Dawson died. You say he wasn't. He told us where he was, and I'm going to look for video proving it today. Do you want to amend your statement? I'd hate to have to arrest you for making a false one."

"You'll never believe anything bad about your dad, will you? When it all comes out, you're going to be so hurt, Jane. I hate it."

"When what comes out?" Something in Elizabeth's manner made Jane think her words had nothing to do with the accusations against her father.

Elizabeth finally looked away. "I'm not going to be the one to tell you."

"You're not making any sense. What's he done that could cause you to turn against him like this?"

"Did you want me to lie about Sunday?"

"What? Of course not! But why would Dad say he was shopping for a rug and tell us exactly where to look for video if he was lying?"

Her brown eyes flickered with what looked like fear. "I don't know why Charles does what he does."

"You sound like you hate him. What happened?"

"I got tired of his lies."

Jane glimpsed the pain in Elizabeth's face. "Was he seeing someone else?"

Elizabeth pressed her lips together. "You'll have to ask him that question. Now, if you'll excuse me, I have to get these flowers planted before the sun kills them. I'm done talking." She turned her back and bent to her task.

Jane frowned. She was sure Elizabeth would open up to her, that there had to be a good reason she'd lied about Dad's whereabouts. This felt unfinished and confusing.

Reid touched her arm and jerked his head toward his SUV. She hunched her shoulders but followed him back to the vehicle.

He turned the air on high. "She knows something, but you won't get it out of her."

"I think she's lying. But why would she do that, especially knowing I might be able

335

to prove it? She looked afraid for a moment. I wonder if someone is forcing her to lie or she'll go back to jail." Did she fear Dad for some reason? Surely he would never lift a hand her way.

"That's what we have to find out. She seemed familiar, but I'm not sure where I might have seen her." He dropped the SUV into Drive. "Where to now?"

"Mobile. You think you could contact your friend with the state police? The stores won't let me view any videos since I don't have any credentials."

He put his foot on the brake and stopped before he pulled onto the road. "I'll text him." He slipped out his phone and tapped the screen. "We'll see what he says."

She buckled up and stared out the window at the clouds beginning to gather in the blue sky. Discouragement clutched her in a death grip. What if she never got her job back? Could she even get another job in law enforcement without a recommendation from Lisa? The even bigger worry was her father. If she wasn't able to prove what happened, her dad would spend the rest of his life in jail. Even worse, he could be executed. Alabama had the highest capital punishment convictions in the nation. If he lived that long. Officers of the law had a rough time in prison. The thought of seeing her dad in an orange jumpsuit was a gut punch.

Her phone had a message, and it was from her dad.

Cops are here to arrest me, but I'm not opening the door yet. I need to talk to you.

"Change of plans. Dad wants to talk to me."

"Can you do that before they arrest him?"

"They're there now, but he hasn't answered the door yet." She shot him a quick text.

Open the door. I'll be there as fast as I can. Don't make this worse with a resisting arrest charge.

She could only pray he listened to her. He was already in a world of trouble.

"Let's head back to his house. Even though I told him to open the door, I'm not sure he will, and I don't want him in more trouble. Maybe Brian will tell me what's going on, and if they have more evidence."

Someone had to know what was going on.

THIRTY

Two squad cars, one local and one from the state police, were parked with bubble lights strobing in front of her dad's house. Brian and Paul were both on the front porch, but the door was closed. The two state guys were at the bottom of the steps.

Jane closed her eyes for a brief moment. She'd hoped he wasn't holed up in there, but he hadn't taken her advice. For all she knew, he was loading an AK-47 inside and wouldn't come out without a blazing gun. She'd like to think he wouldn't be that stupid, but he hadn't behaved in a normal manner for days.

"Looks like you were right," Reid said. "He isn't coming out. I'll stay out of the way with Will and Parker."

She got out the passenger side and called to the officers. "Let me get him."

Paul turned and scowled. "We've got this, and you're not even a police officer any

338

longer, let alone in charge."

"I realize that, but if you want him in custody, I can bring him out, and you can arrest him." She kept her tone even and reasonable.

"She's right," Brian said. "It will be at least an hour before we get any more help from the state. It would be suicide to break down the door and go in with guns. We need a SWAT team."

Paul's scowl deepened, and he clenched his fists before he grudgingly moved out of the way. "Make it quick or I'm calling in more help."

Which would likely mean bloodshed. Her dad had an arsenal worthy of a small army on the property. There was an underground tunnel to the bunker, and if he reached it, he could be holed up in there for days. Weeks or months even.

She pushed past Paul and Brian and used her key to unlock the dead bolt, then pushed open the door. "Dad, I'm coming in."

"Go back!" Dad's voice sounded as though it was coming from the kitchen near the stairs to the basement. He was likely about to head for the tunnel.

She stepped inside and closed the door behind her as Paul made a move to come after her. She threw the dead bolt again. The last thing she needed was Paul stirring the pot. "Stay back, I'll bring him out!"

She walked toward the back of the house. "I'm alone, Dad."

The basement door was open, and she started down the steps. "Dad?" The mildewy odor made her wrinkle her nose. A distant door clicked, and she picked up the pace. "Dad?"

She reached the basement floor and stepped behind a shelving unit containing home-canned goods. As she expected, the door to the bunker was closed. She tried to open it. Locked. It was only a delay since she had a key, but what was Dad up to? She dug out her key and unlocked the door, then opened it to a pitch-black space.

She flipped on the light and illuminated a two-foot-by-five-foot tunnel. "Dad?"

Since she was short, she only had to duck a little to make her way along the cold, dank space. It grew narrower the farther away from the house it got, and she felt breathless by the time it widened again. Drawing in a relieved breath, she burst through the last door into the entry to the bunker, which was brightly lit with LED lights. She shut the tunnel door behind her and threw the dead bolt on the six-inch metal door designed to withstand an attack. If he'd wanted to do the same to keep her out he could have, so he must have wanted her to follow.

The door to the outside was cracked open a bit. Had he gone into the bunker or had he left the building? Intuition drew her to the heavy exterior door, also thick metal, and it creaked as she opened it the rest of the way. She caught the faint roar of a four-wheeler.

He'd flown the coop.

She exhaled and shook her head. He knew better, so why would he run instead of facing what was happening, especially after calling her over? Her dad had never been one to run from a fight.

She wasn't about to go back into that tunnel, so she hurried along the path back to the house. A misty rain began to fall, and thunder rumbled overhead. She picked up her pace and ran.

By the time she reached the front porch, the downpour was drenching her hair and clothing. Lightning struck several yards away, and she bounded up the porch.

Brian and Paul were sitting on porch chairs and the state guys were in their car. Paul leapt up when he saw her. "Where is he?"

"Gone." She tried to wipe the rivulets of water from her face, but without a towel, all she did was smear the moisture around.

"You let him go?"

"He was escaping when I got in. I tried to catch up with him, but he threw locked doors in my way several times and reached his four-wheeler before I could stop him."

"That's a crock. You let him go!" He reached for the handcuffs at his waist. "I'm arresting you for obstruction."

Brian got between the two of them. "Hold up there, Paul. You know Jane better than that. Charles had a head start before she even got here."

Paul tried to shoulder past Brian, but Brian held him in place. "You're acting stupid. You'll be the one in trouble if you do this. I'll contradict your statement. And I ran cell data. Charles wasn't with Gary then."

"That's not proof. He might not have had his cell phone on him." Paul gritted his teeth and released his grip on the cuffs. "Lisa will hear about this."

"You think the mayor's going to let you run wild in the town? Think again. She wants the law upheld, and you're not a one-man show. She only suspended Jane because she had no choice. You're wrong if you think she won't hold you to just as high standards."

Paul huffed and stepped back. "Get out of here, Jane. I don't want to look at your face. And stay out of my investigation."

Jane retreated down the steps to the driveway. There were a million things she could have said to Paul, but he wasn't in any mind to listen. Where would her dad have gone? She needed to bring him in or things would go even worse for him.

Maybe Scott Foster would know. Dad likely would have contacted him when he knew the police were about to arrest him. Though she couldn't see Scott advising her dad to run, he might have gleaned something of her dad's intentions.

She dashed through the rain and threw herself into the passenger seat. She turned to Reid. "Let's get out of here."

The old WWII battleship, USS *Alabama,* was one of the most popular attractions in Mobile, and the gunmetal gray ship had always been an iconic sight for Reid when he drove through this area. "My buddy should be in a state police car."

The sun was low in the sky, and the air held the fragrance of the sea. Gulls cawed and swooped overhead looking for bits of bread.

Reid scanned the parking lot. "There he is." He pointed out the slightly built guy with gray hair getting out of the police car. "Will, you stay here with Parker. Jane and I won't be long."

"Can I go see the ship while you're talking?"

"We won't be that long." Reid got out into the sultry air left over from the earlier downpour and they hurried toward the state policeman.

"Thanks, buddy," Reid said. "I don't suppose you had a chance to study any footage?"

"I did, my friend." Morgan passed along a couple of black-and-white photos. "I recognized Charles Hardy right off. The time stamp reads 2:00 p.m. I found another one when they were exiting at 4:00 p.m. so they were at Lowe's for two hours."

Reid stared at the two pictures. They clearly showed Charles with Elizabeth. She'd lied. He handed them to Jane, who gave a sharp exhale.

"Brian ran the data on Dad's cell phone on Sunday, too, and he wasn't with Gary. This is proof Dad was telling the truth."

"Looks like it."

The cop car beside them squawked, and Morgan leaned in to grab the radio. "Gotta go. Hot case." He sprinted for the big ship to his right.

Jane's phone dinged with a message as she turned back toward Reid's SUV, and she gasped as she looked at her phone. "Harry is missing!"

"Our Harry? The senator's grandson?"

Jane nodded and ran for the vehicle. "I'll call the senator."

He slung himself behind the wheel and waited for her to make the call and decide their destination.

Will leaned forward in the backseat. "What's happened to Harry?"

"We don't know yet. He's missing."

From her side of the conversation, Jane was being put on hold until she could be connected with the senator. He turned down the radio so she could hear once the conversation started. It seemed like a long time, but it was only about ten minutes before Jane finally spoke.

"Senator, it's Jane Hardy. I just got word about Harry. What's happened, and how can I help?" Jane listened to a lengthy statement on the other end. "We're at the memorial now. I'll be right there." She ended the call and gestured to the ship. "They were having an outing here after a fund-raising luncheon today. Harry had been pestering her to see the USS *Alabama.* They finished the tour of the ship before they went into the airplane hangar for the other exhibit. She took a quick call but said he was only out of sight a few minutes while he was in line for the flight simulator. Now she can't find him and is afraid he's been kidnapped."

"Let's go in there." Will's voice was urgent. "Maybe he's just hiding. He'll come out for me."

She stared at him. "He probably would, and maybe Parker can sniff him out. Come on!"

They got out and ran for the entry. Several state police cars came screaming into the parking lot, and several officers already had the entrance to the exhibit blocked off. Jane explained she'd just spoken to the senator and had been invited inside. An officer verified that before he motioned them on back.

Reid had been here before so he walked them through the airplane displays back to the flight simulator where he spotted Senator Fox and her cadre of state policemen. Other cops milled through the planes and exhibits looking for the boy.

Fox spotted Jane and motioned her and

Parker to come closer. Reid and Will followed.

"I don't see how anyone could have taken him. It was so fast." Her voice trembled.

"Has there been any word on your daughter?" Jane asked. "I never heard about the kidnapper's demands."

"That's because he never called back. My life has been on hold waiting. Fanny's vanished without a clue. I can't lose Harry too."

"Do you have anything that belongs to Harry? I can have Parker search."

The senator looked down at the dog. "I'm afraid I don't have anything of Harry's with me."

"Dad, I want to search for him," Will said.

"What's that?" the senator asked.

"Harry and Will became good buddies. Will thinks if he's hiding, Harry will come out if he calls."

"I'm willing to try anything." The senator motioned to a policeman. "Take this boy around the hangar and let him call out to Harry."

"I'll go with him." Reid wasn't about to let his son out of his sight.

Reid followed Will and the officer into the nooks and crannies of the hangar. They checked out the flight simulator, and Will's voice grew increasingly plaintive as he called for Harry.

"I don't think he's here," Will said.

Reid's intuition told him the same thing. Someone had taken the boy. But who? And how?

They rejoined Jane, who was still with the senator. "No sign of him," he told them.

Tears pooled in the senator's eyes. "Why would someone take Fanny and Harry? It makes no sense."

"Unless they thought you wouldn't do what they wanted unless they also had Harry," Jane suggested. "You might be getting another call now that they have him. They might know you and Fanny have some estrangement but that you love Harry dearly."

"I love Fanny too," the senator shot back. "She's the one who's pulled away."

"Of course." Jane nodded. "I didn't mean that you didn't love her. This might be more about leverage and power over you."

"I won't pay a ransom, of course. The police wouldn't let me. Surely they know we're never allowed to negotiate with kidnappers." She wrung her hands and swayed on her feet. "They have to find them. Can you help?"

"I'll do my best, Senator." Jane hesitated.

"One thing you should know is that I've been suspended as chief."

The senator nodded. "I heard something about that. Ridiculous. I'll call Mayor Chapman myself and ask her to reinstate you. I think she'll listen to me. Just find my family."

Reid caught her eye and gave her a discreet thumbs-up. Paul wasn't going to be happy.

THIRTY-ONE

The text from Lisa came when they were a mile from the police station.

Resume your duties as police chief. Lisa

A smile curved Jane's lips. "It's official. Even the mayor can't buck the senator. I mean, I guess she could, but she wouldn't."

"Congratulations." Reid's voice was even, almost deadpan.

"You don't approve?"

He didn't look her way. "You're a great chief, but the weight on your shoulders just quadrupled. And Baker isn't going to make this easy for you."

She flicked her wrist in a dismissive wave. "I can handle Paul. I've been doing it for years."

Reid pulled into the lot and parked. "Here comes Baker now. Looks like he needs some of your special handling."

The detective wore a thunderous scowl, and he hadn't even seen them yet. His stalk toward his car warned people to get out of his way.

Jane got out into the shimmering heat. "Paul."

His thick neck swiveled toward her, and he approached with fisted hands. "You have something over Lisa? Some kind of dirt?"

"The senator's grandson has been kidnapped. You find anything helpful?"

"The senator. I see. She had you reinstated, didn't she? Smart move, Hardy."

"I won't allow insubordination from you, Paul. Get your head out of your butt and act like a professional. I know you don't like this, but it's something out of your control."

"And you plan to get your daddy set free, too, don't you?"

"I intend to follow the law. That's all I've ever done, but you can't see past your hate and jealousy. For your information, my dad's alibi checks out. We have footage of him in Lowe's for two hours that Sunday afternoon, right during the time the witnesses saw my dad's boat go out."

He ripped his badge from his shirt and threw it on the ground, where it spun in circles before settling onto the pavement. "I quit. I'm not working for you, and I'll make sure this whole town knows why. You won't be able to stick your nose in the coffee shop without getting booed."

She lifted her chin in a steady gaze. "I think you overestimate your influence, Paul. Clean out your desk."

"You clean it out."

He stomped to his car, but she followed him and snatched the keys from his hand. "The car is department property. You'll have to call someone for a ride. Or walk."

Red ran up his face and his eyes bulged. His hands came up into claws, and he started for her, but before he could reach her, Reid stepped from behind her and grabbed his arm, then spun him into a headlock. "You need to go home and cool off."

Jane hadn't realized Reid had gotten out of the SUV with her. "I can handle him, Reid. I'm stronger than I look. Let him go."

Reid released Paul and shoved him away. Paul stumbled and went down onto one knee on the hot pavement before he sprang back to his feet and turned to face them. He still looked dangerous.

Paul glared at both of them. "This isn't over."

Jane felt suddenly tired. This hostility had played out so many times over the years.

352

"Why do you hate me so much, Paul? I've never done anything to you."

He gave an inarticulate noise, then stomped across the street. She watched him enter the coffee shop with a violent thrust of the door.

"That guy's deranged," Reid said.

"He's had a burr under his saddle for a long time. I've wondered a few times about my sanity in taking this job." Her legs trembled a bit as the rush of adrenaline subsided. "But let me fight my own battles. I'm not some helpless southern female, you know. This is my job."

"And you're good at it. I apologize if my actions implied I didn't think you were capable. My feelings got in the way of my common sense."

Feelings? She held his gaze for a long moment. The expression in his eyes made her breath catch in her throat. What did he mean? Because she was afraid she was beginning to feel more for him than irritation. A lot more.

She turned away before she said something she regretted. Or he did. "I want to see what's happened in our drive down from Mobile. Maybe they've found Harry."

Together the three of them entered the building and went to her office, where she turned on her computer and had Parker lay down by her feet. She called Brian to her office.

The big guy was grinning as he strode though the door. "Welcome back, Boss. I thought old Paul was going to have a heart attack when he heard the news."

"He quit too." Jane told Brian about the scene in the parking lot. "I would have had to suspend him for insubordination if he hadn't."

Brian rubbed his big hands together. "Man, I would like to have seen that. Who you going to hire in his place?"

Hiring someone. Ugh. She hated interviews. "I'll have to write up an ad. You got anyone in mind?"

"Yeah. A buddy of mine wants to move out of Pensacola to a smaller town. He's a detective there."

That would make it easy. "Have him send me a résumé. Any updates about the senator's grandson?"

He shrugged. "We got nothing. Whoever took the kid managed to get out of the parking lot. State boys are going over video now to see if they can ID the perp and get a description. Maybe a vehicle too. But it'll take time."

And Harry might not have much time.

While she knew the full burden of this was on the state police, Jane had felt a connection to Harry and to his grandmother. She wanted to be part of the team that found him.

The sandwich had long ago dried to a brick along with the other sandwiches Fanny's captors had brought. She'd been in a stupor after three days with no food. Though she'd forced herself to drink the bottles of water, she hadn't been able to force down the meals.

She lay curled on the gritty mattress and prayed for death. Nothing she tried had worked. She was useless as a mother, useless as the protector of her son. She deserved to die just as Harry had. Because there was no way her little boy could have survived this long on his own.

She wanted to cry, but there was no moisture left. *Oh, God, let me be with Harry now.*

The smell of the cellar was potent with mildew, and it permeated the cot as well. Would she ever feel sunlight? She wanted to step into heaven and catch Harry in her arms.

A creak on the floor forced itself past her despair, and she wobbled to a seated position as the door opened for a few brief seconds. It was probably more food she didn't want. Food would make her stay here longer, away from rejoining her son.

At a wail her eyes widened, though she couldn't see anything. "Harry? Harry, is that you?"

"Mommy?" His voice trembled.

She crawled out of the cot and nearly fainted from the sudden movement. "I'm here, Harry, right here. Come to my voice, honey." She tried to move in his direction, but she was so dizzy she staggered like a drunk.

Then his hands were around her knees.

She knelt and gathered him into her arms. Burying her nose in his neck, she drank in his familiar scent. "Oh, honey, I was so scared. You ran just like I told you. Where did you go?"

She couldn't lift him in her weakened state, so she scooted with him on the floor back to the cot, where she pulled him onto her lap. His small arms circled her neck, and she wanted never to let him go again. But what did their captors want? Harry would be frightened. He hated the dark.

He nuzzled into her neck. "I ran fast, Mommy. I had my backpack so I had some snacks with me. I hid in the woods and slept there until I got too hungry. Then I found the road and walked to town. You always said to find the police, so I did. There wasn't anyone at the desk, so I found a closet to hide in. A big kid helped me."

"A big kid?"

"His name is Will."

The only Will she knew was Reid's son. Was it possible Reid and Will had protected Harry? If so, how had he ended up here? "Then what happened?"

"Grammy came to get me. She was sad because we couldn't find you. She had lots of people looking for you."

"I'm sure she did."

Her mother had been right all along about Gary, and if she ever saw her mother again, Fanny intended to tell her so. And apologize for being such a jerk to her.

It didn't take any prompting for Harry to continue his tale. "We were looking at the ship, and I wanted to see inside an airplane. There was a bad man in there, and he stuck me in a sack."

She had so many questions, but Harry wouldn't know the answers. "And they brought you here." She felt him nod. "Did you recognize anyone?"

"No, and I didn't even cry when the man said he'd bring me to you." His arms tightened around her neck. "I missed you so much, Mommy. Don't ever leave me again."

"I won't," she promised, though she had no idea what the future held.

If Reid was involved, he'd turn over every stone to help her. And her mother loved Harry. People were looking for them. She had to keep Harry calm until they found them.

The door opened again, and a cold voice said, "We're moving you. Don't scream for help, or I'll kill the boy."

THIRTY-TWO

Jane wanted to be out scouring the countryside for Harry, but there were no clues on where to look. She sat at her desk with the stench of burned coffee wafting from her cup. Will was in the conference room playing an online video game on a spare computer, and Reid lounged with his legs out in the chair opposite her. Parker rose and stretched, then lay back down again at her feet.

They were all frazzled and exhausted. In a short time, the three of them had come to love little Harry, and his abduction brought back the horrible feelings she'd had when she learned her baby had died. Tears hovered near, and she only kept them at bay by forcing herself to concentrate on her computer screen.

Reid grimaced at the coffee he swallowed. "It all goes back to Gary's death. It has to. First Fanny and now Harry. What does the abductor want? If we can figure that out, we might find them."

She nodded and rubbed her aching left temple. "And could Nicole's death be related at all? She seemed to have been targeted by the vigilante, and her death was more manslaughter than murder, but what if it's connected?" She shook her head. "There was no Kennedy half-dollar left, but maybe he was scared off too soon."

"Who's working the vigilante cases?"

"Brian was heading them up, but he's been busy with Gary's murder. I'm sure Dad looked into them some too. He was a very hands-on chief." She called up the vigilante file and began to pore over it.

Her headache eased a bit as she studied the various cases. "Huh, this is interesting. Fanny gave me a list of her friends who might have known about Gary's arrest for embezzlement. When I put it beside other victims of the vigilante, Elizabeth's name pops up. They were all part of a cooking club."

Reid rose and went to look at the computer over her shoulder. "And we know she lied about Sunday."

She studied the list again. The cooking group was comprised of all women, and Elizabeth's name was the only one she recognized.

"How well do you know Elizabeth?"

"She's been with Dad for ten years. Strangely enough, he met her when she got out of jail."

"You mentioned she had a parole officer. What did she do?"

"She killed her abusive husband. Dad said she never should have been charged because the whole town knew he'd used her for a punching bag for years, but the trial had a change of venue to Mobile, and jurors didn't know how mean Gus was. She was found guilty of manslaughter and not murder, and the judge only sentenced her to two years, but she shouldn't have gone to jail at all."

"Does she carry a grudge about it?"

Jane thought about it. "I've heard her get upset about people getting off for much more serious crimes, but I don't know that I'd call it a grudge. I really should talk to her again."

Reid rose and stretched. "I'm famished, and you need to eat. We can take a quick break at the Irish pub."

She wanted to keep searching, but he was right. The words were running together, and she was finding it hard to focus. Food might help.

■ ■ ■ ■

Mac's Irish Pub was packed for a Tuesday night, but Reid had managed to score a back-corner spot away from the hubbub. He was starving.

Jane glanced at her watch, then looked out the window toward her office in the twilight. "I really can't be gone long." She'd left Parker sleeping in her office.

"You have to eat." Reid hadn't liked how much coffee she'd downed all afternoon without any food. He'd tried to get her to eat a sub sandwich, but it had stayed on her desk half open. The only way to get food in her was to get her away from her computer.

Will sniffed the air. "It smells great in here. I can't remember the last time we had Irish food. What's good?" He glanced at Jane expectantly.

She pushed the menu away unopened. "I always get the shepherd's pie. And they have homemade root beer." The server approached, and she gave him her order.

Reid stacked his menu on top of hers. "I'm going to get that too."

"I think I'll have the Irish lamb stew and root beer." Will stacked his menu, too, then handed the three to the server.

The ambiance of the place was a fun, Irish vibe with signed dollar bills all over the walls and ceiling. The wide plank floors and heavy wooden tables and chairs gave it an Old World appeal. The servers wore green, and the delicious aromas of meat, garlic, and potatoes made Reid's stomach rumble. He hadn't eaten much more than Jane, though he'd choked down half of his sub sandwich.

The server brought their drinks, and Will grabbed his root beer and took a long swig. "Ah, it's great." He leaned forward and fixed Reid with a stare. "You think she's done?"

It took a few seconds for his comment to register. Reid shrugged. "I don't know, son. I never would have expected Lauren to pop up this way and demand money, so I can't predict what she'll do."

"You should get an attorney, just in case she doesn't back off." Jane stood. "Scott Foster is sitting right over there by himself. I'll ask him to join us. I won't say anything about your situation. You can just evaluate whether you'd like his help. No pressure."

Reid watched her approach a small table in the corner and speak to a man in a gray suit with an erect posture and kind eyes. The guy stood and grabbed his briefcase from the table before he followed her back to their table with his drink in hand.

"Scott, this is Reid and Will Dixon. Guys, this is my dad's oldest friend and my godfather."

They shook hands and murmured platitudes before Scott pulled out one of the chairs and joined them.

One look told Reid why the name Scott Foster had seemed familiar. He'd been one of his father's trusted advisors, just like Jane's dad. A rock formed in the pit of Reid's stomach, even though he was sure there was no way the guy would recognize him.

"Have you spoken with your father?" Scott asked.

Jane nodded. "I did." She told him about trying to get to her father and convince him to give himself up. "Has he called you?"

"Not since yesterday." Scott took a drink of his root beer and eyed them over the rim of his glass. "He believed at first this was a planned plot to take him down. Yesterday he started talking about it being a distraction to what was really going on — that the adversary wanted the police too focused on his arrest and the murders so they didn't figure out the real target."

Reid glanced at Jane, and she was frowning with the same bewilderment he felt.

How could a federal indictment and a murder charge on top of it be merely a distraction? Maybe her father was delusional. He certainly wasn't acting rational with his escape from his compound.

She wiped the moisture from her mug of root beer. "Any idea what he meant?"

"Not really. Honestly, I thought maybe he was paranoid. It had to be a shock to be accused of such heinous crimes when he's spent his life bringing people to justice."

"I'm examining his files now to see what he was investigating before he retired."

Scott lifted a brow. "You believe him? He's been acting very erratically."

"I know my dad, though, and he'd never kill someone. Or take money. That's not his nature."

"Everyone has secrets, honey," Scott said.

"Elizabeth said the same thing. You know what secrets my dad has kept?"

"Those are his to tell, not mine." Scott drained his glass as the server brought their food.

"From the cult? You were there too."

"Like I said, they are your dad's secrets to tell or keep."

Reid exchanged a glance with Jane. Those who knew her dad best seemed to think there was something she should know, but no one was willing to tell her. Could Charles be sick? A brain tumor could explain his odd behavior, though Reid was probably jumping to conclusions. It might be as simple as wrestling with the horrendous lie Charles had told Jane when he'd dragged her from the compound.

They fell silent except for thanking the server as he put their plates in front of them. Reid's mouth watered at the sight and smell of the large shepherd's pie in an iron skillet. The server promised to bring more drinks before he left them alone again.

"Oh, before I forget." Scott reached for his briefcase and opened it, then pulled out a greeting card envelope. "Happy birthday, Jane. I know it's not until tomorrow, but I wasn't sure if I'd see you with so much happening." He handed it to her.

"Thank you, Scott. It's very sweet of you." She opened it, read the card, and extracted a gift card to a local golf course. "I haven't had a chance to play in over a month, but I'll put this to good use."

So she loved golf. Reid never would have guessed.

"My birthday is tomorrow too," Will said.

Pain lodged in Jane's eyes but she smiled. "I can't think of anyone I'd rather share a birthday with."

"It's pretty cool."

Reid's fingers closed around his fork, and he prayed for the conversation to change. The last thing he needed was for Will to jump to the right conclusion, but it might have already happened. He could see the wheels turning on his boy's face.

Jane picked up her spoon. "Are you planning to do anything fun?"

"Dad took me on an early shrimping trip. You might not think it was fun, but it was great. I might talk him into another outing."

"I always liked to go fishing with my dad. We haven't gone in a while."

Jane's phone rang, and she picked it up. Her smile faded. "It's Dad."

THIRTY-THREE

The gate to Fort Morgan was closed, but Jane directed Reid to park anyway. "We can duck under it."

It didn't surprise her that her dad had chosen this place to meet. Out on the tip of Mobile Point on the Gulf Shores peninsula, the old fort had seen its fair share of battles during the Civil War and even more battles during the incarnation before when it was Fort Bowyer during the War of 1812. The pentagonal-shaped masonry fort had been the site of fun days with her dad when they'd first moved here. She loved wandering through the batteries and corridors. It closed at five, but she knew her way around the point well. The corner bastions rose protectively above the masonry walls.

Scott had opted to come with them. The four of them got out of Reid's SUV and ducked through the barricade to the fort. She'd put Parker on alert, and his head swiveled from shadow to shadow as she led them down to the beach. The point was dark tonight with clouds scudding across the moon.

The four of them had bolted down dinner before coming out here to meet Dad. They still had a few minutes before his expected arrival at nine. She stared out over the dark water looking for a boat, but the only craft plying the waters tonight was a shrimping trawler heading out. He'd said to meet at the point, so she'd assumed he meant here and he'd be coming by boat, but maybe she'd misunderstood him.

"The last time I was out here was right after the Deepwater Horizon spill," Reid said. "Horrible, horrible tragedy, yet it's all so beautiful now."

"Two thousand and ten," Scott said. "The beaches came back, but we always worry about another oil spill."

Deepwater Horizon had been called the greatest ecological marine disaster in history, but there was little evidence of it now, a decade later. Jane hoped never to see black beaches like that again.

Reid touched her elbow. "You doing okay?"

"Yes." She was surprised to hear her voice tremble. Maybe she wasn't doing as well as she'd thought. This past week had been more than a nightmare.

"Maybe your dad will turn himself in."

"I don't think so. While he didn't say what he wanted, his tone was flinty and determined. I think he might have information for me."

"About what?"

"I wish I knew."

A flashlight beam back at the nearest fort bastion drew her attention. She pointed it out. "Look. Maybe that's Dad."

"Or it could be a night watchman," Scott said.

"I have to find out. You all can stay here and wait to see if Dad comes."

She and Parker started for the fort, but Reid loped along beside her. "You should stay with Will."

"He's fine with Scott. I don't want you going in there alone. There are too many places for an ambush."

"My dad wouldn't hurt me, and I've got Parker."

"Someone else might want to get you out of the way, and Parker is no match for a bullet."

True enough. She could tell he wasn't going back so she picked up her speed and hurried to the fort, where she showed him a secret entrance she'd used for years. Their shoes crunched loudly on the ground and rocks in what seemed an eerie silence. An owl hooted somewhere, and Parker uttered a low growl at the sound. She put her hand on his head. The darkness made the fort seem ominous and scary, though she loved it in the daylight.

"Do you see the light?" she whispered.

"It's gone. Should we call out for your dad?" His breath was warm against her ear, and she resisted the temptation to move closer to his comforting bulk.

"Let's wait a second."

His hand closed around hers, and she curled her fingers into his grip. She bit back a scream when a figure loomed from one of the batteries.

She recognized her dad's outline, and Parker's tail wagged. "Dad, you scared me to death. You should have given me better instructions on where to meet you."

"I wasn't sure if your phone was being monitored."

More paranoia or did he have a legitimate reason for his caution? "What's this all about? You need to turn yourself in. Scott is here, too, and he can make sure you're treated fairly."

Her dad snorted. "Fairness? I don't think

the guy who's doing this cares about fairness."

"Who do you think is framing you?"

He grabbed her arm and drew her into the darkness of one of the rooms used for storing ammo back in the day. The complete darkness enfolded her, and she reached out to find Reid's steady grip. He was there instantly with a warm press of his fingers.

"Dad?"

"Yeah, I'm here. Just trying to decide how much to tell you. I don't want to immerse you in the mess if I don't have to."

"You *have* to tell me all of it. This is too important to hide."

His sigh came from the darkness to her left. "Maybe so, maybe so. They took Harry, didn't they?"

The hair on the back of her neck prickled. "Harry, the senator's grandson? That's part of this?"

"It's part of everything." His hard fingers closed on her arm in the darkness. "The senator is in danger. Don't let her go anywhere to retrieve Harry or Fanny. It's a setup."

This all sounded like a paranoid delusion to Jane. Why would the senator be in danger? The kidnapper hadn't even asked anything of her yet. "Okay, I'll check it out.

But what about you? You need to turn yourself in."

"I can't let you take me in. If you do, I'll be found dead in a cell."

"Has someone attacked you?"

"No, but I can't go to jail."

More delusions? Jane didn't know what to think.

A call came from outside their enclosure. "You there! Show yourself and come out."

A guard. Jane turned toward the voice. All she had to do was explain, but before she could speak, a bullet zinged against the brick behind them, then zipped past her ear. It was no guard.

"Get down!" Reid threw himself at her and tackled her to the stony ground.

She heard her dad's footstep moving to the entrance, and seconds later, a scuffle sounded. She struggled to get up. Reid instantly released her, and she drew her gun to go after the shooter.

"Take cover." Crouching low with her gun at the ready, she moved out into the parade ground with Parker a few feet out in front of her.

The moon had come out, its light giving a ghostly illumination to the open spaces and looming structure around the grounds. Where were her dad and the shooter? The grass was empty of bodies, and she saw no movement.

"Dad?"

Her phone dinged, and she glanced at the message from her father.

Get out of there. You're the next target.

At least he'd escaped. She motioned for Reid to come with her, and she rushed to make sure Will and Scott were all right before she called the Gulf Shores police. This was their jurisdiction, and she wanted to make sure the attack was noted.

Not that she had any idea who the shooter was or what was going on.

Later, Reid tossed and turned a long time before he went to sleep. Jane could have been killed tonight, and the thought left him clammy. He finally drifted off and awoke with a start at a noise. He rolled over and looked at the bedside clock: 2:00 a.m.

His bedroom door stood ajar, and he saw the faint glimmer of light from downstairs. His bottomless pit of a son must be scrounging around in the kitchen for something to eat. Reid rose and went down the stairs. Instead of the kitchen light, he found the lamp on by the sofa in the living room. Will

374

sat looking at pictures.

Reid stopped and watched for a long moment. This whole thing had rattled his boy, and he wished there was some way to reassure him that life would be okay.

Will glanced up and saw him. "Did I wake you?"

Reid entered the room and dropped into the armchair opposite the sofa. "You couldn't sleep? It was an eventful day."

"Yeah." Will returned his gaze to the pictures in his hand. "I figured it out, Dad."

"Figured what out?"

Will lifted his head again and locked gazes with Reid. "My mom. I know who she is. It's Chief Hardy, isn't it?"

Reid's mouth went dry. That comment about the birthdays must have been the key. He didn't want to admit it, but he wasn't going to lie. "Yes."

"She doesn't know who I am." Will's voice trembled. "She doesn't act like she knows who you are."

"She doesn't. Like I mentioned, I've changed a lot, and we were really young." He rubbed his shaved head. "Even my best friend might not recognize me since I'm so hairless." He grinned.

"When are you going to tell her?"

"Soon." He should have done it when he

kissed her. No, before he kissed her. She would be livid when she found out the truth, and he couldn't blame her.

"I'm not sure I want her to know."

"Why not?"

Will's tortured gaze held Reid's. "What if she doesn't like me? She just thinks I'm some random kid trailing around with you guys. For all I know, she doesn't even like kids."

"She likes you, Will. She's told me several times you're a great kid and that I've done a good job raising you on my own."

Relief filled his son's eyes. "She said that?"

"She did. I-I think she's going to be overjoyed to discover you're alive."

"Her dad lied to her. So did you."

Reid wanted to protest that he hadn't lied — that he just hadn't told her everything the second he landed in Pelican Harbor. But that was a type of lie, wasn't it? "Her dad told her you died. I didn't see her before she left or I would have told her the truth."

"But you didn't tell her when you first discovered her."

"No, I didn't, and it's going to be hard for her to hear. I'm not looking forward to the fireworks."

Will chewed on a thumbnail. "Maybe

she'll cut us both off and refuse to have anything to do with us."

"I don't think so. I think it's more likely she'll sue for custody rights." He gave a rueful grin. "I'll be jumping from one courtroom to the other. It seems everyone wants you."

"I won't leave you."

His son's softened gaze warmed Reid's heart. "I'll allow her visitation rights — I want her to get to know you. You could stay weekends or whenever you like. I won't make it hard on her or you. She doesn't know you now, but it's not her fault. I think she'll be a good mother."

Will sank back against the sofa. "This picture." He raised the one of Jane in the trees. "I recognized that determined expression. And she was short, like she is now. When she said her birthday was the same as mine, I just knew. It explains why you wanted to do that documentary. You wanted to get to know her."

"Yes, I did."

"You wanted to know if you could trust her. Can you?"

The boy was perceptive. "I don't think she will try to take you away from me, if that's what you're asking. Her dad is going to face her wrath. I will, too, but I'm a secondary target. And she'll want what's best for you. She's not the vindictive type."

"No, I don't think she is." Will stared back down at the picture. "Can I tell her?"

What felt like a giant fist closed around Reid's chest. While he didn't think Jane would want to hurt his boy, what if she rejected his statement at first? It was risky. But staring into Will's pleading eyes, he was powerless to refuse.

"How about we start it together? I'll tell her who I am and she can get her anger out at me before you tell her."

"Won't she immediately know I'm her son?"

Reid shook his head. "I don't think so. I'm realizing I have a problem with lies of omission. I don't like hurting people, and I don't really like confrontation. I had to deal with it from my father so much that I tend to go the other way."

"I get it." Will yawned and rose. "I'm going back to bed. When can we tell her?"

"I don't think we should do it while she's knee-deep in two murder investigations. Hopefully a few more days and things will be settled enough that this news isn't more of a weight on her shoulders."

"You don't think she will be happy?"

Reid regarded his son's uncertain expression. "I think she'll be delighted and honored to know you're her son. I was afraid she'd be distracted from her duties by wanting to be with you, but I'll let you make that call, Will. You're old enough."

He chewed his lip, then nodded. "I can see your point. I can wait a few days."

The boy was becoming a man in record speed. And a good man at that.

THIRTY-FOUR

Jane sat on her balcony with *The Screwtape Letters* on her screen and Parker at her feet. " 'To decide what the best use of it is, you must ask what use the Enemy wants to make of it, and then do the opposite.' What the heck does that mean?"

The town was mostly dark except for streetlamps and a few late-night bars spilling light out onto the water.

The senator still hadn't called her back, and she couldn't help worrying about what her father had said. The senator was in danger. Maybe she should text that to her since she hadn't called back. She picked up her phone from the stand beside her, and it rang almost instantly with the awaited call.

"Senator Fox, any word on Harry?"

"Yes, finally. I'm on my way to my retreat to —" The words became too garbled to make out what she'd said.

Jane looked at her phone to make sure it

was still connected. "Senator, you're breaking up. Don't go anywhere to get Harry. It's a setup."

There was no answer, and she looked again at the screen. The call had ended. She immediately called her back, but it went straight to voice mail. "Don't go, Senator! It's a setup. You're in danger."

She tossed her phone down. Just great. If the senator's phone was in a dead spot, there was no way of knowing when she'd get the voice mail. *Retreat.* Hadn't she heard the senator had a cabin in the woods around here somewhere? Who had told her that?

Paul.

She felt sick at the thought of calling him to ask. He'd gloat and preen that she had to go to him for help, but what other choice did she have?

Her gaze fell on the words on her screen again, and she remembered the quote. Her own self wanted to have nothing to do with Paul, but the better thing was not to worry about who got the credit or what she had to do to save a life.

She snatched up her phone again and called Paul. It was nearly two thirty so he wouldn't be happy to be awakened.

"Yeah." Something crashed in the background, and he swore. "What do you want?"

"I need your help."

"Oh, that's rich. You call me in the middle of the night after kicking me out on my ear?"

She wanted to point out he'd quit, but she held her tongue. There was no time to argue. "The senator is in danger. Her call was garbled, but I think she said she was on her way to her retreat. Didn't you tell me she has a cabin along the bay in the Gulf National Islands Seashore?"

The area was privately owned, and mere mortals didn't own homes there, but the senator could land a chopper there or take a boat out to her place.

"Yeah, yeah, she does. I can show you."

To his credit he didn't try to bargain. "I'd appreciate it. I think this is all coming down tonight, and I need to get out there. I'll try to secure a boat."

"Did you notify Brian?"

"Not yet. I'll call him and have him meet us. Oh, and Paul? Bring your firearm. This is apt to be dangerous. I'll meet you at the dock."

"Got it."

He ended the call, and she called Brian, who didn't sound sleepy at all. He said he'd be there in five minutes. Brian had probably been at one of the bars. She picked up her gun.

Reid. He had a boat, and he'd want to be in on this. He wasn't law enforcement, but something in her wanted him with her. She dithered for several seconds, then placed the call.

"Jane, are you okay?" He didn't sound sleepy either.

"I need your boat." She told him what was happening.

"I'll be there in fifteen minutes. Pick you up at the dock."

"Don't bring Will. It's too dangerous."

"Of course not. Should I bring my pistol? I have one."

"It might be a good idea."

"Be there shortly."

She ended the call, strapped on her gun, and exited onto the balcony with Parker on her heels. From here she could see Brian standing just off the pier. She hurried down the steps and across the street past the bar to the marina and the dock. The slap of the waves against the boats' hulls mingled with the sound of a boat motoring to its berth.

She stopped beside Brian. "Sorry to interrupt your night."

He shrugged. "No problem."

"We're going on Reid's boat. I called Paul too."

Brian stopped. "Paul? He's not an officer anymore."

"For tonight he is. He knows where the senator's beach house is, and I need him."

"Boss, you're one of a kind."

Running steps pounded on the dock behind them and she turned to see Paul barreling toward them. He looked grim and determined.

He squinted at the bobbing vessels. "You find a boat? I can call a buddy."

"Reid is bringing his." She heard a motor and saw lights approaching. "That's him now, I think."

The boat pulled up to the dock, and the three of them hurried toward it. She told Parker to jump aboard, and Reid helped the dog land safely, then took her hand and helped her aboard. Brian shoved them off after they were all on deck.

Brian looked alert and focused. "You think Harry is there?"

"I think there's an ambush there. Call Baldwin County Sheriff's Department and have them send backup."

Brian made a face. "And what if your dad is wrong, and we're pulling them out to a wild-goose chase?"

He was right. Dad had been so vague, and she hadn't been able to question him. The

384

four of them were armed. That should be enough to rescue the senator, who was likely bringing state police with her anyway, but she shouldn't take any chances.

"Just call them."

He shrugged and pulled out his phone, then placed the call and made the request. He ended the call. "Okay, let's go."

The salty wind tangled her hair, and she brushed it out of her eyes as she turned to Paul. "How long will it take us to get there?"

"Fifteen minutes. Tell us what you know, if you don't mind."

Paul with a contrite tone? Would wonders never cease? "You're not going to like the source, but just listen, okay?" She launched into what had happened to Fanny, then Harry's abduction, before she told them what her dad said. Paul tensed but said nothing at first.

Brian whistled. "So your dad is saying all of this is part of some kind of plot against the senator? Seems dicey at best, Jane. I'm not tracking very well."

"I know it seems convoluted, but I've been thinking about it. What if my dad stumbled onto something that meant he had to be silenced before he could upend their plan?"

She could see by Brian's expression he wasn't buying it. Paul betrayed no emotion at all, so she could only imagine what he thought. Only Reid seemed to believe her.

Paul gestured. "The senator's place is dead ahead. It looks empty."

"Can you dock us down the way, Reid? Close enough to walk but not so close anyone knows we're here?"

"Yep."

She strained to see the cabin through the darkness as Reid brought them close to a dilapidated dock sticking out into the water from some old mooring long ago. Trees marched along the front of the property at the edge of the small spit of sand, and she glimpsed a boathouse at the edge of a small inlet that veered into the forest.

Brian looped the rope around one of the rotted beams and helped her step onto the dock. "Careful. It doesn't look safe."

This whole night wasn't going to be safe.

Reid didn't like the way they filed along the beach toward the structure. The moon had come out from behind the clouds, and the water intensified the illumination. Someone could see them, but the trees and brush were too thick to get through in any kind of timely manner, and he sensed Jane's urgency.

He felt it too. Harry had stolen his heart,

and if the boy was up ahead, afraid and in danger, he wanted to get to him as quickly as possible.

Jane was leading the way and she paused, holding up her hand. "There's a path through the woods here. Let's take it so we're concealed from the light."

The tangle of vegetation was close enough to brush Reid's arms as he and the other men followed her. "You have any idea how the senator is arriving?"

"She didn't say, just that she was on her way to her retreat. I think this has to be the place she meant. There's nowhere to land a chopper as far as I can tell, though, so I'm guessing she's coming by boat. We should hear it approaching."

Jane started for the house again. "We need to scout around outside. We don't know where these guys are, and we know so few details. We obviously can't go busting into the house without a warrant. Let's split up and circle the house. Everyone have their radios ready?"

Paul touched the mic clipped to his shoulder. "Ready to go."

"Me too," Brian said.

"You go with Paul, Brian. Reid, you come with me. I don't want anyone wandering around without a radio. Set your frequency, Paul."

Paul fiddled with the mic on his shirt. "Got it. Where do you want me?"

"You go around the south side of the house. Reid and I will go across the back to the boathouse. I want to make sure it's empty. If you hear a boat coming, give me a holler."

Paul nodded, and they moved closer to the house until they were standing on the perimeter of the woods and the lawn. Night sounds enveloped them: frogs croaked and splashed in a body of water nearby, mosquitoes hummed by Reid's ears, a hawk's screech was followed by the terrified squeak of a mouse. Predator and prey. Which one were they tonight?

Reid had an uneasy feeling they might be prey. Though he heard no human sounds or movement, the night pressed in with a sinister embrace that raised the hair on his forearms.

He was carrying, though, and he touched the gun at his waist for reassurance. If Jane needed him, he would be there to protect her.

Jane motioned for him to follow her and Parker. They left Brian and Paul behind and crept toward the back of the house. The floor-to-ceiling windows on the back turned blank, dark faces onto the massive deck that boasted an outdoor kitchen and a hot tub. A small inlet of water glimmered in the moonlight. The boathouse beside it wasn't large, but a smaller boat might fit. The dew drenched his sneakers as they made their way across the tall grass that hadn't been mowed in several weeks.

They reached the boathouse on the right side of the home, and he peered into the first window. He shook his head and whispered, "Doesn't look like anyone's in there. No sign of the senator's boat."

Jane nodded and moved toward the front of the house with Parker on her heels. As they approached, Parker crouched and uttered a low growl. Reid yanked out his gun, and Jane did the same. He strained to hear anything above the sound of surf striking the shore.

Someone was out there. He could feel their presence as clearly as the wind rippling the dog's fur. Jane felt it, too, and she held up her hand. He stopped and waited as she sidled to the front corner of the house and peered past it at the boardwalk extending from the front door to the dock.

He moved close to her, but there was no movement out there. Maybe they were inside. That would make sense. If they were, had they seen the shadowy movements in the yard?

His straining ears finally detected the sound of a boat engine at full throttle. Lights rounded the shore to their left, and Reid pointed them out to Jane, who nodded. They watched the boat as it slowed on its approach to the dock. It was smaller than he'd expected, and only one head was visible as it docked at the pier. He'd hoped the senator would have brought an army with her, but if this was a trap, she'd likely been told not to bring police.

Would she have been gullible enough to come alone?

Love made people do stupid things.

The moon shone on the senator's head as she stepped aboard the pier and stared toward the house. He didn't see a gun in her hand, but then he hadn't expected her to come armed. Could she have arranged for the state police to be swarming in by land? He heard nothing that might give credence to that hope.

She tied up the boat, then walked slowly toward the house. He heard a sound from the other side of the house and knew instantly an attacker was coming for the senator. Several shots rang out from that direction, and Jane's radio sprang to life as the senator hit the dock on her belly.

"Officer down, officer down," Brian's voice screamed.

"Go! Take care of the senator," Reid told Jane as he leapt into the yard and ran toward where he'd heard the shots.

THIRTY-FIVE

Reid's breath heaved harshly through his lungs as he ran around the back of the house toward where Jane had stationed Brian and Paul. *Officer down* were the words no one wanted to hear when on a mission. Since Brian reported it, that meant Paul was down.

He could only pray Jane would be all right on her own. Logically he knew she was well trained and an extremely competent law enforcement officer, but cops died every day in the line of duty. He couldn't lose her.

Gun in hand and running in a crouch, he rounded the corner of the house. Brian huddled over Paul, who wasn't moving. Looking to the left and right, he saw no one else, and no more shots had been fired.

Paul lay on his back with one leg slightly curled. He'd flung out both arms as he fell, and his eyes were closed.

Reid dropped to his knees beside Paul and

touched his carotid artery. No matter how he probed, he felt no pulse under his fingertips. He touched Paul's chest and felt sticky moisture in the middle. He'd been shot cleanly through the heart.

"He's dead." Brian's voice was even.

Reid stood and looked toward the darkness of the woods. "Did you see what happened?"

Brian still had his gun out and gestured toward the woods with it. "A guy came out of the trees with his gun blazing."

Reid tried to remember how many shots he'd heard — two or three maybe? Was the shooter even now circling to attack Jane and the senator?

Brian glanced toward the water. "Where's Jane?"

"She went to check on the senator. Fox was facedown on the dock. I don't know if she was hit or not." Reid gestured to Brian's mic. "You might let her know what's happened here." It would reassure him just to hear Jane's voice.

"I don't want to give away her location. She'll join us when she can. There could be a shooter watching them."

Reid looked at the prone figure on the ground. "There's nothing we can do for him, so we'd better go help Jane. You know there are at least two men out there. Jane's alone." He turned toward the water.

"No."

Reid turned back at the hardness in Brian's voice. He was aiming his gun at Reid's chest. "Brian?"

"Drop your gun, nice and easy."

Reid eyed his face and knew he had no chance to fire first. "You killed Paul?"

"He needed killing. Now drop the gun."

Reid let the weapon fall to his feet. "Why would you be part of this?"

"Kick it toward me. Gently."

Reid did as he was told but didn't kick it too far. He might be able to dive for it.

Brian gestured to the woods. "That way."

At least Brian wasn't going after Jane, but that didn't mean someone else wasn't. Or was Boulter in this alone? Maybe there weren't any other shooters.

Reid glanced down at the man on the ground. "What about Paul?"

"There is no Paul. He's gone, man. Now move."

With a last glance at the unwavering gun, Reid started for the shadow of the forest. "Where are we going?" *Please, God, keep Jane safe.*

"You'll see soon enough."

"You're part of the plot to kill the senator?"

"I'm not part of it — I *am* it. I've been planning it a long time, and no two-bit journalist is going to ruin it for me."

It was cooler in the trees, and mosquitoes quickly buzzed Reid's ears and swarmed his arms. As Brian forced him deeper into the woods, he searched for some kind of weapon. A tree branch, a rock, anything. While he saw possible items he could use, there was no real opportunity to attack.

At least if something happened to him, Will knew the truth. Jane would take good care of their son. He didn't want to leave his boy, but if it happened he had peace about it.

"Do you have Harry and Fanny or are they dead?"

He shrugged and didn't reply.

Reid clenched his fists. "Why take him?"

"Leverage."

The path to the beach was just ahead, and Reid expected Brian to take them to the boat. Instead, he pointed out what appeared to be a deer trail that veered deeper into the forest. The brush was thicker here, too, and there was barely enough room to force their way through. Brambles tore at Reid's skin, and Brian swore several times behind him.

Maybe this would be a good opportunity to make a run for it.

The idea had barely formed when Reid heard a cough just up ahead. Too late for action.

"Elizabeth, that you?" Brian called.

Elizabeth? Charles's girlfriend? Reid strained to see through the darkness and made out the faint glow of a lantern.

"Over here, Brian."

They broke through into a clearing that held a cabin. Moss grew on the shake roof, and the lean-to porch lurched to the right as it still maintained contact with the structure. Another light shone through the dirty window of the tiny house.

Elizabeth was sitting on a four-wheeler, and she wasn't alone. The other seat held Daryl Green. Jane's intuition had been spot-on.

Daryl frowned when Reid stepped into a shaft of sunlight. "That's not the senator. Why'd you bring this guy? He's of no use."

"He was about to wreck the whole plan. I had to bring him. And Paul's dead."

Elizabeth bit her lip. "No one else was supposed to be hurt. We had it all planned out. What happened?"

"Charles figured it out. He called Jane and told her the senator was in trouble. Jane tried to call Fox and heard she was going alone to her retreat. Paul knew where the house was, and here we are. The best-laid plans."

"She'll be looking for you."

Brian shook his head. "She has no idea I killed Paul. She'll think the killer took me and Reid." He grinned. "And she's half right."

"That just means she'll be searching for this guy even harder. She has a soft spot for him." She gestured toward the deer trail. "Maybe you can lure the senator away from Jane?"

Reid took a step forward. "Jane won't fall for that. She'll do whatever it takes to protect the senator. Besides, Baldwin County deputies are on their way. Your little plot is over."

Brian laughed. "You don't think I really called them, do you?"

Reid took a step back. "You lied."

"Yep. No one was on the other end of that call." Brian glanced at Elizabeth. "He's right, though. The senator's safety will be Jane's first priority. She won't bring her to us. I'll take care of Reid and go get Jane and the senator."

"No!" Elizabeth wet her lips. "I never agreed to be party to all this murder. Paul is dead, and now you're going to kill the senator and Jane. I only went along with this to stay out of jail. This has grown into something much bigger and more serious."

"You're in too deep to back out now." Brian smirked at Reid and reached behind Elizabeth for a coil of rope. "But killing him can wait, just in case we need him."

Crouching down, Jane dashed to the fallen senator who lay unmoving on the dock. She knelt at her side and touched her back. "Senator, are you hit?" Parker was on the senator's other side, and he whined and nosed at the senator's hand.

Senator Fox lifted her head a fraction. "No, I'm okay. What's going on?"

"My dad told me it was a trap. I think our phone connection was cut off before I could tell you. We've got to get you to safety." Jane helped her up. "Stay low. We'll try to make it to your boat and move offshore."

She strained to hear anything from the direction Reid ran, but there was nothing. He had to be okay. So did her officers. Pushing away her worry, she turned and looked out to the water. No boat lights as far as she could see, but that didn't mean someone wasn't out there with their lights off. It was a gamble, but she had no choice. The senator was an open target here.

The senator stared toward the house. "I can't leave if there's a chance Harry and Fanny are in there. Have you checked inside?"

"No, but I doubt the kidnappers brought them. There just would be more details for them to track. The main goal here was to get to you."

"Why? What do they want?"

"I don't know that answer yet, but I'm going to find out. Do you have state police officers on their way?"

The senator bit her lip. "The caller said if I came alone they wouldn't hurt my family. They said they meant no ill will toward me or my family and just wanted to talk. But they clearly lied. I felt a bullet whiz by my head."

"Shots were fired on the south side of the house too. I've got an officer down."

"Oh dear."

Jane's sentiments exactly, especially when there was nothing more from Brian or Reid. She tried to wrap her head around an intelligent woman like the senator coming out here in the middle of nowhere without backup. The police had surely told her not to trust a kidnapper's word. She must have been so driven by love that she didn't care what happened to her.

But would Jane have acted any differently if she'd thought she could have saved her baby? No matter how high or hot the flames, she would have plunged back into that cabin in a heartbeat if she'd thought her son was in there. A mother's love overcame any fear.

Jane felt exposed out here on the pier and tried to stand in a way to block line of sight to the senator. The shooter could be creeping around for another try.

She gestured to the boat. "You get in the boat and take it out into the bay. I'll see if I can find your family."

"By yourself?"

Jane guided her toward the boat. "We have to keep you safe. I don't have a signal here so if you can get one, call the Coast Guard when you get offshore and let them know where you are. I don't know how big this is or what's going on. And stay alert for any boats cruising without lights. Ask the Coast Guard to notify the state police as well. We need backup."

Senator Fox nodded and stepped into her boat. "I've got a gun."

"Keep it ready."

Jane untied the rope and shoved off the vessel before she turned back toward the still-dark house. She hadn't heard anything more about her fallen officer, and her lungs felt tight as she went for the trees and sidled closer to the front of the house. Gun in hand, she went into a crouched position and rushed forward. Parker wasn't growling so she didn't think anyone was close by. She peered into a dark window and could only make out the rough outline of furniture shrouded in sheets. The senator must not come here a lot.

Nothing moved inside. She sidled along the edge of the house to the back door. Though desperate to know how the men were, her first duty was to rescue Harry and Fanny if they were here. She eased up the deck steps and approached the back door. When the doorknob turned easily in her hand, her pulse sped up.

Someone had been here. The doorjamb was busted and the house didn't feel empty. It could be her nerves on high alert, but she didn't think so. She pushed open the door and stepped on broken glass as she made her way into a sunroom. The moon streamed through the windows and illuminated the shadowy humps of furniture. She spotted the door into the rest of the house and crossed the space to look into a family room. Nothing moved inside. She opened the door and stepped inside.

The place smelled stale and dusty. She moved past the furniture toward the open kitchen. She heard nothing, not a cough, not a shoe scuff, not a breath. Maybe they had left here and gone into the trees. The kitchen wall was to her left, and she ran her fingers over the surface until she found the light switch. It was a gamble to switch on the lights, but in the dark she'd never be sure the place was clear.

No. She withdrew her hand. She'd be an obvious target to anyone outside. She'd have to clear the house in the dark as best she could. At least Parker would warn her.

THIRTY-SIX

The house was empty.

As she exited it Jane checked her phone. Still no signal. What was keeping her backup from the sheriff's department? She hoped the senator had a signal and could call for help from the Coast Guard.

She touched her mic. "Brian, you copy?"

Only static answered her, and she went around the corner of the house to the south. She stopped and assessed the danger. No sounds but the music of the forest. Nothing moved but the breeze.

"Brian? Reid?" she called softly. "Paul?"

She swept her gaze over the tall grass. She drew a sharp breath when she saw the body lying near the trees. On high alert she approached Paul and knelt to touch him. Parker whined beside her, another bad sign. Paul's skin was already cooling, but she had to be sure and sought a pulse. Nothing. Moisture glimmered on the front of his shirt. He'd been shot in the chest.

Would she find Reid and Brian dead nearby too?

She struggled to draw a breath. They couldn't be dead. And she'd heard no other shots.

She rose and checked her phone again. No signal. She could get to the boat and summon the Coast Guard by radio, though, make sure the senator had contacted them and was safe.

She started down the path they'd taken to the house and followed it back to where it wound toward the beach. The cool ocean air touched her face when she emerged from the trees and hurried across the sand to the boat. She hadn't been sure it was even still here. For all she knew, the shooter could have taken it or shoved it away from shore.

She and Parker reached the dilapidated pier when something or someone crashed through the vegetation. Dropping to her knees by a post, she brought up her gun and aimed it toward the sound. Parker wasn't growling so she wasn't as concerned as she would have been if he'd been bristling. Brian's broad shoulders forced through the thick brambles, and he stumbled to his knees as he hit the sand.

Jane leapt to her feet and rushed toward

him. "Brian, are you okay?"

Before she could help him to his feet, he sprang up and came toward her. "I'm okay." He looked past her to the boat. "Where's the senator?"

"I sent her back out in her boat. I hope by now she's called the Coast Guard."

He took a step closer. "Can you stop her from calling? They're going to kill Reid."

A fist closed around her heart. "What are you talking about?"

"I barely escaped. We have to get back to save him. If they find out more law enforcement are out here, they'll kill him. Fanny and Harry too." His eyes blazed with urgency.

She pulled out her phone. "I've got a signal."

"Call her and tell her to come back."

His story wasn't making sense, and something in his manner sent chills running down her spine. "I can't deliberately bring her into harm's way. You know that, Brian. I'll call the sheriff's office myself and see where our backup is, then I'll go with you."

His eyes went cold, and he brought up his gun. "They were never called. Toss your gun down."

"B-But you —"

"Pretended to call them," he finished for

her. "I never spoke to anyone. Your gun."

She let her firearm fall from her fingers. "You're behind this? But why?"

He grinned and didn't answer. "I've got another idea." He gestured at her with his gun. "Call the senator and tell her we're coming to get her."

She lifted her chin. "No. I won't be party to this. You'll have to kill me." She put her hand on the dog's head. "Parker, take!"

The dog whined and looked at her as if to ask if she was sure. Before she could repeat her command, Brian yanked her arms behind her back and tied her roughly with a rope he pulled from his backpack. He took a handkerchief from the other pocket and stuffed it in her mouth. It tasted of cinnamon gum. She tried to yank her arm out of his grip, but he shoved her to the sand, then plucked her phone from her pocket.

"If you want something done, you have to do it yourself." He placed the call.

Parker was dancing around, whining and barking. He didn't know what to do. Brian was a friend and had often brought him treats. Parker had never been ordered to attack a friend before. It was training she should have made sure he had.

Jane held her breath. *Please don't answer, please don't answer.* She tried to push the cloth out of her mouth with her tongue, but it was too big.

"It's not Jane, Senator. This is her detective, Brian. She gave me her phone to use, but she wants you to stay put until we join you. We've rescued your daughter and grandson." He went silent, listening. "Yes, it's a miracle for sure. They're both fine, but they're asking for you. Yes, I'm sure you'll be glad to see them too. Oh, did you call the Coast Guard? Uh-huh, that's good. No reason to bother them when we have this under control. We've got a boat, and we're heading your way with your family. See you in a few minutes."

His smirk was wide but humorless when he stuffed the phone into Jane's back pocket, then pulled the cloth from her mouth. "I knew she'd listen."

Jane struggled to sit up and pulled at the rope. It was too tight for her to get much wiggle out of it. "Why would you do this, Brian? You're my best detective. I trusted you."

"Yeah, yeah. You don't really know me." He grabbed her arm and yanked her to her feet, then shoved her toward the boat. "I'll have to hide you in the hold until I have the senator subdued." He propelled her along the rickety pier to Reid's boat. Parker followed, whining the whole time. "You and the senator are going to suffer a little accident at sea. Reid will be assumed dead with you since it's his boat, and none of your bodies will ever be found."

He threw her to the boat deck and ordered Parker to jump. The dog obeyed, but his tail was tucked and his ears were down.

Stumbling along the deck with Brian, she fell to her knees several times, but he yanked her back up. The boat reeked with the stench of shrimp and fish. He pushed her into the hold. She fell down the steps and banged her shin and arms several times on the way. Stunned, she lay in the darkness for several seconds before she struggled into a seated position.

If she was going to save the senator, Jane needed to get loose and find a weapon. Parker might be the only weapon she had, but she'd be hard-pressed to get him to attack Brian.

The blasted mosquitoes were going to drive him crazy. Reid shifted on the hard ground and tried his bonds again. Still too tight, but he might have loosened them a little. His face and arms itched almost unbearably, and he was thirsty.

Elizabeth had a propane cooktop going

408

and was stirring something in the glow of the small flame that smelled like chicken soup. She hadn't looked at him since Brian left them carrying a backpack. Getting to her was his only chance of getting free to help Jane and the senator.

The moon came out from behind the clouds and gave him a better sense of the layout. He spied an outhouse and had an idea.

"That smells great. Do you suppose I could have some water and go to the bathroom?"

She looked up, and he saw moisture on her cheeks. "So far he's killed Paul and Gary. He tried to kill Charles, but he missed." Tears tracked down her cheeks in a steady stream that shimmered in the moonlight.

"You okay?"

"What do you care?" She stared sullenly at the pan of soup. "It wasn't supposed to be like this. Brian lied to me. This is way worse than the trouble I was already in."

"What trouble was that?" He wrenched on his wrists again. Still tight.

"Brian figured out I was the vigilante, but I was only trying to bring a little justice to town! No one was really hurt, but I had to help him if I didn't want to go back to jail."

Reid stared at her and remembered what Jane had told him. "Why would you help him set up Charles? You didn't love him anymore?"

She stared down at her hands. "He'd asked me to leave and said it just wasn't working. He gave me a month to find another place to live." She shook her head. "I should have known he was never going to marry me."

"Why not just leave like he asked? Why punish him?"

"Everyone gets away with everything! It's not fair. He needed to pay for taking ten years of my life with no intention of making our relationship permanent."

She was justifying everything in some twisted way. "So you wanted him thrown in jail for something he didn't do? Where's the justice in that?"

She went white. "When Brian first came to me, I didn't think it through really well. All I could think about was that I didn't want to go back to jail, and I didn't owe Charles anything anymore." She wrung her hands. "Besides, Brian promised no one else would be hurt — that it was just about justice for him and his family. That resonated with me too. You don't know what it's like in there. I'd rather die than go back."

Reid nodded. Jane hadn't mentioned Elizabeth's last name was Spicer, but he remembered it all now. "I wanted to do a documentary on that case because I believed you shouldn't have been sent to jail. The trial was moved to another venue because the jury pool was too sympathetic. My producer picked another case, but I never forgot yours."

She studied him a long moment. "You're telling the truth."

"I am. Your husband was a commercial fisherman, right? You even had bruises from the last time he hit you, but the prosecution claimed they were made during the so-called murder. But you killed Nicole. Did you kill Gary for hitting his wife?"

She shook her head wildly. "Nicole was an accident! I had no idea she was allergic to feathers, but when she died, Brian was going to charge me with murder. I'd never get out of jail."

"What about Gary?"

"I had nothing to do with Gary's death. Gary had seen Brian taking stuff from the evidence room to Daryl Green, who was selling it and putting the money he got in a bank account in Charles's name. They both wanted revenge on Charles. Gary tried to squeeze him for money, but Brian knew the guy would tell Charles sooner or later, so he needed to get rid of him."

"Woman, you never shut up." Daryl groaned. "You can handle this." He started the ATV and roared off onto the trail.

Reid watched him unlock the cabin and enter. "Why not just kill him and deep-six the body? The wedding dress and mutilation was extreme."

"Brian thought he could eventually tie the vigilante incidences to Charles. He thought muddying Gary's identity would make it more fun." She shuddered. "He and Daryl took Gary out on Charles's boat where they killed him and put the body in the shrimping waters knowing he'd eventually be found."

He strained at the bonds again. "Jane found some stuff in the files Charles had. She knows you knew all the victims."

Elizabeth nodded. "Charles was suspicious, too, but Brian had all the evidence. He promised to destroy it if I'd help him. I thought it had to do with convincing the senator to back some legislation, but after he took Harry and Fanny Dawson, I realized it was all about assassinating the senator."

"Do you know why he wants her dead?"

She rolled her eyes. "It's all he talks about.

She was a prosecuting attorney before she became a senator, and she was behind his dad's conviction. He wants revenge on both her and Charles."

"Why Charles?"

"Charles gathered the evidence, and it was his testimony that put Brian's dad in prison."

There was a lot more to know about the story, but the past five minutes seemed like hours. What was happening with Jane? Reid twisted the rope again, and it moved a little more.

He sent Elizabeth a placating look. "Could I use the outhouse? You've got a gun there. You can tie me up when I come back out."

She chewed her lip and glanced toward the trail to the woods. "You'll have to be quick. Brian is pretty scary. Now that I know how dangerous he is, I'm not sure he won't shoot me and feed me to the fish like he plans with everyone else."

"It won't take long." Reid struggled to his feet and turned his back to her so she could remove the rope.

If she put the gun down and released him, he could run for the woods before she was able to snatch it up and fire. And even if she moved faster than expected, he was willing to gamble that she wouldn't shoot him in the back.

She dropped the gun to the ground, and her fingers plucked at the rope. "It won't loosen. I'll have to cut it." She picked up the gun and moved to the fire. After a moment's hesitation, she put the gun in the waistband of her jeans, then picked up a knife and carried it back to him.

He felt the cold steel touch his wrists and tensed before the bonds fell at his feet. His hands were numb and tingling. It would be a while before he could hold a weapon of some kind, and his legs and feet were stiff as well, but he had to make a move. Jane could be looking down the barrel of Brian's gun right now. There was no time to waste.

He leapt past her and ran for the woods. She shouted but didn't shoot. The coolness of the tree line welcomed him, and he tore through the brambles and thick brush. His harsh breath stuttered in and out of his chest until he stopped a moment to see if she was giving chase.

There was no sign of her behind him. He glanced around to get his bearings. The beach was to the west, so he located what he thought was the deer trail again and loped into a run.

Jane needed him.

Thirty-Seven

Jane's arms ached from being tied behind her, and she was dizzy and disoriented as the boat moved through the dark waters. It was time to get free. She'd practiced this maneuver of getting her hands in front of her back in the academy, but she'd never had an opportunity to use it in the field. Being so small and dexterous made it easier, but it was far from simple.

She squirmed around until she was sitting on her hands. Flexing her shoulder muscles to make her arms as long as possible, she shuffled and moved until she had her hands at her thighs, then at her calves and down to her ankles until she got her feet through the loop made by her tied hands. Her shoulder and back ached from the exertion, but she forced herself up and reached out with both hands to find the light switch.

She blinked in the sudden illumination. The berth contained a galley with a small bank of cabinets, a table that transformed into a bed, and a head. There had to be a knife or something sharp down here somewhere. She stepped to the cabinets and wrenched open the first upper one. Plates, metal pans, nothing to cut with. The other cabinet held towels. She knelt to check the bottom ones. It wasn't until she opened a small drawer that she found a fishing knife. She moved it around in her hands until she had the blade against the rope. She sawed it back and forth for what seemed like forever.

The engine throttled back, and the boat slewed sideways a bit as it began to slow. She heard a woman's voice and knew they must have reached the senator's boat. There wasn't much time. With renewed urgency she sawed with the knife. So close. The blade finally broke through the top of the rope, and her bonds loosened. She quickly unwrapped them from her wrists and tossed them to the floor.

She needed a better weapon than this pitiful knife that could barely cut through butter. Reid had a concealed-carry permit, so maybe he had a gun here somewhere. She pulled out every drawer, upended the cushions on the benches, and went through the tiny cabinet in the head. No gun.

She picked up the knife again. There was

no choice but to go up there and do the best she could with it. If only she had her phone to call the Coast Guard. Her chest was tight as she eased up the ladder rungs and poked her head above the hatch to the upper deck. Brian was tying the two boats together. The senator stood on the starboard side ready to board Reid's boat.

Jane glanced around for Brian's gun, then spied it tucked into the back of his waistband. There was only one, so he must've left her gun on the sand. Was there anything she could use to hit him over the head? Another glance around didn't turn up a possible weapon. She would have to bide her time.

She quickly went up the rest of the ladder and crouched down in the bow. With any luck Brian wouldn't look here. Her gaze fell to the deck, and she saw a fire extinguisher attached to the side. It might do as a weapon.

She released it from its caddy and hefted it in her hand. Good and heavy. It would take the right circumstances to be able to use it before he pulled his gun and shot her.

The boat rocked a bit, and the senator's voice was louder. She must have stepped aboard the ship. "Harry? Fanny?" The senator's footsteps came closer. "Where are they?"

"They're in the berth. The little guy was really tired."

"Poor little man. This has to have been hard on him. Did you find out who took them and why?"

"Sure did. Do you remember a guy you sent to prison by the name of Karl Boulter?"

"Cop killer from Pelican Harbor? He was on death row for a while, but someone killed him in prison, I think. What's he got to do with this? I think he's been dead seven or eight years or so."

Brian's dad? This was about revenge? Jane dared a peek out of her hidden spot, and Brian had his back to her. Should she try to ambush him? She gauged the distance. Too far to throw the canister, and he'd hear her coming before she got two feet. Plus, the senator might see her and give away the attack without meaning to.

Patience. The right time would show itself. She ducked back down and crept along the bow a little closer to the two of them.

"What you might not know is that his wife and daughter died in a car accident the day he was sentenced to death. Some say it was suicide."

"I'm so sorry. That's terrible."

"You don't know the half of it. He had three kids. Two boys as well as the girl. Do you want to know what happened to the boys?"

Jane peeked up for another look and saw a glint of metal in Brian's fingers. A coin of some kind. Maybe a Kennedy half-dollar?

The senator sidled away a step. "I'd rather see my family right now."

Brian smiled. "Chief Hardy felt a lot of guilt. He helped one of the boys start a business in town. Paid for the other one to go to police academy, and that one eventually got hired at Pelican Harbor a couple of years ago." He held up the coin in his hand. "Karl Boulter loved Kennedy half-dollars and always had some in his pocket. I think he liked them because they were minted the year he was born — 1964. I like to have them on me too."

Jane snuck another peek. The senator must have been figuring out something wasn't quite right because she continued to sidle away from Brian.

"I don't understand what that case has to do with this. It was a long time ago."

In a smooth movement Brian snatched the gun from his waistband and brought it up to center on the senator's chest. "I don't suppose things like that bother you. My dad

419

wasn't guilty. Charles Hardy framed him, so I'm returning the favor. He's wanted by the FBI, and he's implicated in Gary Dawson's murder. He'll soon be in jail, and he'll suffer the same fate as my dad. His daughter will be dead as well, and when you're dead, my revenge be finished."

"W-What about my daughter and grandson?"

He grinned. "It might be better if you didn't know."

"No!"

He gestured with the gun. "Let's go back to your boat. That's a better place to end this. Don't worry. I'll make your death fast. It will be much briefer than the pain you brought my family." He shoved her toward the yacht.

His boat was gone.

Lungs burning, Reid stood on the rickety deck and looked out to the water. Some of those boat lights might be from his boat, but he couldn't tell from the distance and in the dark. Jane and the senator were not here, and he guessed Brian had taken them aboard Reid's boat. At least he prayed he wasn't going to find their bodies somewhere here on the sand.

Reid scanned down the deserted beach

and saw nothing. No people, no lights, no boats close enough to hail for help. Maybe he could call someone from the senator's house. It was all he could think to do. He crashed back through the vegetation, then took off in a run along the trail to the house. He didn't think Elizabeth would come after him. In fact, she'd probably escaped herself. She would if she was smart anyway. Reid doubted Brian would let her live.

He wished she'd told him where Fanny and Harry were being held. He'd seen the cruelty in Brian's face, and he didn't trust that the detective hadn't already disposed of them. Elizabeth seemed to think they'd be allowed to live, but Reid wasn't counting on it.

It seemed an eternity before he stepped back into the clearing where the house stood. Paul's body was where they'd left it so no one had been here. "Jane?"

Only bullfrogs answered him. He went inside the house in search of a phone. It smelled of disuse and dust, and he felt along the wall for a light. The switch was near the door, and he flipped it on, then blinked at the sudden glare of light. It was mostly a big open room filled with dust cloth–draped furniture. The senator must not come here a lot.

He walked through the place and found a landline, but it had no dial tone. He searched for some kind of weapon, but there was no gun or rifle in the place — probably because of the possibility of theft clear out here in the wilderness.

Jane needed him. But how would he get help or reach her?

He started to leave, then saw a kayak up in the rafters of the boathouse. Stretching up on his toes, he managed to grab hold of it and drag it down to the floor. A paddle was strapped to the side of it, and it looked seaworthy.

He put the boat into the water, then stepped into the kayak and picked up the paddle. Out in the bay the waves were bigger than he'd expected, probably left over from the storm. Splatters of rain hit his face as he steered the kayak out toward the middle of the bay where he'd seen the boat lights.

The lights drew nearer as he paddled into the bay, and he could make out two boats tied together. The one presenting its starboard side to him was his boat. He squinted in the dark and prayed the clouds would part so he could see better. The moon had been out earlier, but another storm seemed to be moving in.

A wave nearly capsized him, but he righted the kayak and paddled closer. The senator's yacht should have a ladder. There it was. Brian's voice was a low murmur, and Reid couldn't make out the words.

Reid went up quickly behind Brian. He stepped onto the yacht's deck, then slid onto his stomach and listened for any sounds that would indicate he'd been spotted. On his belly he crawled toward the wheelhouse. A whine caught his attention, and he spied Parker crouched under the captain's seat.

Reid reached out and ran his fingers through the fur on Parker's head. He looked around for a gun or a knife, but the senator didn't have any weapon stashed that he could find. He reached up and grabbed the VHF radio's mic, but before he could key it in and send out a mayday, Brian's voice came toward him. He dropped the mic and crawled to the bow where he hoped to remain out of sight until he could get the jump on Boulter.

Was Jane here with him, too, or just the senator? He'd seen no signs of Jane, but with Parker here, he hoped she was somewhere close.

THIRTY-EIGHT

Jane had to move fast. The senator was in the yacht's berth, and Brian was walking toward the rope attaching the two boats together. He was planning to come get her and take her aboard the senator's yacht too. The minute he got over here he'd see her.

Considering her options, she looked over the side of the boat into the dark waves lapping the hull. Gators were known to be in the bay sometimes. Sharks too. She let go of the fire extinguisher and threw one leg over the railing. After taking a deep breath, she lowered herself over the side of the boat. The shock of cold water made her gasp, but she struck out in strong strokes for the bow and swam to the yacht, where she paused to figure out the easiest way to reach the deck. The anchor chain caught her eye first, and while there might be a ladder around the starboard side, it was impossible to know how much time she had. Brian could discover her missing from the boat's berth any time.

She grasped the anchor chain and began to walk and pull up the side of the boat. Her arm and leg muscles burned by the time she'd maneuvered herself up four feet, but she gritted her teeth and pressed on. Inch by inch, she climbed until her palm gripped the upper rail. She hauled herself over and lay gasping on the deck. She thought she heard the senator shouting for help from belowdecks, but it was unlikely any boater out here would hear her.

If she could get the yacht free from Reid's boat, she could leave Brian behind and call for help on the radio. She rose to her knees and looked around. When she saw no movement, she rose and started for the wheelhouse, then caught motion from the corner of her eye. She ducked down.

Brian, his face set and angry, leapt from the boat back to the yacht. He no longer had his backpack. He untied the two boats and shoved away from Reid's boat.

And she was still weaponless.

A boat this size would have multiple fire extinguishers, but she hoped for something a little more lethal. The yacht slewed in the water and moved away from Reid's boat. She peeked up and saw Brian at the wheelhouse. Where did he plan to scuttle the yacht? She was sure that was his plan. Scuttle the boat and let the senator drown. It would seem to be an accident.

But what would he do about her being missing? The answer was a boom followed by a flash so intense it imprinted red on her eyeballs. Flames shot along the deck, and the crackle of burning wood made her wince. The thick smoke rolled toward the yacht, and she gagged at the stench.

Reid's beautiful boat was burning. Was he even still alive somewhere on shore? She had to cling to that hope.

If she'd stayed, she would have been killed. Brian's exultant expression in the light of the flames made her shudder. He thought he'd won. She couldn't let that happen. She scanned the area in earnest for a weapon and found a speargun. Perfect. She checked to make sure it was ready to fire, then crept along the deck toward the wheelhouse.

She heard a sliding, clicking sound to her right and whirled, speargun up, toward the sound. She gaped and blinked, unable to believe her eyes for a moment. Reid stood with Parker at his side. A warm tide of joy washed up her neck and heated her cheeks.

Reid's gaze locked with hers, and relief

curved his lips. He held his forefinger to his mouth, then jabbed his thumb toward the wheelhouse. She nodded and sidled toward Brian, who sat in front of the wheel with his back to them. Reid dropped to his belly and crawled quickly toward Brian on the other side.

She brought up the speargun and aimed it at Brian. "It's all over, Brian. I wasn't aboard Reid's boat."

Brian jerked so violently he nearly toppled from the chair. He sprang to his feet and whirled to face her with his gun drawn.

His gaze locked on the spear in her hand. "Drop it. I can shoot you before that spear hits me."

Which was true. Out of the corner of her eye, she saw Reid rise from the ground and leap onto Brian. The two tussled for the gun as she ran forward. Parker barked and ran around them as if he wasn't sure who to bite. Jane held the speargun in position, but with the men rolling around, there was no opportunity to stab Brian.

She stepped past the men and grabbed the radio. "Coast Guard, mayday, mayday. Senator Fox's yacht has been boarded, and we need help." She read off the coordinates, then left the handset dangling as she backed away.

The Coast Guard was answering her, but she couldn't hear them above the grunts and blows being bandied between the two men. Brian was big and powerful, and he was slowly winning the battle for the gun. Jane brought up the speargun and was prepared to shoot her detective if he came up with it pointing at her or Reid.

Brian rolled atop Reid and held the gun aloft. Jane's finger twitched on the trigger, but it was hard to overcome her training and shoot a spear into his back. She glanced at her dog, who was still showing signs of distress. He didn't know what to do.

"Parker, gun!" He'd been trained to wrest a gun from an attacker's hand.

Parker's whine turned to a growl, and he lunged for Brian's wrist. He sank his teeth into the fleshy part of Brian's hand.

Brian screamed and tried to shake off the dog's strong jaws, but Parker hung on, worrying Brian's hand like a rat. The gun dropped to Reid's chest, and he grabbed it, then rolled Brian off of him.

He sprang to his feet with the gun in hand. Jane ran to Parker and grabbed his collar. "Release, boy. We've got this."

With a final growl the dog unclamped his teeth. Blood poured from Brian's wound, and he cradled his right hand in his left.

"He bit me." He looked at Reid holding the gun, then at Jane with the spear in her hand. His shoulders sagged.

Jane strode forward and slapped cuffs on him. "You're under arrest for the kidnapping and attempted murder of Senator Fox. And I'm sure myriad other charges will follow."

Now to find Harry and Fanny. Her gaze went to Reid, who was staring at her with longing. She wasn't aware of moving until she was in his arms.

Reid closed his eyes for a moment and inhaled the fragrance of Jane's hair, something with vanilla and coconut. "I thought I'd lost you," he murmured.

"I was sure you were dead." Her voice was choked. Her grip was tight around his waist.

He brushed a kiss across her forehead, then dipped lower to capture her lips. They were soft and warm with promise.

Brian made a sound of disgust, and Jane pulled away. Her eyes were luminous, and her full lips tipped into a smile. "I'd better get the senator out of the cabin." She nodded toward lights headed their way. "Here comes the Coast Guard."

He didn't want to let her go, but he forced himself to release her grip. "I'll get the senator. You're the law on the ship so you can talk to the cavalry."

He walked through the dark to the stairs that led to the berth and unlocked the door, then yanked it open. "Senator Fox, are you all right?"

Looking pale and disheveled in the dim berth lighting, she appeared immediately. "Do you have my family?"

"Not yet, but Boulter is in custody, and I'm sure Jane and the Coast Guard will get him to talk. I know the identity of the other conspirators as well. Daryl left, and Elizabeth might have as well."

Senator Fox came up the stairs. "Let's go there now."

"In just a few minutes. Jane can transfer Boulter to the Coast Guard for safekeeping, and if we can find Elizabeth, she might lead us to Harry and Fanny."

"I've got a dinghy we could take now."

He understood her urgency. "It should only be a few minutes. Jane needs to tell the Coast Guard what's happened." He steered the senator to the side of the yacht where floodlights illuminated the deck. Jane was remanding Boulter into Coast Guard custody.

"I have to find the senator's family," Jane said. "I'll pick this guy up in a few hours,

430

and we'll explain everything. For now just know he kidnapped the senator with the intent to kill her and me."

Reid tuned out the discussion and looked out across the dark water toward the shore. He saw no glimmer of lights anywhere along the shoreline, but then the campsite was farther in from the water and sheltered by the trees. There was no way to get in there except by foot because of the terrain.

Jane touched his arm, and he put his hand over hers as the motor of the Coast Guard boat intensified to a roar. "There's a lot to tell you, Jane. You won't believe the identity of Brian's accomplices." He moved to the wheelhouse and started the engine.

The senator followed them and sank into the chair beside Jane. "I'm so frightened. He really meant to kill me. What if he's killed Fanny? He said he hadn't killed her yet, but I don't trust him."

"I don't think the woman who has them will harm them." He told Jane and Senator Fox about Elizabeth and how Brian had coerced her into helping after discovering her vigilante attacks.

Jane's eyes widened when he told her about Brian and Daryl's conspiracy to frame her dad. "So much hate." She put her hand to her mouth. "I can't believe Elizabeth would do something like this. And Brian." She turned to the senator. "I heard him telling you this was all about revenge for his father. My dad tried to help those boys too."

"He was marked by tragedy at such a young age," Senator Fox said. "When you let rage and anger grow, it consumes you."

"I wonder if Troy had any inkling Brian was so eaten up with thoughts of revenge."

Reid squinted through the dark and spied the old pier coming up. "You'll have to ask him." He docked the yacht and tied it up, then helped the women and Parker disembark. "The camp is this way."

He led the way through the dark forest and found the deer trail. The senator brought out her phone and handed it to him with the flashlight app on, which helped push back the shadows. Jane slipped her hand into his, and he squeezed her fingers and kept her close.

He smelled the camp before he saw it — a mixture of fire and soup. "Senator, you should wait here. Let me see if Elizabeth is still here."

Jane put her hand on his arm. "You stay with the senator. I'll check out the camp and see if Daryl or Elizabeth are still around."

Ever the capable cop. He stayed at the tree line and watched as Jane, gun in hand, stepped into the clearing. Nothing stirred but the wind. The camp stove still sat in its place with the battered pot still on the burner. The campfire had burned out, and only a wisp of smoke curled from its ashes. The door to the cabin was shut.

Jane walked across the clearing to the cabin and mounted the steps. She rapped on the door. "Elizabeth? Are you in there? It's Jane."

Reid strained to make out the sounds coming from the cabin. Cries maybe? Jane tried the door, but it was locked. She stepped to the window and peered in, then turned toward Reid and the senator.

"It's Fanny and Harry. They're tied up inside. I don't see Elizabeth."

Reid and the senator ran to join her. "Harry!" Senator Fox called. "Harry, it's Grammy. You're safe."

Reid bounced up the rickety steps to the door. "Stand back."

He made a running start and crashed his shoulder into the flimsy door. The jamb splintered under the weight of his body, and he fell into the cabin and toppled to the floor.

"Wait, Senator," Jane called, but the senator didn't stop. She raced past Reid.

Reid blinked in the dark cabin and saw Harry and Fanny chained to an old iron bedstead that looped through the foot rail and ended in a padlock. He scrambled up and went to see how to free them.

Senator Fox sat on the bed and scooped up her grandson in one arm and reached for her daughter with the other. "Get these chains off," she told Reid.

"Let me see if there's a key around. If not, we'll need a bolt cutter." He looked around the nearly empty cabin and didn't see a key.

Jane reached toward a hook on the wall. "I think this is it." She plucked a key loose and brought it to Reid.

He inserted it into the padlock. "It fits!" The key clicked, and he disentangled the padlock from the chains.

With Harry still in her arms, the senator helped Fanny wobble to her feet. "We're going home."

Jane touched Reid's arm. "Okay, Captain America, let me take a look at that shoulder."

But sore muscles were nothing compared to the joy he saw on those three faces. He put his arm around Jane and pulled her into his side. "Let's enjoy the moment, just for now."

He knew she wouldn't look at him with that same admiration for much longer.

THIRTY-NINE

Had Brian ever been who she thought he
was? Jane stood behind the one-way mirror
with Reid beside her and watched Brian sitting at the interrogation table. Since she'd
been one of his targets and he was a police
officer, the state boys had taken over the
case and would be here soon to interrogate
him. Elizabeth and Daryl had been picked
up as well and awaited their own interrogations in other rooms. Daryl was the one who
had shot at them at Fort Morgan.

The scandal would reverberate through
the state.

She glanced at Reid, who was prepping
his video equipment. "This will be a crazy
documentary for you."

He froze for a moment, then turned to
look at her. "You want me to scrap the
whole thing?"

Did she? She examined her churning
thoughts mixed with the shame of knowing

436

she'd swallowed the lies Brian had told her. She shook her head. "It's an important lesson about the masks people wear. I considered Brian a friend, and all the time he was seething with rage." Her voice trembled, and she cleared her throat. "Is there anyone who doesn't wear a mask? I'm beginning to think there isn't."

She sensed him stiffen. "I didn't mean you. But wow, all of this has really rocked me. Dad was right all along — someone was out to get him."

Reid watched Boulter in the other room. "I feel sorry for Brian's brother. He was shaken by what Brian had done."

"I wish he'd told me Brian was angry — maybe talking it out would have helped."

"That level of rage and hatred usually isn't something you can talk out. It takes God doing a work with forgiveness. We usually can't do it by ourselves."

Maybe he was right. She sure hadn't been able to get anywhere on her own feelings.

Brian rose from the table and strolled to the glass. He pressed his face against it and gave a flat grin that didn't reach his eyes. "I know you're back there. You've won, Jane. That make you happy? Your family has taken everything from me."

"No, it doesn't." He couldn't hear her,

but the rage in his eyes was heartbreaking.

"I might have missed out on justice at the moment, but it has a funny way of slapping you in the face when you least expect it. One of these days your dad will pay for what he did."

Reid's camera was rolling. "He seems sure his dad was innocent. Do you know the case?"

"Very well. A dash cam caught his dad in the act. There was no question of his guilt, just like there's no question of Brian's now."

Brian turned as the state detectives entered the room. He thought he was entitled to his hatred, and she didn't see that ever changing.

Will's jaw flexed, and he stared at Reid. "I want to tell her today. That's the only birthday present I want."

Today was his boy's fifteenth birthday and Jane's thirtieth. With all that had happened, Reid hadn't retrieved the new video game he'd bought from upstairs. And he hadn't dared to buy Jane anything for fear of moving too fast. Besides, even if he had, the minute she heard who he was, she would throw it back at him.

Reid poured the last mug of coffee and set it on the tray with the beignets before he answered. Will was the only one who'd gotten any sleep last night since he and Jane had arrived here only an hour ago. With his eyes burning from lack of rest, and fatigue slowing his movements, Reid didn't feel up to the trouble that was surging toward him like a rudderless ship.

The sun was up but just barely. He glanced out the window to where Jane sat on the dock at the Bon Secour River. The water glittered with color from the sunrise, and her hair had a pinkish tint. He'd tried to imagine her reaction, but no matter how he tried to spin it, he didn't see this ending well in spite of the obvious feelings growing between them.

For the millionth time he wished he'd announced who he was the minute he'd hit town, but he hadn't known her well enough to trust her. He did now. He knew she was a good person with a heart big enough to embrace Will with a mother's love without trying to take him from Reid.

But he hadn't been sure back then.

He doubted the distinction would mean much to her.

"Will, she's had a rough night. So have I. I think it would be better to let us all get a little rest first."

Will's shoulders slumped. "You think she

439

will be mad, don't you?"

"You were," Reid pointed out. "Of course she's going to be mad at me. There's no way around it."

"You didn't tell her I was dead. Her dad did." Will's gaze went far away as he looked out the window. "When can I meet my grandpa?"

"You want to meet him? After he —" Reid snapped his mouth shut.

"After he left me and lied to her. Yeah, I know. But I have a grandfather. That's pretty cool. Maybe he'll take me fishing."

Reid's chest squeezed. His boy had missed having extended family in so many ways that Reid hadn't noticed. He'd tried to be there for Will, but it hadn't been enough. Hard as this was going to be on all of them, he knew it had to be done.

Just not this moment.

The door opened, and Jane stepped inside with Parker. "Where's our coffee and beignets? I'm starving."

Reid picked up the tray. "I was about to bring them out, birthday girl." He tried to put a light note in his words and desperately prayed Will wouldn't say anything. Not today.

"Aw, thank you. The mosquitoes are feasting on me so let's eat inside. There's another

440

storm brewing, too, and I felt a couple of drops of rain. I thought I might curl up on your sofa and take a nap."

Without waiting for a reply she went past the breakfast bar into the open living room and dropped onto the sofa. Reid set the tray of food and drinks on the coffee table, and she reached for a beignet. Powdered sugar dusted her lap as she devoured the sweet treat in three bites.

She gave a small moan of delight. "They're still warm."

"I had them delivered so they'd still be hot. It's not much of a birthday cake, but it was the best I could do for you and Will."

She smiled at his son. "That's right — today is your birthday too. Happy birthday, Will. I bake a mean German chocolate cake. I'll make one for us to share after I have a nap." She slanted a grin at Reid. "I might let your dad have a piece, too, if he doesn't wake me up too early."

If only they could stay in this cocoon of closeness. The minute she heard the truth it would all change.

"Does your dad know what happened yet?"

"I called him. He was shocked about Brian, hurt too, I think. He did a lot for those boys over the years." She wiped her fingers and took a sip of coffee before she set it on the end table beside her. "I'm chilly. You have a throw somewhere?"

"You bet. Lie back on the pillow and I'll cover you."

"I'm so tired." She curled up on the sofa with her head on a decorative pillow.

Reid grabbed the throw on the opposite sofa arm and shook it out to cover her. Something fell from its folds, and he stopped dead. The pictures he'd given Will. The throw dropped from his hand, and he felt queasy at the thought of her seeing them.

She'd surely recognize herself. And the boy he used to be.

She scooped them up and glanced at them, the smile freezing on her face. She took in her long-ago self standing by the trees. "Where'd you get this?"

All the explanations dried on Reid's tongue, and he lost all coherent thought on how to make her understand.

"You were investigating me?"

"No, no, it's nothing like that."

She sat up and threw off the blanket. "Then where did these pictures come from? I haven't seen them in years."

Reid swallowed the boulder in his throat,

but before he could speak, Will stepped forward. "Let me, Dad."

FORTY

Jane's hand trembled as she held the picture, and an overwhelming wave of nausea hit. The reminder of who she used to be hit hard on the heels of her triumph in saving the senator. Why did Reid have this? She'd trusted him, and he'd been investigating her. Did he intend to expose her past?

The shame of who she used to be circled her, hemming her in and squeezing her chest.

She gulped in several calming breaths and reached for Parker. He whined and crawled up into her lap as if to comfort her. She rested her chin on his furry head.

Will clutched his hands together in front of him. "I know this is a shock, Chief."

She eyed the boy's tentative smile and couldn't return it. What did Reid's kid have to do with this? Had it been his idea to investigate her?

She licked her lips and struggled to think

444

past her furiously racing thoughts. "What is there to explain? I think I need to talk to your dad. This is between him and me."

Will's chin came up, and he held her gaze. "Actually, it's not. You see, I'm your son."

Your son.

The words made no sense. She stared at him. Her son was an infant laid to rest in a hasty grave long ago. Her son was a baby with black hair and dark, questioning eyes. Her son had wound himself around her heart the same way his tiny fingers had clutched her index finger.

She swallowed. "My son is dead, Will. Is this some kind of mean joke?"

His dark eyes earnest, Will stared back and gave a small shake of his head. "It's true. Today is my birthday, just like yours. My dad had those pictures of you. He's Moose."

Moose.

The long-ago name was like a splash of cold water in her face. Her gaze traveled to Reid standing behind his son. "That's impossible."

"It's true, Jane. I know I look very different now." He rubbed his shaved head. "All that hair is gone. You never saw me without hair on my head and face."

A trickle of belief began to snake into her heart. No wonder she'd been so taken aback when Reid had kissed her. No wonder her thoughts had drifted to those long-ago days at Mount Sinai.

Her gaze went back to Will, and she rose on wobbly legs. "It's true?" She reached out a shaky hand to touch his cheek, a cheek that wasn't as petal soft as it had been fifteen years ago.

"I-It's true. You're my mom." Will's eyes filled with moisture, and his Adam's apple bobbed as he struggled to hold back the emotion.

"Can I hug you?" she whispered.

He nodded and opened his arms. She stepped into them and clutched him as he bent down over her in a protective grasp. Where she'd once held him to her chest, he now held her to his. Was this a dream? If it was, she didn't want to wake up.

Her little baby was alive and well. Growing big and strong like his father. Most of all, he was a fine young man. Respectful, hardworking, and kind. He'd turned out the way she'd dreamed he would when she first held him in her arms so long ago.

She pulled away and looked up at him. "How long have you known?"

"Just a few days."

Anger began to simmer again when she realized what all this meant. Such a huge lie

446

had wrecked her. It had left a sense of sadness that had been impossible to overcome.

Her fingers curled into her palms and she looked at Reid. "You lied to my dad!"

He shook his head. "That was all Charles. Your mom brought Will to me just before the attack on the compound started. I saw your dad on my way to getting Will to safety. He knew Will and I were fine."

The blood dropped from Jane's head, and she felt faint. Her dad would never lie to her about something so important. Would he? Was this heinous lie what Elizabeth had meant when she talked about secrets?

The strength vacated Jane's legs, and she sank back onto the sofa as a flashback of that terrible day swamped her with pain and terror. Fire, screams, gunshots. Her baby. Her mother. So much taken from her that day.

She forced the images out of her head and looked up at Reid. "He lied to me to get me to leave with him?"

"I'm afraid so. For a long time I thought you'd died in the raid. Then I saw you on TV about six months ago when you testified in a trial I was following." His shoulders slumped, and a sigh escaped his lips. "If it's any consolation, I didn't recognize you either, but my dad had a list of all the cult members so I've always known your real name."

A lie of omission, this time from Reid. "Why didn't you tell me the truth when you first came?" She gritted her teeth so hard her jaw ached.

He spread out his hands in a placating gesture. "Think about it, Jane. I didn't really know you during that time. We weren't together much. And after you left me and our son, I wasn't sure I could trust you."

"Trust me? Of course you can trust me." Her gaze went to her son again. "Oh, I see. You thought I might try to get custody of Will?"

"Some women would. They wouldn't care what it did to the kid or the father."

"I would never try to come between you and Will. You two have a special relationship."

"I know that now, but I didn't when I first met you."

He sounded tired, and he rubbed his forehead. "We were going to tell you after your nap today."

She didn't know if she believed him or not. How could she trust him or anyone now? Her own father had told the most painful lie imaginable. All these years she'd thought her son was dead. It was almost too much to take in.

She managed to make her wobbly legs obey her enough to rise to her feet. "I've got to talk to my dad."

Will held out his hand. "Are you mad at me?"

She took his hand. "What? Oh, honey, of course not. This wasn't your fault." She saw the hurt in his face and pulled him into another tight embrace. Everything in her wanted to sit here and talk with her boy, but she had to find out why her father had done this to her. "I'll come back later, and we'll talk about the future. I want to be with you as much as you'll have me." She skewered his father with a glare. "As long as I don't have to be around your dad."

Ignoring the hurt that settled in Reid's eyes, she called Parker to her and rushed for the door. How did she even accept what had happened?

Reid felt as though he'd just escaped from a war zone. Jane's anger had been everything he'd expected, but it was what he deserved.

He glanced at Will sitting on the sofa and staring off into space with confusion clouding his dark eyes. "She's entitled to be mad at me, Will. Things will be fine between the two of you." He forced a lighthearted note into his voice. "And hey, you'll get a dog out of it too. Parker already loves you."

Will blinked and sat back. "I wish she hadn't been so mad at you. How am I supposed to handle it if she starts bashing you?"

"She won't, son."

"She just did."

"It was just the shock speaking. She won't want to make you uncomfortable or do anything to keep me from letting her see you. She doesn't really have rights unless I give them to her."

Will's brows rose. "You wouldn't stop me from spending time with her, would you?"

"Not for anything. But she won't want open war between us either." Reid glanced at the clock on the wall. "You hungry? I could make omelets or we could go to the Brew House for coffee and a breakfast sandwich."

"I don't want anything."

"I don't want you to stay home and mope all day on your birthday. We could go out on the boat." Too late he remembered his boat's fate. "Scratch that idea. One thing I didn't mention was that Detective Boulter blew up our boat."

That got Will's attention. "Our boat sank?"

"It burned, then sank. I doubt we'd find

more than a charred board or two in Mobile Bay. I could rent a boat so we could see if there's any sign of it."

"I don't think I could stand to find anything."

"Basketball? You and I could go to the schoolyard and shoot some hoops."

"Yeah." Will brightened and rose. "I guess I could do that."

"But you'll need breakfast."

"Anything to poke food down me?"

"Hey, you're a growing boy."

Will trailed after Reid to the kitchen. He perched on a bar stool while Reid whipped up omelets and hash browns. The scent of coffee and food made Reid's stomach cramp, and he realized how hungry he was. Jane had gone off without food. He hoped her dad would feed her.

What was happening over there? Would Charles lie to her again? Would he try to convince her the consequences of that night had been Reid's fault?

"You're frowning," Will said.

Reid started to make an offhand remark, then caught himself. Truth. He needed to let Will inside, to understand what he was going through too. "I'm worried Charles might not tell her the truth."

"You have no way to prove what happened

that night, do you?"

"Nope. Her mother isn't around to corroborate what happened. Charles could spin her a line a mile long. He's her dad, and she's more apt to believe him than me."

"I don't know — my mom is pretty sharp. She wouldn't be a police officer for long if she didn't recognize lies."

My mom.

Hearing his son say the words lifted Reid's spirits. While he might be on Jane's mud list, his son's life was about to expand in amazing ways. He'd mourned Will's lack of a mother's love, and Jane would lavish it on their boy. He vowed not to stand in the way of Will experiencing everything Jane wanted to give him. His son never should have been subjected to Lauren, and his real mother could heal that pain. She would be an excellent mother, and he would give her the space she needed to learn the ropes and find her way to a close relationship with Will.

He owed her that much.

He slid Will's breakfast to him, then picked up his own plate and came around the end of the island to join his son. They ate in companionable silence.

"Could we stop and get her a birthday present before basketball?" Will asked.

"Sure. Any idea what you want to get her?"

"She likes books about Rome. We could stop at the bookstore and see if they have anything new."

"I know why she likes books so much. We weren't allowed to read books in the cult. We could read the booklets we used to reel in new members, but we weren't even allowed to read the Bible. She had some contraband books she hid in a hole in her closet. I found them once and put them back so she wasn't worried I'd turn her in."

Will pushed away his empty plate. "That's really sad. No wonder she's always reading. Would she read a real book? I know she's always got her e-reader."

"Her apartment is full of books. I think she just likes her e-reader so she always has a book with her. She'll treasure anything you get her."

"I want to use my own money."

Will earned his own money by yard work, mowing, and occasionally acting as a shrimping assistant for a friend in New Orleans. Reid had no idea how much the boy had saved, but he nodded. "Whatever you want."

He ate the last of his omelet and put the plates in the dishwasher. "Let's go see what we can find."

It would be Jane's first birthday gift from her son so it needed to be special and something she'd always remember. Maybe a book wouldn't be that memorable, but he had to let Will make that decision.

No apology from him would be enough to erase Jane's anger, and he wished he could see her look at him the way she did last night one more time.

FORTY-ONE

Jane got out of her vehicle in front of her father's house and let Parker out of the back to run and chase squirrels. Her dad's truck was parked at the side, so she knew he had come home once he knew the truth was out. It would take a few days to totally clear his name, but those involved would be turning on each other to plea bargain. The scandal would take months to die down, and even then, people would talk about it for years.

Her dad wasn't in the house, so she walked along the tree-lined path to the bunker and pressed the buzzer. "Dad, it's me." The heavy metal door clicked to the unlocked position, and she pulled it open and stepped inside to walk down the long incline to the bunker.

The smell inside was a mixture of gunpowder and steel from all the guns and shelves. The space was huge. Twenty-foot ceilings soared overhead, and rows and rows of shelving held canned goods and other staples. A room behind this one held his armory. It would make the ATF salivate to know how much he'd accumulated down here. All legal, though.

She found her dad stacking canned goods on a shelf. He looked perfectly normal even though he'd been running from the law for days. Dressed in his usual jeans, boots, and plaid shirt, he worked methodically without looking at her.

She stopped and folded her arms over her chest. "Rotating stock?"

"Yep." He stopped what he was doing to stare at her a long moment. "You did a fine job, Jane. Better than I could have. I'm proud of you."

Her eyes burned, and she blinked back the moisture. Too little too late. "I want to talk to you about Mount Sinai and the day we left."

He set the last can on the shelf and picked up the box of older cans. "That was a long time ago. What's the point? Why bring it up now?"

She grabbed his arm as he started past her. "The point? The point is you *lied* to me. My baby didn't die. Moose didn't die. And what's more, they are right here in Pelican Harbor!"

The color drained from his face. "That's not possible."

"Reid Dixon is Moose. His son, Will, is *my* son. He's your grandson." Emotion cut off her words for a long moment. She swallowed down the pain. "He's wonderful, Dad. Wonderful! And I missed out on fifteen years with my own baby. All because you lied to me."

He carefully set down the box and sighed. "I knew you'd never come with me, Jane. I didn't want you to stay there and be swallowed alive by the false teaching. By then I knew it was all a lie. And even more than that, I really thought everyone was about to die. I had to get you to safety. Can't you understand that?"

"We could have taken him with us! There was time. You'd just seen him with Will. You knew where he was."

"There was no time to rescue him. And I didn't trust your mother. She would have convinced you it was the best thing for the baby for you to stay. You know how persuasive she always was."

"I can't believe you're defending your actions even now." Her chest squeezed with the need to inhale fresh air, to get away from his self-congratulatory tone. He still believed he'd been right. How delusional. Hadn't he noticed the fog of pain that clouded her eyes and never left? Did he have any idea how much his monumental lie had cost her?

All he'd seen was his own desires. He'd gotten everything he wanted — a new life away from the cult and her mother. She'd paid the price for him to have a career and this compound he loved. How completely selfish of him.

She turned and ran for the door. He called after her, but she ignored him. She couldn't breathe in there with his deceit choking off her air. Was there no one she could trust?

She should have asked her father where her mother was now. He probably knew. Maybe he'd known all along where to find Reid and Will. But no, he'd been shocked to discover they were in town.

She called for her dog as she ran to the SUV, and Parker reluctantly left his squirrel chasing to trot along at her heels. She reached her vehicle and let him into the backseat, then collapsed in her seat. She didn't know what to do with the emotions churning her gut and making her hands shake. For the first time the thought of faith, true faith, felt like a spring of fresh water to cool her burning cheeks. But she'd left God behind long ago, and she doubted he'd care to hear from her now that she was in the worst trouble of her life.

Will was her son. Jane was still processing it and trying to imagine how her life was about to change. She tried to focus on the wonder of that and let go of the rage vibrating just under the surface. She couldn't dwell on it or it would swallow her whole.

She entered Pelican Harbor city limits and was driving past the school when she spotted Reid's SUV in the parking lot. Two tall figures were shooting hoops, and she recognized Will's rangy form immediately. She whipped into the lot and watched them for several minutes. She was sure she would always feel this jolt of wonder when she looked at her boy.

Her baby was alive and wonderful. It was hard to wrap her head around how that tiny infant could have been transformed into this handsome specimen of young manhood. Her gaze traveled to Reid, and the smile dropped off her face.

Lies, so many lies. Her entire life had been shaped and transformed by lies. Her career was all about digging out truth and bringing justice, but it felt like a futile exercise now when she'd discovered how wrong she'd been about so many people.

Reid stopped and looked toward the lot.

He nudged Will, and they both walked toward her vehicle. Her chest compressed, and she blew out a breath, then inhaled several times to calm herself. She didn't want to spoil this moment with Will. Anger toward his dad could derail their relationship. She'd always despised the way divorced couples trashed each other and the kids had to pay for their unhappiness.

Parker had seen them, too, and he gave a happy woof, his tail wagging. She got out and opened the door for him. He bounded off to greet Will and Reid. Will petted him, then stopped at their SUV to extract a bag. He smiled her way, a big grin that nearly split his face, and her heart seized at the joy it brought her.

Several steps ahead of his dad, he trotted toward her, then stopped a couple of feet away. "Hi. Um, Mom. Is it okay if I call you that?"

Mom. She'd never dreamed she'd hear that word directed at her. Tears gathered in her eyes again, and she reached blindly toward him. She couldn't speak with such happiness enveloping every cell in her body.

Will clutched her to his chest, and she sobbed against his shirt. He patted her back awkwardly, then turned slightly toward his dad as if to ask, "What do I do with her?"

She sniffled and lifted her head. "I'm not usually an emotional wreck, Will, and I promise to try not to embarrass you like this ever again." She stepped back and grasped his forearms. "My son. I still can't believe it. I love you with all my heart, Will. I'm new to this mothering business, but I'm a fast learner. I'm sure I'll make mistakes, but never doubt that I've loved you from the moment I looked into your wrinkled little face."

Tears gathered again, and she shoved them away as best she could. She dropped her hands and glanced at Reid. "Can I have him spend the night?"

It galled her to have to ask him anything after he'd hidden Will's existence from her. His brown eyes processed her request, and she bit back the threat to take him to court if he didn't agree. That wasn't the way to start a distant but cordial relationship for Will's sake.

Reid shoved his hands in his pockets. "He can stay with you anytime he wants."

She couldn't look him in the eye and kept her gaze somewhere around his chin. "Thank you." The words nearly choked her.

Will thrust the bag into her hand. "I-I got you a birthday present. They couldn't wrap it. I hope that's okay."

461

"Aw, honey, I don't care about that kind of thing." She peeked inside the Two Turtles Bookstore bag and pulled out a copy of a book on Roman history. "I haven't read this one."

"It's new." He sounded anxious.

Her first gift from her son. "I'll treasure it. Thank you." She hugged him again but made it quick in case he thought she was too touchy-feely. Other people she knew complained about how their teenagers didn't want to be touched. It would be hard on her if he ended up being like that.

She forced herself to look at Reid again but still couldn't bring her gaze up to meet his. "Can I take him now?"

"Of course. I'll drop some clothes by for him." He reached a hand toward her. "Jane, I-I'm so sorry. I want us to get past this. Can you forgive me?"

She turned away so she didn't have to deal with the yearning in that gesture. "Maybe. I'm going to try, but I can't deal with it today." The falsely bright note in her voice stabbed her with its hypocrisy. She didn't want to be the kind of person who put up a fake front, but she couldn't handle any more until she got control of her rampaging thoughts.

She felt his gaze burning into her back as

she walked to her SUV with Will and Parker. All the budding feelings she'd had for Reid still churned inside, and she couldn't forget that kiss. That wonderful, amazing kiss that felt like coming home. What did it really mean after all this? She wasn't sure when she could take those feelings out and examine them. It would take all her energy to figure out this new relationship with Will. That had to be her priority right now.

She'd have to talk to Reid eventually and resolve what had happened, but not today. Maybe she could figure out a way to get past it, but not with her tall son walking beside her. Today was for discovering the wonders wrapped up in this handsome boy next to her.

A NOTE FROM THE AUTHOR

Dear Reader,

I visited the Gulf Shores area for the first time in 2017 and fell in love with the area. The blue water, the wildlife, the thick dunes spoke to me. We were having dinner with the England family, and sixteen-year-old Isaac began to recount his adventures aboard a shrimping boat. He talked about all the things the nets would bring up and mentioned they'd even snagged a washing machine.

My weird mind immediately conjured up a body in a refrigerator. I ultimately decided on a big ice chest for the discovery, but that conversation was the jumping-off spot for the series. I've been interested in the cult experience for a long time, too, and after noodling on the idea, I decided Jane had too much baggage to resolve in one book. She was worthy of an entire series, just like Bree Nicholls from the Rock Harbor series.

I hope you enjoy the book as much as I loved writing it. Let me know what you think — I love to hear from readers!

Love,
Colleen Coble
colleen@colleencoble.com
colleencoble.com

ACKNOWLEDGMENTS

My great thanks to the England family from the Gulf Shores area. Isaac's recounting of his experiences on a shrimp boat was the jumping-off spot for this series, and Amy selflessly hauled me all over the area to experience the flavor of southern Alabama. You all are awesome!

Seventeen years and counting as part of the amazing HarperCollins Christian Publishing team as of the summer of 2019! I never take my great fortune to land there for granted. I have the best team in the industry (and I'm not a bit prejudiced), and I'm so grateful for all you've taught me and all you've done for me. My dear editor and publisher, Amanda Bostic, makes sure I'm taken care of in every way. My marketing and publicity team is fabulous (thank you, Paul Fisher, Kerri Potts, and Allison Carter!). I'm truly blessed by all your hard work. My entire team works so hard, and I wish there was a way to reward you all for what you do for me.

Julee Schwarzburg is my outside editor, and she has such fabulous expertise with suspense and story. She smooths out all my rough spots and makes me look better than I am. I learn something from you and Amanda with every book, so thank you!

My agent, Karen Solem, and I have been together for twenty years now. She has helped shape my career in many ways, and that includes kicking an idea to the curb when necessary. She and a bevy of wonderful authors helped brainstorm this new series. Thank you, Denise Hunter, Robin Caroll, Carrie Stuart Parks, Lynette Eason, Voni Harris, and Pam Hillman!

My critique partner and dear friend of over twenty-one years, Denise Hunter, is the best sounding board ever. Together we've created so many works of fiction. She reads every line of my work, and I read every one of hers. It's truly been a blessed partnership.

I'm so grateful for my husband, Dave, who carts me around from city to city, washes towels, and chases down dinner without complaint. My family is everything to me, and my three grandchildren make life wonderful. We try to split our time between

Indiana and Arizona to be with them, but I'm constantly missing someone.

Most important, I give my thanks to God, who has opened such amazing doors for me and makes the journey a golden one.

eg and he is not distressed. What would you have done past situation?

8. ... and ... her ... begin a ... you think it was so hard for ...

DISCUSSION QUESTIONS

1. Jane's past shamed her, and she never wanted to be gullible, especially about faith. How might the world's view of God steer her away from real faith?
2. Reid came to town with a heavy secret. What would you have done if you were Reid?
3. How do you think Jane's past led her into law enforcement?
4. Have you ever known anyone who had been in a cult? What did you think about them?
5. Jane had a strong desire for family, but she was afraid of rejection so hadn't tried to find them. What would you do in a situation like that?
6. Jane often feels inadequate to the job of chief of police. Have you ever felt you weren't up to what was expected of you? If so, how did you handle it?
7. Reid found himself being less than hon-

est, and he hated dishonesty. What would
you have done in his situation?
8. Jane found it hard to forgive the lies. Why
do you think it was so hard for her?

ABOUT THE AUTHOR

Colleen Coble is a *USA TODAY* bestselling author and RITA finalist best known for her coastal romantic suspense novels, including *The Inn at Ocean's Edge, Twilight at Blueberry Barrens,* and the Lavender Tides, Sunset Cove, Hope Beach, and Rock Harbor series.

Connect with Colleen online at
colleencoble.com
Facebook: colleencoblebooks
Twitter: @colleencoble
Pinterest: @ColleenCoble